STOLEɪ H

Best wishes, Sandy!
The world is only
a plane ride away!
Freddie Remza
— 2015 —

BY FREDDIE REMZA

outskirtspress
DENVER, COLORADO

The Stolen Brooch
All Rights Reserved.
Copyright © 2015 Freddie Remza
v2.0

Cover Photo © 2015 thinkstockphotos.com. All rights reserved - used with permission.

Outskirts Press, Inc.
http://www.outskirtspress.com

ISBN: 978-1-4787-5001-7

Library of Congress Control Number: 2015900024

Outskirts Press and the "OP" logo are trademarks belonging to Outskirts Press, Inc.

PRINTED IN THE UNITED STATES OF AMERICA

DEDICATION

In Memory of

Charlene E. Day
(1949-2013)

If I let my mind go quiet, I can hear your voice.

Rest in peace, my Huckleberry friend

Whenever I've journey to other parts of the world, I've discovered people are not too different from each other—the Chinese woman holding the hand of her grandchild, the Nepalese boy chasing after his brother, the Thai woman selling vegetables in the market, the young South African girls jump roping in the schoolyard. We all have basic needs, desires, and joys. I invite you to come along as an armchair traveler to Thailand, China, South Africa, Nepal and Vietnam because a book is the next best thing to being there.

Freddie Remza

Thousands of candles can be lighted from a single candle, and the life of the candle will not be shortened. Happiness never decreases by being shared.

Guatama Buddha

SIGNIFICANT CHARACTERS

Jim McGregor	NYC Editor
Allison Wagner	American journalist
Lan	Nurse/counselor at a woman's Safe House in Bangkok
Yen	Novitiate at Thai Safe House
Mae Chi	Supervising nun at Safe House
Sarut	Thief
Deng	Sarut's partner
Keerati	Clerk in jewelry store
Naai Montri	Shady exporter/importer
Ashwin	Allison's guide
Marubo-dekka	Japanese detective
Chaidee	Detective from Chiang Rai
Wattana	Undercover agent in Chiang Rai
Police chief	In charge of investigation in Bangkok
Virote	Kidnapper
Man with tattoo	Kidnapper

Chapter 1

THE PURSUIT

Dolby Theatre
Hollywood, California

"And the winner of the documentary film category goes to . . . The Orchid Bracelet."

THE FLOODLIGHTS FLASHED across the audience and settled upon the people representing *The Orchid Bracelet*. The audience applauded as Jim McGregor and his team made their way to the stage to receive the Oscar. Jim accepted the trophy and walked to the microphone.

"Thank you, Academy, for this wonderful honor," Jim said. "I don't need to tell this audience that behind the scene of any movie are many people who laboriously put together a production."

He turned around and pointed to the six people behind him. "Here they are. At this time I would like to introduce one of these fine people to you—a talented journalist who wrote and produced this project, Allison Wagner."

Jim handed the Oscar to Allison and gestured towards the mike. Feeling a little out of place in this room of celebrities, she walked up to the microphone. "I went to Vietnam to gather information on how this country has changed since the end of the war. Without realizing it, I became entangled in a human trafficking scheme that forced my eyes wide-open. Sure, I heard about trafficking and of its atrocities; but unless you put a face on it, you can conveniently erase it from your mind."

Allison walked over to the young Vietnamese girl elegantly dressed in her newly purchased evening gown. Taking her hand, she pulled her center stage. "May I introduce Lan. This young woman took a terrible situation and used it to help others. I could not be more proud of her; and so, I accept this award for all the Lans in the world, and there are many. Yes, they live in places like Vietnam, Cambodia and Thailand. Somehow we Americans can process that, but human trafficking knows no boundaries and has no socioeconomic restraints. Human trafficking can be found right in our own United States. That quiet house at the dead-end of a middle-class neighborhood, the apartment next door, the farmhouse with the flower boxes—all are possible settings. We need to educate our children—boys and girls—of the dangers they may unintentionally encounter. Lan had no idea the day she left her small village in the Mekong Delta that the better life promised her would turn into hell. For you, Lan, I accept this Oscar."

3 Months Earlier

New York City

The sign on the door read *Jim McGregor, Editor*. It often hung slightly crooked which drove Allison crazy; so before knocking, she reached out and straightened it like she had done many times before.

"Come in, Allison," beckoned the raspy voice on the other side. Years of smoking had done that to McGregor and after much coaxing from his wife, he gave the habit up three years ago.

The petite, honey-blonde reporter entered the room holding her first mug of coffee of the day. "Jim, what's up already? I barely got my coat off when you called."

"You're going to like this, Allison. Remember the assignment you had in Vietnam several years ago?"

"Sure, will never forget. Why?"

"The documentary you helped orchestrate on human trafficking is nominated for an Academy Award."

"Are you kidding?" Allison placed her mug on Jim's desk and quickly slid into the chair opposite his. "Okay, tell me more."

"Just got the word last night. It appears we're going to Hollywood."

"Am I dreaming? Tell me this is all real."

Jim smiled. "A little excited, are we?"

"Beyond excited—when are we going? Who's coming with us?"

"You, me, and the tech crew . . . won't be until spring so you'll have plenty of time to prepare the acceptance speech," Jim half-heartedly joked. Nearly three decades older than Allison, Jim had been somewhat of a mentor to this thirty-something reporter. He often described her as intuitive, if sometimes not annoying, beyond her years.

"Allison, I've called you in today for two reasons. We hope to piggy-back on this recognition by collaborating another story. You did such an excellent job that I suggested we send you to collect the information."

"What's the storyline? Where will I be going?"

"Close to where you were before—Thailand. We're interested in getting behind both Thailand's successes and recent conflicts. You will need to focus on the advances made in their infrastructure that other Southeast Asian countries seem to have difficulty achieving."

Allison nodded her head. "You mentioned conflicts. Are you referring to the problems centered on the government?"

"Absolutely, I would like you to spend time in both Bangkok and northern Thailand, not as a journalist but as a tourist."

"Why a tourist?" Allison asked with a puzzled voice.

"You'd have a better chance of infiltrating amongst the people if they thought there was no hidden agenda. You know, get the inside story about their desires and concerns. There's also a real curiosity about life in the hill country— the area in The Golden Triangle. If you agree to accept this assignment, I'll give you an expense account and a local person as a guide for a month. Think about it and get back to me tomorrow."

"I don't need to think about it—when do I leave?"

Jim laughed as he got up from his chair and walked over to the table covered with papers, unopened manila envelopes, and stacks of folders waiting to be filed. From the pile, he pulled a fairly thick folder and handed it to her. "Read through this. Be ready to leave in two weeks."

"Perfect—it'll take me that long to finish my current project. Hey, I just realized Lan is living in Bangkok. I'll have to contact her."

"Lan?" asked Jim. "Oh, the young girl you managed to

rescue from the brothel in Cambodia. What's she doing in Thailand?"

"She took advantage of my offer to finance her schooling and recently completed her degree in clinical counseling and nursing. This past year she's worked at a Safe House in Bangkok counseling trafficked girls from Vietnam and Thailand. You know, Jim, after all she went through, she can relate to their problems and fears."

"I would think working in that field might keep wounds open and prevent her own healing."

"No, in any situation where rehab is needed, identifying with the problem and sharing personal stories with those afflicted can only be a win/win for everyone involved."

Jim nodded in agreement and fell back into his worn leather chair. The once animated man looked old showing deep wrinkles in his face and a rounded back that replaced the square shoulders of his younger days.

"How have you been feeling, Jim?" she asked.

"Good, why do you ask?"

"No reason, only that you look a little . . . you know . . . tired."

Jim swung his chair around and glanced out the large window behind him. "Yeah, I've been somewhat on the tired side. Age is creeping up on me as it does all of us." He turned back around and looked up at her. "Hey, I just had an idea. How about if we bring Lan over here for the awards ceremony? I can't think of anyone better to accompany us. I'll talk to the director of the Progley Foundation to see if funds could be released for that purpose."

Allison recognized Jim's clever divergence but chose to ignore it. "Really?" she said. "Now that would be a class act."

Chapter 2

LAN

"WHEN IS YOUR friend coming?" asked the Mae Chi.

"She's in the air right now and will be in Bangkok to-morrow morning. I'm beyond excited over seeing Allison again."

The Mae Chi pulled the white sleeves of her robe up and dipped her hands into the hot dishwater. She gently swished the rag around the plate and handed the clean dish to Lan. "Is this the lady who made it possible for you to attend school?"

Lan placed the dried dish onto the short stack ready to be put away. "Yes, without her I'm afraid I'd still be in Vietnam working in my grandmother's restaurant. Actually, I'd most likely still be in Cambodia working in Madame Kolab's brothel. She did so much for me that I could never repay her. So I did what she suggested—repay by giving to those who have a need."

The Mae Chi smiled and patted Lan on the shoulder. "Which is what you've been doing the past year. We are lucky that Yen brought to your attention our mission here at the Safe House."

"Well, after everything was over, Yen and I became close." Lan reached for her wrist and twisted the delicate orchid bracelet she always wore on her right hand. "It was this bracelet that bonded us. If Yen didn't tell Allison and my Uncle Trung about finding it, the probability of them locating me would have been slim. It's incredible how everything came together like it did."

"Did I hear my name?" asked the young novitiate, entering the kitchen.

"You sure did, Yen. We were discussing how my bracelet connected the two of us."

Yen's face grew somber as she remembered that difficult time in the silk factory. "And now Allison is coming. I hope to get the opportunity to talk to her because I never had the chance to thank her for what she did for me."

"She knows you're here," said Lan. "How would you like to come with me to pick her up at the airport tomorrow morning; that is, if you can be excused?"

The Mae Chi smiled. "If Yen wants to go, it's fine by me. We can switch our morning schedule to accommodate the change. I suppose, Lan, you might enjoy several days off to spend with your friend?"

"Really? Is that possible? I wanted to ask but didn't want to inconvenience anyone."

The Mae Chi walked over to the door, turned around and said, "No inconvenience, be off and enjoy. Just be sure to return, okay?" She looked at her watch. "Oh, it's getting late. I better prepare for meditation."

Lan walked over to the stove and poured herself a cup of tea. "Do you want a cup?" Yen nodded her head and sat at the large table set up in the center of the kitchen.

"We've come a long ways, haven't we, Lan? Do you think about the other girls? I've wondered what's happened to them. I know Kim and Thien are back with their family."

Lan took a sip of the tea and placed the cup gently in its saucer. "Ah huh, and I heard Linh is still living and working as a nanny with that French family in Cambodia."

"Linh wrote me awhile back," Yen said. "She's so happy living with them. She said they are her family now."

Lan nodded her head in agreement. "It's just as well after what her family did to her—sell her off to work in the silk factory. I can't blame her for not wanting anything to do with them. Her little boy must be four-years-old now."

Yen placed her chin in her hand and said, "Much like us, Linh's in a good place."

"Oh Yen, I am so sorry. How thoughtless of me," she said as she remembered that Yen's demise was not too different from Linh's."

"No need to apologize, Lan. As I said, we all are in a good place now."

At that moment, the chimes rang out calling everyone to the meditation room. Lan grabbed the two cups, placed them in the empty sink, and the girls hurried off to join the others.

Chapter 3

THE REUNION

"THERE SHE IS! Sa-wat-dee-kah," yelled Lan, waving at the Westerner, pulling a suitcase behind her.

"I'm here! It's been such a long time," Allison said as she grabbed ahold of Lan and gave her a big hug. "You're all grown up, Lan. How have you been? Are you enjoying your work here in Thailand?"

"Allison, I'm so excited to see you. My work here in Thailand is so fulfilling. Look, do you remember who this person is?" Lan asked, pulling Yen over to her.

Allison looked at the young Buddhist girl wearing the white robe. Her face was perfectly round, accentuated by the shaved head that characterized all Buddhist novitiates in order to rid themselves of any outward beauty. "Hmm . . . not sure. So I know you, huh? Wait a minute—are you Yen?"

Yen smiled. "You remember me even though I have no hair?"

Allison said, "Of course, I do. Just because your beautiful braid is gone, I can still see your sweet face. You can't chase that away. Now that I remember, you wanted to join the Buddhist nunnery. Are you happy, Yen?"

"Very much so, but here in Thailand women are not acknowledged or ordained as nuns as they are in Myanmar and Vietnam."

"I didn't know that, Yen. But your head is shaved and you're wearing a robe."

Yen grinned and patted her head. "In Thailand, we are known as Mae Chi. We take the eight precepts from a monk, but without any formal ordination ceremony."

"I see you have white robes instead of the pink."

"Yes, that distinguishes us from a nun. We are not recognized by the Thai government and don't have the same privileges a monk or a Vietnamese nun would have; but like a nun, we are not allowed to vote in civil elections."

"Do you live in a monastery?" asked Allison.

"Some do, but their role is like a servant or staff member. Those of us not attached to a local monastery are expected to provide for ourselves. The order I joined lives at the Thai Safe House where we've counseled and helped trafficked girls."

"What a wonderful service you are providing, Yen."

"I owe so much to you and Lan's uncle."

Allison laughed. "I guess we tracked you girls down much like a momma bear looking for her cubs, huh? That jerk, Banh, got what he deserved. Lan, your Uncle Trung told me he's still in jail. I hope they keep him there for a long time."

Lan grabbed Allison's luggage and led the way to her car. "How about some lunch and then we'll drive you to the hotel?"

The girls got onto the highway that lead from Bangkok's International Airport and started the long drive into the city. As Allison looked out the window, she viewed a city quite different from Ho Chi Minh. Everywhere she looked she noticed high-rises that framed a variety of elevated highways. The buildings were contemporary; but as she took a closer look and peered downward, she saw many corrugated shacks with tin roofs. Cranes stretched like metal giraffes showing the progress new construction brought with it. Unlike the thousands of motorbikes that invaded the streets of Vietnam, here there were cars. Everyone seemed to own either a Toyota or a Honda. If they weren't driving their own vehicle, they were in a yellow and green taxi.

"Allison, I bet you're thinking Bangkok is different from Ho Chi Minh," Lan said as she steered the vehicle into the passing lane.

"You read my mind. This place has the same energy found in New York City. I'm guessing you've adjusted to this new life."

"I have. I do miss the quiet of Con Quy Island; but right now, I could not go back."

Allison looked to her left in time to spot a polished chrome train speed by. "Is that part of Bangkok's subway system?"

"We call it the Sky Train," Yen said from the back seat of the car. "Commuters who can afford it, take the Sky Train to avoid this traffic congestion."

Lan pointed to a series of elevated walkways that stretched over the road. "These link the Sky Train stations to the newly built shopping malls and offices."

"Another choice we have is the underground which we call the MRT," said Yen. "Many people prefer this because it's more affordable than the Sky Train."

Allison nodded her head in surprise as she realized her misguided assumption that Bangkok would be in an earlier stage of development. She opened her notebook to record her first impressions of this large Southeast Asian city. As they approached the city center, she noticed how the new started to mix with the old. Deteriorated apartments blended with modern condos. High-rises stood amongst typical concrete buildings found in other Asian cities. She noted wooded areas and sometimes an empty lot scattered with garbage. Similar to Western cities, billboards competed with apartment houses and glass paneled buildings for space. This glass reflected the traffic which came to an abrupt crawl.

"We're not far from your hotel, Allison," said Lan, "but first we're going to this neighborhood restaurant that a lot of business people enjoy. Do you like Thai food?"

"Sure, sounds great," said Allison. "Anything over the airplane food I've been eating the past twenty-three hours."

Upon leaving the highway, she spotted the typical narrow shops with garage-type doors to close things off after business hours. Resembling Vietnam, these stores shared sidewalk space with street vendors selling baskets, ice cream, and cheap jewelry. Street after street, the scene repeated itself until, as if resulting from the wave of a magical wand, a more modern and sophisticated boulevard suddenly appeared.

Pointing to the right side of the street, Lan said, "We are entering Silom Road. Many of our older neighborhoods are being bulldozed and replaced with these tall buildings."

"How long has this been going on, Lan?"

"I wasn't here when the development started, but from what I heard much of what you see took place in the past decade. Here on Silom Road you will notice the greatest concentration of offices, upscale department stores, and hotels. Bangkok's increased tourist trade has resulted in a growing number of restaurants and hotels."

"When did Thailand start capitalizing on the tourist trade?" Allison asked, jotting down notes.

Yen replied, "I heard it was around the time of the American War with Vietnam."

"Hmm . . . really? Now that's interesting."

"Yes, I guess with the war going on in the 70's, many American soldiers came into Bangkok for their R&R causing the hurried construction of hotels, nightclubs, and bars," said Yen. "Many of these buildings were not built well which brought on the question of whether destroying the old historic buildings justified this."

Lan said, "As a result, now we have these concrete and glass high-rises. Personally, I don't think they can compete with the earlier teak buildings of Siam, topped with their curly, curved roofs."

Allison said, "I know what you mean. Sometimes the easier and cheaper fix is to demolish and rebuild without taking into account the centuries of historic loss."

Lan sighed. "That's the sign of the times." She pulled the car alongside the road and parked in front of a small restaurant with a large, bronzed Buddha in front. "We'll eat here, okay? Today we'll spend time in this neighborhood and tomorrow I will take you to the older section of Bangkok—much better, you will see."

After a fabulous Thai lunch of deep fried chicken wrapped in Pandan leaves, Lan and Yen drove Allison to her hotel. "I suggest you take a shower and get some sleep," said Lan. "Is 9:00 good for tomorrow's pick-up?

Allison laughed. "You must be a mind-reader. Nine o'clock is perfect."

Chapter 4

BANGKOK

"SAWADDEE TORN CHAO" (*good morning)*, Allison. How did you sleep?" asked Lan.

"I slept quite well, thank you."

"First Thai lesson . . . you say, 'Dee, kob-khun-kha'. Kob-khun means thank you; but because you are a lady, you always say kha at the end whether you are addressing a man or a woman. So it's kob-khun-kha. If a man says thank you, he says kob-khun-krub."

"I better write all that in my notebook as I'll never re-member it. Lan, I do have a question for you. Everyone I've run into greeted me this way." Allison put the palms of both hands together and bowed her head. "It didn't matter who it was—the housekeeper, the breakfast greeter, or even a person entering the elevator. Am I expected to return that gesture?"

Lan laughed. "Yes, the Thai people are always smiling and showing respect whether you are coming or going."

"I don't recall that being done in Vietnam."

"You're right about that. The Thai people call this greet-ing the *wai* which is their way of paying respect. Next time, notice the higher the hands are raised, the greater the respect is shown. It's always proper for a younger person, or some-one of lower status, to be the first to wai. Then the senior person can return the gesture."

"So tell me, how is it done?" Allison asked.

"For greeting most people, you bow your head and with the palms together, touch the tips of your thumbs to the heart. For a teacher or someone of higher status, the hands go to the mouth. If you are greeting your parents, the fingers go to the nose; but to a monk or Buddha, the hands are elevated to the forehead. If lucky and you are greeting the King or royal family, then always bow with the hands over your head."

"Hmm . . . that's very interesting. The greeting to the royal family is of a higher level than your Buddha. I can see I've got a lot to learn."

"Chai *(Yes)*, but you don't have to know everything this minute, right? Everyone here knows you are a farang. I've been here for over a year, and I'm a farang."

"What's that?" Allison asked as the car pulled out into traffic.

"It's a foreigner. People here will look at you and call you that. 'She's a farang,' they will say."

A short time later they were on a two lane road that didn't just have Toyotas and Hondas mixed in with taxis and cheap buses, but also tuk-tuks and motor bikes. Few traffic lights existed, and the scene could adequately be described as chaotic.

"So I thought we'd go to the Grand Palace today. How does that sound?" asked Lan.

"The Grand Palace—is that where the royal family lives? Is it possible to go inside?"

"No, the royal family has not lived in this palace since 1925. Now it's pretty much used for dignitaries from other countries. You know, until it was designated as the Thai capital in 1782, Bangkok was nothing more than a fort built to protect the country from its enemies coming up the Chao Phraya River."

"Is that the river that runs through Bangkok?"

"Yes. This place turned into an island city after the digging of many canals. King Rama I decided to build the royal palace as the focal point—like a city within a city. What we'll be visiting is not just a palace, but a collection of about 100 buildings within its walls. The Wat Phra Kaeo, which means Temple of the Emerald Buddha, is included and is the country's most important temple."

"I'm guessing the word *wat* means temple."

Lan nodded. "You will be hearing that word quite often."

The two girls strolled up to the gate that separated the Grand Palace from the rest of the city. They paid their entrance fee and began the long walk leading to the temple.

"Okay, tell me why this is such an important temple?" Allison asked.

"What makes this important is the Emerald Buddha. I find it interesting that the Buddha is not actually made of emerald, but carved from a single piece of green jasper. It's only 27-inches which is not tall compared to the other Buddhas you'll be seeing, but its importance is not in the size. I think you mentioned you'll be visiting Chiang Rai."

"Yes, after I leave Bangkok I'm traveling north."

"Well, this Emerald Buddha was first discovered in Chiang Rai. The legend has it that lightning struck and split open an old chedi resulting in its discovery."

"What's a chedi?" asked Allison, slipping off her shoes and placing them on a rack next to the temple door.

"A chedi is another word for stupa. They are tall, dome-shaped structures housing the relics of the Buddha."

"You've aroused my curiosity, Lan. What happened when this Buddha was found?"

"The King ordered it to be taken to Chiang Mai, but the elephant carrying it refused to travel. The king took this as an omen and instead placed it in the city of Lampang. Eventually, the statue ended up in Laos. When the Thai king's army defeated the Lao in the late 18th century, he triumphantly brought the Emerald Buddha back to Thailand and placed it inside the Wat Phra Kaeo."

Allison stood for a moment and soaked up the warmth of the morning sun that reflected off the wat's roof. The gold-leafed pillars framed the blue and gold mosaic patterns that covered the temple's façade. Looking closer, she saw tiny pieces of colored glass inside these mosaics. Appreciating the craftsmanship, she realized how difficult a task it would be to duplicate this masterpiece. Two giant demons called yaksas stood guard at the door of the wat. Lan briefly explained that the yaksa's role was to bar the entry of any evil spirits.

Allison stopped to take a photo of one of the statues. Its shoes, curved at the toe, revealed the Siamese clothing style of a time long since gone. The dress of each yaksa matched the gold and blue mosaics of the temple's façade. A golden hat, ending with a spire resembling that of the cheti, accentuated the pair of piercing eyes on its demonic face. Each yaksa was armed with a wide club that extended down to the base of the pedestal.

"Utterly beautiful," was all Allison could say.

"When we go inside, we are not able to take photos, Allison. The rule we follow for any of the temples in Thailand is if you see sky, you can take a picture. If you don't see sky? Well then, not allowed."

The inside of the temple was high but not wide. In the center was the Emerald Buddha which sat upon a tiered altar resembling a massive wedding cake. Beneath this Buddha were several rows of gold-plated figurines that alternated between the Sitting Buddha and the Garuda.

Back outside, the girls slipped on their shoes and walked the grounds to locate the Grand Palace which turned out to be in sharp contrast.

"This looks so European," said Allison. "If I had to compare it to something, it would be a snowy-white Buckingham Palace with gold spires."

Lan laughed. "Yes, I agree. The architecture of this building is definitely a blend of European and Thai styles." They walked along the stone path bordering the plush green grass until they came upon what looked like dancing trees with its branches sculptured into rounded balls. Everything was impeccably groomed.

As they headed back to the gate, they encountered a group of five soldiers dressed in fatigues, boots, and helmets. Each carried a rifle that rested over his left shoulder. "Are they here because of the recent demonstrations against the government?" asked Allison.

"Yes, we've had several episodes."

"Could we go to where these demonstrators are camped out?" Allison asked.

Lan stopped and looked at her friend. "No, you don't want to go there. Not a smart thing to do."

Just as she was about to insist, she remembered Jim's words. *You're presenting yourself as a tourist, not a journalist.* So instead she nodded in agreement, but secretly decided to slip out later and go on her own.

Chapter 5

SARUT AND DENG

"WHAT DO YOU mean you can't find her?" asked the Thai man as he threw his cigarette onto the floor and butted it with the toe of his boot.

"No kidding, Deng. You don't understand. I had her in my view at the airport until she disappeared on me."

"Sarut, we are talking millions of bahts *(Thai currency)* here. You've got to get it back. Explain again how she ended up with the brooch."

"Listen, Deng, I sat next to her on the flight from Tokyo. She told me she was off to Bangkok to visit a friend. I asked if anyone was traveling with her, and she said she was alone. I tried to ignore her, but she kept chatting away. Why do some American women always like to talk to strangers?"

"Did she tell you about the friend?"

"No, and at the time it didn't seem important."

"Well, there's your first mistake."

"I tried to ignore her by pretending to be asleep. It was when she got up to use the bathroom that I came up with the idea. You see, I worried someone at airport security would discover the brooch on me. I figured by the time I arrived in Bangkok, the store would be aware of its disappearance and the scrutiny of passengers departing from Tokyo would be tight. I figured this lady was my solution. Besides being an American, her innocent appearance would not raise any suspicion. Security would let her through especially seeing her travel didn't begin in Tokyo."

"So what did you do with the brooch? Where did you put it?"

Sarut sipped his coffee, shook his head and looked straight at Deng. "The cabin was dim and everyone was asleep. When she left her seat, I reached for her backpack that rested on the floor. I spotted a slight rip in the main compartment's lining so that's where I put it."

"You stuck it inside a ripped lining?"

"Yes, Deng, that's what I said. I put it inside the lining. I didn't want her to see it, so I thought that was a perfect spot. I planned on grabbing the bag in the airport's Arrival Hall, thinking she'd be distracted."

"Okay, Sarut, what went wrong with this brilliant plan of yours?"

"What I didn't count on were the three other planes that showed up at the exact time as ours. It was crazy. People were in lines everywhere. She had to go through the foreigner line at customs while security directed me through the Thai citizen line."

"You didn't know that would happen?" asked Deng.

"No, I didn't remember. I guess I forgot."

"So what you're saying is you didn't think this out, did you?"

"Hey, security was tight coming here, and I needed to make a quick decision. It would be all over if customs found that brooch on me. I took a chance and by the time I got through, I could no longer find her. She vanished."

Deng banged his fist on the table causing the coffee to spill. He stared at Sarut and shook his head in disgust.

"Sarut, check this out." Sarut picked up the newspaper laying in front of him and read the headlines:

VALUED THAI BROOCH
STOLEN FROM TOKYO JEWELERS

Pointing his finger at him, he said, "All that planning and all that risk—for what, I ask? We have nothing. What am I going to tell Naai Montri? Bangkok is a city of millions of people. How are we going to find this American woman and the brooch?"

"I have an idea. The girl asked me many questions about the Red Shirt protests—you know, the stuff behind the demonstrations. I tried changing the subject, but she wasn't interested in any other topic. I think if we go to the site where the Red Shirt demonstrators are camped, we might see her. It might be a slim possibility, but we have no other ideas, right?"

"I don't want to get mixed up in politics, Sarut. What those damn Red and Yellow Shirt people are doing—I can't be bothered! What did you tell her about the demonstrations?"

"I told you I tried changing the subject, but she kept asking."

"Well, did you tell her anything?" Deng asked as he waved to the waiter requesting the bill.

Sarut finished his coffee and stood up to leave. "Stuff like how the Red Shirts want to keep Yingluck in office, while the Yellow Shirts want a re-election because the last one was rigged. I say we go and look around the encampment. I have this strong feeling we'll see her there; and Deng, be sure to wear a red shirt."

"I'm not wearing any red shirt. This government protest is a total disruption of business."

"Deng, I don't view it that way. I see these protests as a distraction, heh? The more the news reporters are occupied with the protests, the less attention will be given to the brooch. Now don't be a stubborn fool—blend in and wear the damn red shirt."

Chapter 6

LUMPINI PARK

THE CAB MOVED slowly as it made its way along the gridlocked streets of Bangkok. Allison sat in the back trying to decide what her plan of attack would be once she arrived. Although the hotel concierge explained that the Red Shirt protesters had set up their tent campsites in Lumpini Park, he tried to persuade her not to go. "So many other good things to do while in Bangkok."

When the cab approached Sukhumvit Road, she caught sight of hundreds of tents set up all over central Bangkok's only green space. Scattered throughout were several stages, port-a-johns, and a variety of food stalls tended by vendors. The Red Shirt encampment resembled a city within a city. Soldiers, dressed in uniforms similar to the ones she saw the day before at the Grand Palace, sat behind camouflaged sandbag bunkers in order to maintain order. The taxi driver informed Allison that only a few days earlier the camp had been under a series of attacks by the Yellow Shirt people. "They might be well-dressed," he said, "but they got ahold of one Red Shirt demonstrator and tortured the poor fellow."

"Was he killed?" asked Allison.

"No, he was a lucky one. He was rescued after being dumped into the river."

"How is all this going to end?" Allison asked.

"Not sure, but I can tell you the leader of the Yellow

Shirts, the military brass, business leaders, and the King's advisers have had little success unseating the Prime Minister."

"Suthep Thaugsuban—is that who's the leader of the Yellow Shirts?"

The cab pulled over to the side, and the driver turned off his engine. "Yes, the leader of the People's Democratic Reform Committee—that's what they call themselves. He promises to replace the current government with an unelected council that would carry out reforms."

"Tell me . . . why are the Yellow Shirts against this current administration? This is a democracy and the people elected the Prime Minister. Couldn't this all wait until the next election?"

"It goes deeper. The Prime Minister is the sister of the former minister, Thaksin Shinawatra, who was accused of corruption. He got on the good side of the poor farmers of northern Thailand by making many advances for them; such as the building of roads, granting them universal health care, and providing loans for schools."

"Why is that a bad thing?" asked Allison.

"That's where the corruption comes into play. The firms hired were owned by his cronies. They all became wealthy, including the former prime minister, while Thailand's debt increased."

"But people re-elected him, didn't they?"

"Sure, all these farmers from up north and other poor peasants banded together and voted for him. When found guilty of corruption by the courts, he escaped and now lives in Dubai. So what did this political party do? They got behind his sister and elected her. People against this government say she is like—what you say—a puppet and does what her brother tells her to do.

Allison thought about what the cab driver just told her and asked, "So are you saying that the Yellow Shirts want her removed because they believe her landslide election was rigged through vote-buying?"

"That's exactly what I'm saying," he said.

"Are most of the Yellow Shirts from Bangkok and the south of Thailand?"

The cab driver nodded in agreement. "The Yellow Shirts are made up of Bangkok's middle and upper classes as well as the southern part of Thailand. These people are also royalists. You know we have a monarchy, but our King is mainly a figurehead."

Allison said, "Yes, much like Great Britain." Allison paid the cab driver his fare and said, "Keep the change."

Thinking this pretty Western tourist was unaware of the currency value, he reached out to return some of the bahts. "You gave me too much."

Allison smiled in appreciation of the honesty of this man. "I want you to have it. You've been very helpful."

"Kob khun krub," the driver said, placing his palms together and bowing his head. Allison stood by the side of the road and watched the green taxi disappear into the city's smog. She felt the small, smooth stone inside her skirt's pocket which she rubbed whenever insecurity overwhelmed her. Like magic, this worry stone absorbed all the tension from her body.

Allison walked around bunkers topped with barbed wire forming a temporary wall around the encampment. Although only mid-morning, Bangkok reached scorching hot temps, and she wondered if the sweat streaming down her neck resulted from the heat or from anxiety—perhaps both.

A man stood on the stage talking to the crowd as they

occasionally cheered. The language barrier proved to be a definite problem for Allison as she had no idea what he said. She spent the better part of an hour walking around and observing people. She singled out one particular young girl sitting on a plastic chair eating what looked like pumpkin in coconut milk. From her, Allison learned that 2010 was the last time the Red Shirts took over Bangkok. The girl explained how they occupied a shopping district in the center of the city for over two months. When a military crackdown was ordered, the city was in flames and nearly 100 people were dead.

"So tell me," Allison asked the girl, "what is the guy saying over the loudspeaker?"

"He's saying that we can't rely on anyone—not the military, not the police, no one but ourselves."

The girl's boyfriend came over and sat by them as they talked. After listening for a little while, he added, "We believe in nonviolence, but we are willing to sacrifice our lives if necessary."

Allison shrugged her shoulders. "Let's hope that won't be necessary."

"Some Red Shirt supporters aren't optimistic about solving this through negotiations, but I hope both sides can compromise," said the girl.

Her friend quickly added, "But if they can't, we will see what happens."

Allison thanked the two and quickly excused herself. She walked amongst the tents and avoided the litter that a temporary community often produced. She wondered why people didn't pick up their trash, but then recognized the lack of available receptacles.

Standing by one of the vendor stalls was an elderly

farmer. Allison walked up to him and asked if he spoke English. He shook his head, but a teenage boy standing nearby overheard the question and said he did. Allison was anxious to get this older man's perspective of what was happening and how he felt about it. "Is this gentleman with you?" she asked.

"Yes, he's my grandfather," the young boy said.

"Could you ask your grandfather why he supports the current Prime Minister?"

The boy posed this question to the older man. Allison waited as the man dramatically spouted his opinions of the Yellow Shirts. Although she could not understand, she patiently listened until the younger teen carefully translated.

"My grandfather said that this administration has done much for northern Thailand. Before, we did not have the services Bangkok has, few people could get medical care, and our children didn't have good schools."

The old man listened to his translated words. He nodded his head and smiled showing several missing front teeth. When the boy finished, the old man continued to talk and then motioned for his grandson to tell this Western lady more.

"My grandfather wanted me to tell you that the Prime Minister and her brother arranged for their towns to have good roads. Several years ago we had dirt paths, but now we have paved roads, good electricity, and even internet."

Allison understood how these improvements could win over the people, but decided she needed to find a group of Yellow Shirts to hear their perspective. They certainly would not be found here at this site.

The sea of people that surrounded Allison could easily be viewed as one solid entity, and much harder to single out any one individual. But it wasn't the crowd that piqued her interest. So she forced herself to focus on each person—their mannerisms, interactions with others, and how receptive each was listening to the speaker. As a journalist, she learned a lot could be learned by stepping back and watching. That was when she spotted him. Was that not the fellow who sat beside her on the plane? Although she never learned his name, she reacted as though she knew him. She wondered if he noticed her, too; but decided possibly not since he quickly turned and melted into the crowd.

"Deng, there she is—over there by that stall talking to some old guy. I'm afraid she saw me."

"Keep an eye on her, but move on and definitely don't strike up any conversation."

After blending into the crowd, Deng said, "Sarut, you were right about coming here. I thought it impossible to find her amongst all these people. We were lucky, but keep your eyes glued because we must not lose sight of her now."

"Do you have a plan?" asked Sarut.

"First, we follow her to see where she's staying—most likely a hotel. You said you didn't get that information, right?"

Sarut shrugged his shoulders. "Didn't realize I needed it."

"I don't see any backpack with her so it must be in the hotel room. If we can find a way of getting into the room while she's gone, we can grab the brooch and no one will know the difference."

"I better not go along, Deng. She will become suspicious

if she sees me, but she doesn't know you. Call me when you find out something."

Twenty minutes later, Deng climbed into a taxi and told the driver to follow the cab in front.

Chapter 7

CHINATOWN

LAN SHOOK HER head. "Going to the encampment by yourself was not a good idea, Allison. How did you even know where to go?"

Amused, Allison thought back to when she first met this young girl. Lan's uncle had accompanied the reporter to Lan's grandmother's restaurant on Con Quy Island in the Mekong Delta. Lan was waiting on tables and came over to greet her uncle. She had graduated from high school and expressed how she planned to accept a stranger's financial help to further her studies. Allison nervously expressed her reservations over this proposal, but Lan paid little heed and ultimately ended up in a mess—a human trafficking mess. How ironic that only a few years later, the roles reversed, and Lan is now chastising Allison for taking on foolish risks.

"I know what you're saying, but really—I had no problems," Allison said, hoping to reassure the young driver as she navigated the car through the early afternoon traffic. "The concierge advised where to go and I called a cab. Pretty much all I did was chat with a few Red Shirt people about why they were in favor of keeping the current prime minister."

"Were all your questions answered?"

"No, not really. I need to talk to people who are not in favor of the current administration—the Yellow shirts."

Lan said, "You should have little problem finding them in Bangkok. I fear this conflict will result in a civil war. Things quiet down for a while only to later explode."

"Much like a dormant volcano," said Allison, "appearing to be extinct but ready to cause damage when least expected."

"That's it . . . exactly. Look, Chinatown is over to your right; that's where we're headed."

The Thai sun was getting quite strong so Allison reached for her purse and pulled out her sunglasses. "It seems all major cities have a Chinatown."

"Yeah . . . here in Bangkok, Chinatown is almost as old as the city itself. You'll find this to be a place for much trade and commerce."

"What kinds of trade are we talking about, Lan?"

"Oh, you'll see crowded alleys filled with gold shops, market stalls, and craft workshops. This road we are on now? It's called Charoen Krung which means *new road*. Not looking too new, huh?"

"I remember my family put an addition onto our house back when I was a kid, and through the years we always referred to it as the new room. I'm guessing a little of that is happening here."

Lan laughed as she slid the car into a parking spot by the side of the road. "The construction of this *new* road took place in the mid-1800s. Before that, would you believe it used to be an elephant path?"

"That's awesome," said Allison. She reached over to the backseat and grabbed her camera and backpack. "Not many places can claim that honor. I know we don't have any elephant paths in America. I'm sure after it became a paved road, it allowed easier access to wheeled traffic."

Lan nodded. "The downside is the river and canals became less important to the city since they were no longer Bangkok's main transportation routes."

"I find that to be a normal occurrence, Lan. In order for progress to happen, some aspects of the old are sacrificed. Sometimes it's difficult to let go of old ways."

Lan said, "Yes, even though the Chao Phraya River is no longer the country's main highway, it's still the main channel for bulk cargoes like rice, sand and cement. Local people still use it, but not like earlier times."

"Where does the river empty?" Allison asked, stepping out of the car.

"Into the Gulf of Thailand about 25 miles south of here. Later today I plan to take you to the Floating Markets. Is that something you'd be interested in?"

"Sounds like a wonderful idea," Allison said, her eyes scanning the long, narrow street. "You know, right now I'm thinking this is not like any Chinatown I've ever seen."

The girls weaved amongst the throngs of people buying and selling. Allison took several photos of the carts lined up like train cars. Unlike the crudely constructed, wooden stalls in Vietnam, these colorful, sophisticated push-carts sat atop of three bicycle wheels–a large one on each side of the cart and a smaller wheel in front. These well-designed vehicles allowed for no wasted space. On the top surface rested a refrigerated chest positioned next to either a stainless cooking pot or a small grill. Tucked to the side of the cart was a folded umbrella that could easily be pulled out and raised to protect from either rain or sun.

The blend of smells predominated the neighborhood as black chicken from one wagon mixed with the aromatic spices of the bird's nest soup brewed from the adjacent vendor's cart. On the next corner, permanent stalls displayed sea cucumbers and shark fins. Allison stopped to photograph the colorful abundance of food paying particular attention to the unique displays.

Pointing to an elongated crème-colored item, Allison asked, "So what's this? I'm thinking, perhaps an intestine?"

"That's called fish maw. These internal gas-filled organs are found in large fish and resemble bladders. Would you like to try it?"

Allison wrinkled her nose. "How do you turn that into something edible?"

Lan smiled, realizing this item would be low on Allison's *must try* list. "Often it's served in soups or stews and is considered to be a delicacy in China."

"Really? Okay then, I'll take your word for it. Now here's something that looks familiar," she said, approaching bins of apples, lemons, limes and tomatoes. "This I can handle."

"Come over here, Allison, I want to tell you about this." Lan stood in front of paper replicas of real items—passports, plane tickets, pants, credit cards and even underwear. "People buy these items for a loved one who passed on. The family places the articles with the deceased so that upon reincarnation the necessities of life will be available."

"But these are only paper versions," said Allison.

"They are actually burned with the body," Lan said, picking up a package with a paper shirt inside.

Allison always found it interesting to learn about the beliefs of people from other cultures. She had concluded long ago that appreciation and tolerance often followed if we'd respect the differences of other countries, even though we may not understand. The practice of paper relics and the ingestion of fish maw fell quite nicely in that category.

Chapter 8

ENTANGLEMENT

"THIS IS A travesty," said the jewelry store owner to the marubo-dekka *(Japanese detective)*. "Tell the marubo what you told me, Keerati."

Keerati shifted from one foot to the next as perspiration beaded on his forehead. With a great deal of difficulty, he managed to explain what happened late that afternoon. "Around 4:00, a man walked into the store asking to see some nice jewelry for his wife. He said he needed a gift for a special occasion. He looked in our display case for several minutes before he picked out three rings, including an expensive 4-carat diamond. He examined them and asked many questions. Then he pointed to the Royal Thai brooch that we've had on display since acquiring it at an auction."

The marubo-dekka interrupted and asked, "Can you tell me why the store purchased such an expensive item?"

"I can answer that," the store owner said. "I became interested in acquiring the Royal Barge brooch as a promotion for our store. I planned to display it for a year, and then donate it to the museum in Tokyo. Until today, we've had much success with many people stopping in to see it. We hope while they are here, they will see something they like to buy."

The detective turned to Keerati and asked, "How was the customer able to steal this brooch?"

"He asked if he could see it up close. I didn't think there

was any harm so I pulled the brooch out, and we talked about it for a while. He seemed interested in knowing the pin's history after I told him how the piece once belonged to Thailand's King Rama V's first wife."

The detective asked, "Were you ever suspicious of his behavior?"

"No, many people come in to take a look at the brooch."

The store owner said, "Keerati, you never should have removed the brooch from the case."

"I understand, but this customer was different—you know, accustomed to fine things."

"How was he able to walk off with it?" asked the detective.

"He distracted me. He told me he had difficulty deciding which ring his wife would like so he thought he'd bring her in to make the choice. He asked for a business card with my name and work schedule so he could give me the business. I gladly wrote that information down, handed the card to him, and he left. As I returned the rings back into the case, I noticed the brooch was missing and could not find it anywhere."

The marubo-dekka said nothing, but studied the clerk's face. He observed the more he questioned him, the more flustered he became. Finally, he asked for a description of the brooch.

"It was in the shape of a Royal Barge with three oarsmen and a Garuda as a figurehead."

The store owner said, "The Garuda had many rubies and diamonds while numerous cuts of emeralds and sapphires were found on the oarsmen. Pure gold accented with diamonds filled out the background."

The detective wrote the description in his notebook. "Sounds like a work of art."

"Definitely," said the owner, "but the main focal point was the four-carat diamond that hung from the Garuda's neck—an exquisite piece of jewelry."

The detective looked up from his notes and said, "I'm sure that in addition to its monetary worth, there's also historic value. How much is the brooch valued at?"

The store owner explained they had documents valuing it over 200 million Japanese yens or about 66 million Thai bahts.

The detective stared at the owner. "Hadn't your store put a policy in place to prevent this kind of thing from happening?"

"Yes, we have strict procedures," said the owner, glaring at Keerati and shaking his head. "Our policy is to show only one piece of jewelry at a time. Before another piece is pulled out, the first one must be secured in the display case. At no time should that brooch ever have been removed from the display case."

The marubo-dekka asked, "So, Mr. Keerati, you didn't follow this policy?"

Keerati looked away. "I've no excuse except the man was friendly and interested in jewelry. He said he needed to leave but would return with his wife. Hey, I was anxious to make a sale."

The marubo-dekka scrutinized the shop and noted the two surveillance cameras. "Are these the only surveillance cameras you have in the store?"

The store owner pointed out one other camera, and the three went into the backroom to view the earlier recorded footage. As described by the clerk, an image of a man shopping for rings appeared.

"Is that him?" asked the marubo-dekka.

"Yes, here I am showing the customer the brooch, and now you see me looking for a business card to give him," said Keerati.

"There . . . see that?" The store owner stopped the tape to focus on the customer slipping the brooch into his pocket. "Now he's shaking Keerati's hand and walking out the door."

"Just like I told you," Keerati said, relieved. At that moment, I hadn't noticed the brooch was missing."

The marubo-dekka jotted down a few notes in his book. "I'll be taking this tape with me as evidence. It appears our thief is of Thai descent."

"The brooch is missing! An American lady has it!" shouted Naai Montri, visibly irritated as he yelled into the phone.

"How could it be missing?" argued the harried voice on the other end.

Montri said, "How the hell do I know! Was I there? No! Do you understand the risks I took pulling this off?"

"Oh, you took risks? What about me? Kee *(shit)*!"

Montri walked over to the sofa and kicked the leg. "That stupid bastard, Sarut, came up with this idea of putting the pin in this American's backpack to get through security, and then lost sight of the farang *(foreigner)* in the airport."

"Montri, I'm finding it difficult to understand this stupidity. It's best I return."

Montri's face turned scarlet red as he pounded the table with his fist. "Look, Big K, the time is not good. Don't do anything stupid. Largone *(good-bye)*."

FREDDIE REMZA

Montri slammed the phone down, stood up and started to pace like a caged animal. It became obvious what had to be done, but it was unwise to carry it out now. It would have to wait. He continued to pace until the ring of his phone interrupted his thoughts.

"Chai," said Montri, agitated.

"Montri, this is Deng."

"Do you have the pin?" asked Montri.

"No, but I devised a plan. I followed the girl to her hotel and into the elevator to find what floor she's on. It's the fifth."

"Good . . . so you know where she is?"

"Yeah—Room 513. I inquired at the reception desk which rooms were available on the fifth floor. Room 516 was and so I took it."

"Good, Deng—I'm glad someone is thinking. How do you plan to get the brooch?"

"It appears she's here for a few nights so tomorrow I will wait for her to leave for the day. When housekeeping arrives to clean the room, I'll break in and search for the bag."

"Is that idiot with you?" asked Montri.

"Who? Sarut? No, we thought it better if the girl never saw me with Sarut so not to raise suspicion. She'd recognize him from the plane."

"Yeah, yeah . . . probably a smart move. Deng, keep this to yourself. When the time is right, I want you to take him out." Montri heard no response, only a dead silence. "Deng—you there?

"Yeah, I am. Are you saying you want me to take out Sarut?"

"When the time is right—be prepared. I'll tell you when. Another problem—Big K is nervous and jerky. I told him to lay low until we find the brooch. You'll have it soon, right?"

"Yeah—I should."

"What do you mean you *should?*"

"Hey, relax! I'll have it."

Chapter 9

THE FLOATING MARKET

"HI THERE, JIM. Allison calling from amazing Thailand."

"Good to hear from you. How's everything going?"

"Not bad . . . I managed to work myself into the Red Shirt encampment and discovered what that's all about. I need to interview a few of the Yellow Shirts to get their perspective. Lan has been so helpful showing me around Bangkok. This city has it over Ho Chi Minh as far as advancement in their infrastructure, but I'm anxious to check out the situation once I get out of Bangkok and into more rural areas."

"What are you up to today?" asked Jim.

"This morning we are going to this place called the Pak Klong Talad Floating Market. I'm excited because I'll be in touch with a part of Thailand's past. It'll be a terrific contrast to the skyscrapers found in modern Bangkok."

"Tell me about modern Bangkok," said Jim.

"To give you an idea, think of how most of Bangkok's business once existed along the river and canals. Since the last half of the 20th century, expansion took place away from these riverbanks and into an area called Silom. One of the streets in Silom is Sathorn Road which used to be a street divided by a tree-lined canal. It changed from this charming street to an eight-lane thoroughfare running next to muddy water contained only by a wall."

"Yeah, sometimes advancements are not necessarily improvements," said Jim.

"You're right," said Allison. "Thailand, with all of its canals, shifted from being a city like Venice into a metropolis resembling Los Angeles. Cars have replaced the boats."

"So much change since the mid-1900's."

"Yeah, it seems the Vietnam War encouraged the advance of Thailand's development because the American soldiers would come here for their R&R. Isn't that amazing? Well, I need to shove off and meet up with Lan. Besides, the housekeeper is here to clean my room. I'll talk to you later or as they say in Thai—largone."

Allison picked up her purse and headed for the door when she thought about exchanging it for her backpack, just in case she made any purchases. She took her wallet out and placed the purse in a drawer she found in the closet. Leaving the room, she told the housekeeper that the room was now all hers.

The maid placed her hands together in the custom wai, bowed her head and said, "Khob khun kha."

From across the hall, Deng peered through his door's peep hole ready to make his entrance into Room 513. The peep hole allowed a distorted, elongated view of a petite woman closing the door of her room. He waited until he was certain the woman entered the elevator, and then slowly opened his door. He walked by Room 513 and observed the housekeeper washing the tub in the bathroom. Pulling the room's key card from the wall slot, he quickly replaced it with a substitute found on the housekeeping cart left unattended in the hallway. This needed to done so not to shut off the room's power. He returned to his room and placed the "Do Not Disturb" sign on his doorknob. Deng decided to wait until after the maid finished cleaning but before she realized someone switched the key card. Feeling a bit smug, what he hadn't counted on was that the American girl took the backpack with her.

"Bangkok has four of these markets," said Lan. "Each is located on a klong as a reminder of how this city use to be."

"So what's a klong?" asked Allison.

"That's the Thai word for canal."

Standing on an overhead bridge that connected one side of the canal to the other, Allison noted the hundreds of boats—some took tourists for rides, several transported fresh flowers, while still other boats were chock-full of produce. Both men and women, wearing straw hats to block the hot sun from their eyes, navigated their way through the murky waters using only one paddle. It was amazing to see how so many boats could be jammed into this narrow channel of water. Alongside the canal, a person could sit upon a plastic stool and eat a breakfast of coconut pancakes or be served rice with seafood for lunch. Intermixed amongst these food stations were wooden stalls tended by smiling vendors anxious to hawk their cheap souvenirs.

"It's good you are here to see this, Allison, because even Thailand's floating markets are beginning to change. Instead of a place where locals come to shop for their daily supplies, the markets are transitioning into a tourist photo-op."

Allison shrugged her shoulders. "I thought the same

thing, Lan. There's no longer an urgent need for the traditional selling of vegetables and fruits from a small boat."

Lan said, "You can see why so many tourists come here. It does make for beautiful photos, don't you think? Check out the colors of the vegetables mixed in with the reds, oranges, and yellows of the flowers."

Allison pointed to a boat unloading a pile of large melon-looking fruit. "What's that called?"

"That's star fruit. You probably don't see that very often in America because it's grown in this part of the world. Come on over and I'll show you how it looks when cut open."

The girls walked to the stall to watch the vendor use her sharp knife to cut across the broad side of the fruit—dividing it into star-shaped slices. She then motioned for them to taste it.

"The whole fruit is edible," Lan said, handing a slice to Allison. "The more yellow the skin, the sweeter the fruit will be—especially if there's a bit of brown along the edges."

Allison bit into the slice. "Crazy! It's a blend of flavors— oranges, grapefruit, and papaya."

Lan agreed. "While the taste is sweet, it also has a tangy flavor. Do you like it?"

Allison nodded as she handed over 30 bahts and placed the star fruit in her backpack. "We can snack on this later."

Deng waited until the housekeeper left Room 513 and made her way into the elevator. Once the coast was clear, he left his room and opened Room 513's door with the stolen key card. Inside was the typical bed, dresser, TV and nightstand. He opened each drawer but found nothing. He went into the closet only to see a few shirts hanging—no backpack. Panic set in after he combed every corner. The backpack was not in the room. So much for this brilliant plan.

Back in his room, he called Sarut. "Look, I saw no backpack. Describe it."

"It's olive green trimmed with some gray. There's a large compartment and two smaller ones. I put the brooch in the larger compartment where the torn lining is located."

"There is no sense mentioning the torn lining when the backpack can't be found. Do you think she threw it out because of the tear?"

Sarut argued that if the bag could not be found in the room, it had to be with the girl. "The hole is small. I'm sure she wouldn't have thrown the bag out because of that. Keep that room you're in and the next time she leaves, do another check. Otherwise, if she's carrying the backpack, follow her."

"I still have the key card so I'll go back and take another look. You know, Sarut, you caused all this trouble losing the 66 million baht brooch, and now I'm faced with the problem of having to find it. This does not sit well with me."

"Deng, she'd recognize me if I helped. Don't be flipping out over this. We know where the girl is, and it's a matter of time before we get that damn brooch back."

"Sarut, there's something else I need to tell you. I talked with Montri and he mentioned Big K is getting crazy over this whole situation. He insists on returning despite Montri telling him to stay where he is. We need to meet somewhere to discuss this problem."

"Kee *(shit)*! That doesn't sound good. I'll meet you at the Tiger Bar tonight at 9:00."

Chapter 10

A PUZZLEMENT

"SA-WAT-DEE-KRAUP, MS. WAGNER, I'm sorry to disturb you, but this is hotel management calling to see if everything is okay with your room?"

"I just got in, but there doesn't appear to be a problem. Why?"

"Could you look around and make sure everything is okay? Your housekeeper reported a missing key card from her cart. She believes it went missing while cleaning your room."

"Oh, let me give you a call back." Allison hung up the phone to search through her things. Nothing seemed to be out of the ordinary until she opened her closet. The purse she placed in the drawer now laid on the closet floor. She remembered placing it inside the drawer that morning because she swapped it for her backpack. Mentally retracing her steps brought her to the same conclusion. Allison sat on the bed and anxiously looked inside the purse. As she recalled, she placed everything of importance in either her backpack or the room's safe. The only items left inside the handbag were the itinerary and written confirmation letter from the guide assigned to her in Chiang Rai. Although everything was there, someone had pulled the letter contents out of the envelope. She rechecked the room in case anything else was missing or moved, but came up with nothing. Allison sat down on the bed and stared at the letter now resting on the desk. *Why did the purse end up on the floor of the closet with the letter and itinerary removed from the envelope?*

Allison reached for the phone and called the hotel desk. "Yes, this is Allison Wagner in Room 513. You called a few minutes ago to ask if everything was fine with my room. Well, I believe someone had been rummaging through my closet. In particular, I found my purse laying on the closet floor. I know I put it inside a drawer."

"Are you missing anything?"

"No, but a letter I had in the purse was pulled out of its envelope. I'm sure someone was in here because it wasn't left that way."

"Okay, I'm sending up security to take your statement and assign you a different key card."

"Had any other rooms been broken into?" Allison asked.

"Not that we are aware. The housekeeper's concern centered only on your room. The key card she found in your wall slot was not the one she inserted."

"How does she know that?"

"The card she put in the wall slot was a master, but the one she pulled out would not open any of the other rooms on the floor. We believe the master may have been swapped with one of the cards off her cart."

"Not sure if I like the way this sounds."

"No worries, Ms. Wagner. We will be resetting all the key cards on your floor, but please continue to look and make sure nothing is missing."

"I don't believe anything was taken, but I'll take another look."

The environment around Tiger Bar could best be defined as grungy. Young women, dressed in seductive clothing, crammed the streets while not-so-young men pursued with hopes of alluring a potential escort for the night. Each girl governed her appointed corner with the intensity of an alpha dog protecting its territory. Earlier, the rain left the road slick with a mixture of oil and water. Cars and motorbikes recklessly dodged each other as they attempted to compete for space and attention. Neon lights—reds, yellows, blues, greens—transformed the night into day and fueled the energy that ignited Bangkok's night scene. Unlike the softness of a rainbow, the colors of the street screamed.

In the center of this chaos was Tiger Bar. An intimidating bouncer stood at the front door scrutinizing the clients as they entered. In Thailand, no one concerned themselves with the legal drinking age, but instead the bouncer's attention focused on the maintenance of order and the prevention of property destruction.

Sarut arrive first. Inside, cigarettes and stale alcohol robbed the bar of most of its oxygen. He walked through the smoky saloon and sat at one of the few remaining unoccupied tables. He ordered a drink, lit up a cigarette, and watched the parade of girls prance across a shoddy stage. Each girl, identically dressed in a bikini bottom and bra-like top, had a number pinned to her chest. If any girl interested a client, he simply pointed out her number. Names were unnecessary.

Loud music riveted the room as the percussionist's beat bounced off one wall onto the next. The competition between conversation and music intensified as the night wore on. People shouted what few words they could until overcome with hoarseness. Dancers gyrated while holding a drink in one hand and a cigarette in another.

Although under normal circumstances he'd be interested in this scene, today Sarut was not. Feeling reasonably nervous, he stroked his chin feeling the growth of three unshaven days.

"Waiting here long?" Startled, Sarut swung around to see Deng standing over him. "Man, you're uptight," said Deng.

"Shia" *(Damn it)*, didn't you hear the news?"

"What? You mean the news regarding the brooch? Yeah, but do I have the brooch? That's the important question."

Deng motioned to the waiter to bring him a beer. Then he settled in the chair across from Sarut and started watching the girls dancing on the elevated stage. "Personally, I'd pick number seven."

Sarut shook his head. "Yeah, well that's not gonna happen tonight."

Deng stared at his frazzled companion. "So what's with the sunglasses and stubs?"

"Deng, they caught me on their surveillance camera. Haven't you seen the clip of me walking out of the store with the brooch? Shia *(shit)*, they keep replaying it."

"And who's to blame for that one? Look, I don't need to have you go crazy on me. Here, read this." He reached into his pocket and pulled out a wrinkled paper with scrawled writing. "While I was in the girl's hotel room, I found a letter written by some guy she hired to take her around northern Thailand. I copied the information. His name is Ashwin Willapana and according to his letter, he's meeting this girl in a few days at the Bodesta Lodge in Chiang Rai.

Sarut pulled out a pen and copied the guide's name and the Bodesta Lodge onto a napkin he found on the table. He folded it in half and carefully slipped it inside a leather money pouch that already held an airline boarding pass and the address of a Bangkok hotel.

"If we don't get the brooch before she leaves, we're gonna have to follow her there."

Sarut nervously picked up the bottle of beer placed in front of him and stared at the label. "Deng, I'm telling you right now that it's too risky for me to go with you. I'll be recognized."

Deng snickered under his breath. "Sarut, what are you good for, huh?"

"How did I know there would be a surveillance camera in that store?"

Deng pointed his finger at Sarut and said, "That's when you should have worn a disguise, Sarut. You wear it while in the store. All stores, especially expensive ones, have cameras. You never considered that, huh? What a ting tong *(stupid)* fool."

Chapter 11

CHAO PHRAYA RIVER

NAAI MONTRI WAS not only a rich man, but he had no principles. Put those two elements together and the results can be quite dangerous. The loss of life mattered very little to him. One day you'd be in his inner circle and invited to his estate on the outskirts of Bangkok; the next, in a ditch with two bullet holes in your head. That's how Naai Montri worked. Everyone who depended on his money and security knew how fickle he could be. Few dared disagree or even challenge his word. Such was the situation when Deng received the call to come to Montri's home. He was ushered into the study where he found the head boss sitting on the couch with a fairly large cat. Although Montri had no love for anyone, he did have a fondness for the cat he referred to as Princess.

Deng wasn't there long before the assignment to get rid of Sarut was given. Sure, Sarut was incapable of pulling anything off without screwing it up, but they had some good times, too. Deng reflected on persuading Montri to reconsider, but then thought better of it. No sense angering Montri further—to do so could be a dangerous move.

"Sure, Mr. Montri, I'll take care of it."

"Good. Be quick about it. He's been identified by the police and they're after him. It's only a matter of time before he's found. Knowing that idiot, he'll spill his guts within five minutes. How you handle it is up to you. Just be clean about it, you hear?"

Princess jumped off the couch and headed over to where Deng sat. Deng was not particularly fond of cats which was evident as he tried to shoo her away.

"What? You don't like my Princess?" asked Montri, insulted. "You should feel honored she greeted you. That's not something she'd normally do. Go ahead, Deng—don't hurt her feelings, pet her."

Not wanting to upset Mr. Montri, Deng bent over and gave Princess a quick stroke resulting in fur immediately attaching itself to his pant legs and jacket. As Deng brushed it off, Mr. Montri laughed. "When you leave, my friend, you will take some of Princess with you, huh?" Realizing that was his cue to go, Deng stood up and walked over to the door while strands of Princess' hair floated around him like pixie dust.

Having left Montri's house, Deng got into his car and immediately called Sarut. "Hey, Sarut, I just finished talking to Montri. Seems he has an assignment for us."

"Deng, I can't be out in public."

"Look Sarut, you won't be. Tonight around ten, I'm swinging around to your place to pick you up in order to discuss this next assignment. Can't talk about it on the phone, you know?"

As planned, later that night Sarut climbed into Deng's car and they headed out of Bangkok.

"What's this new job about?" he asked. "Is it about the American girl?"

"Yeah, we have to meet up with one of Montri's guys to figure out our next move. He insisted you be there."

Sarut smiled feeling somewhat relieved. "Oh yeah, so Montri's no longer pissed about the brooch?"

"Nah, I covered your ass and told him we knew where the brooch was and will get it," Deng said, pulling the car into an empty lot next to the river. "Okay, this is where we meet this guy. I see he's already here."

The two got out of the car and walked over to where the other vehicle waited. The door opened and a fellow got out and threw his half-smoked cigar on the ground.

Sarut said, "Hey, Keerati, when did you get back from Tokyo? Deng, why didn't you tell me Keerati was the guy we're meeting?"

"Thought I let it be a surprise," Deng said.

"Yeah, it's a bit of a surprise for me, too," said Keerati, glancing over at Deng with a puzzled look on his face.

Deng smiled and nodded his head. Keerati shrugged his shoulders and pulled a gun from his hidden holster. Realizing what was about to transpire, Sarut yelled, "Hey, what's going on? Come on, fellows, let's talk this over."

Deng put his arm around Sarut and said, "This is nothing personal," and quietly walked away. After three muffled shots and a continuous flash of light, Sarut fell to the ground.

"Nice going, Keerati."

"You didn't tell me the guy with you would be Sarut," said Keerati.

"Hey, you're the one who decided to return to Bangkok." Deng playfully punched him in the arm. "Thought you could use a job."

Deng grabbed a cable from his car, wrapped it around Sarut's waist, and attached it to his hands.

"Why are you going through that trouble?" Keerati asked. "He's dead."

"It'll weigh him down. Now give me a hand and we'll drag him to the boat." They pulled Sarut's body aboard a longtail boat that was stashed under a tree near the riverbank, started the motor, and went out to the middle of the river where the two judiciously made their deposit into the murky water.

"Today was such a lovely day, Lan," Allison said as the two girls walked along the Chao Phraya River. "The Wat Arun" has got to be one of the most stunning temples I've ever seen. Just when I think this is my favorite, you take me to another one. What other surprises do you have, huh?"

Lan laughed. "My favorite time of seeing Wat Arun is at sunset like we did last night on the riverboat. I'm glad we were able to visit the place this afternoon."

"What can I say other than—spectacular. You know what really intrigued me? From a distance you see this lovely blue and gold mosaic pattern. Then when you get up close and focus on the finer details, what you notice are fragments of porcelain plates and bowls. I've never seen anything even closely resembling that. And there is such a feeling of tranquility. I see why it's called the Temple of the Dawn. These ancient temples are well-tended. It's quite impressive."

"This area of Bangkok is called Thonburi, Allison. Remember when I told you about the canals that were built in order to protect the city? Well, even though most of those canals have been filled in and replaced by roads and highways, Thonburi has actually kept more of its canals than any other area in Bangkok."

"Progress is good," Allison said, "but it's also essential to keep some areas as they've always been. Seeing the painted, rickety shacks along the riverbank hidden in the shadows of the tall glass and steel buildings—what a contrast."

"The river people have their own culture, and it's not unusual to see them doing laundry at the edge of the river or lounging in hammocks on porches that look as though they will fall into the water with the slightest breeze."

Allison gazed into the rapidly flowing river sadly realizing her days with Lan would soon be over, and she would be on a plane headed for Chiang Rai. "Lan, not often can you witness first-hand the old clashing with the new as right here on the river. Look, on the roof of most of these shanties are satellite dishes. That totally intrigues me."

The girls continued watching the activity along the river until the noise of a longtail boat averted their attention. Colorful, yet simple, these boats reminded Allison of the gondolas of Venice. "I can see how all of this resembles what life was like when Bangkok was considered the Venice of the East."

Lan agreed. "It's a shame to think that someday this could all be gone."

Up ahead Allison spotted an adult elephant being ridden by a rather young man. They stopped to watch as the elephant went from person to person waving its trunk. At first Allison was amused, even took a few shots with her camera, but she soon became disturbed when it became apparent the elephant was forced to beg for money. The elephant rider knew who to approach—anyone resembling a tourist and there were plenty here along the river. The elephant rolled its trunk, grabbed a bill and swung it up to the mahout sitting on his back.

"You know, Lan, this all doesn't seem right—elephants

should not be in a city setting involved in this type of activity."

Lan nodded her head in agreement as they both moved on from the crowd that started to form around this exquisite animal—forced to solicit money. As the girls approached their car, they noticed some commotion taking place further down the river. The sirens of several police cars screeched announcing their arrival amongst a small gathering of excited people.

"Do you think there's an accident?" asked Lan.

Allison stopped a man coming towards her on a bike. "Kho thot *(Excuse me)*, what is going on down there?"

The man stopped his bike, turned around to take a look, and said, "I'm not too certain, but I believe there's been a drowning. They pulled this guy out of the water. Pretty sad, huh?" He hopped back on his bike and took off down the road.

"Hi Jim, good to hear your voice. I had a great day with Lan. We saw another unbelievable temple and viewed the city from the river last night. Bangkok definitely has one foot in the past and the other in the present. It's anyone's guess which one will win out for the future. My guess? The present—unless a civil war breaks out between the people supporting the current administration and those wanting a change. That could set Thailand back like so many other countries involved in war."

"When are people going to understand that negotiations are better than violence and turmoil?" asked Jim. "I understand the lack of tourist trade has taken a heavy toll on Thailand. Have you seen evidence of that?"

"I have. I'm not seeing many Americans over here except for the occasional tour group passing through. The temples are crowded but pretty much with Asians. Lan tells me the vendors that depend on the tourist trade are really hurting. I feel their desperation every time one approaches hoping to sell a piece of jewelry or a postcard. These people can be borderline as far as harassment goes; but when I do make a purchase, there's genuine gratitude. My problem is I can't buy from everyone. By the way, have you heard anything about Lan attending the Oscars?"

"I'm still working on it," said Jim. "Did you say anything to her about it?"

"No, I don't want to raise her hopes and then dash them if it doesn't materialize. I know if it does come through, she'll be excited. She's dreamed of coming to the United States, but never believed it would really happen."

"So are you ready for Chiang Rai?" asked Jim.

"I leave in two days. I have to be honest with you, Jim, I'm uncomfortable in this room after discovering someone broke in and went through my things. So far I haven't noticed anything missing. I'm grateful my passport and money were locked in the safe."

"That could have been a real problem if someone took off with your passport."

"Jim, could you hold on for a moment?" Allison reached for the TV remote to turn the volume up. Then she picked up the phone and said, "When Lan and I were walking along the river this afternoon, we stumbled upon a drowning. Looks like BBC is about to report on it."

The body of a young man was washed up along the banks of the Chao Phraya River early this afternoon. At first it was believed to be an accidental drowning, but upon further investigation, the police determined the man had been murdered. They found two gunshot wounds to the man's skull and one to his chest. Wrapped around his waist and wrist was a steel cable. At this time we are not certain if this death is related to the civil conflict taking place in Bangkok. Anyone having information, please notify the police. Displayed is a photo of the victim recently identified as Sarut Wongsawat.

"Jim, I'm back. You're not going to believe this, but the drowning was actually a murder. They showed a photo of him and I swear the victim was the same guy who sat next to me on the plane from Tokyo. Matter-of-fact, I think I actually spotted him at the Red Shirt encampment the other day. Isn't that odd? "

Jim said, "Hmm . . . pure coincidence, I'm sure. Keep me posted on the details."

"They're reporting he may have been heavily into the political scene which surprises me as he acted uninterested in the conflict while on the plane."

"You said you found a letter in her room from some guide she hired?" Montri asked.

"Yeah, an Ashwin Willapana. He sent her an itinerary and arranged for her to stay at the Bodesta Lodge in Chiang Rai. Hey, I've got an idea—leave the rest up to me, Boss," said Deng. "As a matter-of-fact, the plan is in play."

Montri snuffed out his cigar and flipped the phone to his

other hand. "That's good, Deng. I'm counting on things to go as planned with no more surprises."

"Sure, a friend referred this guy, Anthony, to help us out. Never met him myself, but talked to him on the phone. I heard he's a regular pro at whatever he touches. He's been filled in on the situation, as much as I felt comfortable telling him, and I believe he's up for the challenge. He's not a dumb-ass like Sarut."

"Okay, but one thing to remember. You're not to let Keerati or anyone else in on this. The fewer people who know, the better for all of us."

Chapter 12

THE YELLOW SHIRTS

THE EMPEROR'S ROYAL Barge was a rather up-scale restaurant unlike any of the other places the girls frequented while Allison stayed in Bangkok, but she wanted to thank Lan for her help in guiding her around this big city. Locating the temples and museums was one matter, but Lan's explanation of what she was seeing proved to be significant. Allison also asked Yen to join them on her last night in town. The supervising Mae Chi *(nun)* at the Safe House gave the young novitiate her permission, and the three now sat and enjoyed each other's company.

Meals in Thailand often consisted of several courses shared amongst the diners at the table. Allison experienced a little indigestion after devouring a meal of lemongrass soup with mushrooms, green curry with pork, stir-fried chicken with ginger, and fried pumpkin with egg. They topped the meal off with watermelon.

"I'm guessing they serve the watermelon to put out the spicy fire now raging uncontrollably in my stomach," Allison said, holding her stomach.

Yen laughed. "I've gotten used to it after living here for over a year. Vietnamese food is not as spicy."

"Allison, not to change the subject, but are you certain the man we witnessed being pulled out of the river yesterday was the same guy sitting next to you on the plane?"

"They showed his picture on TV and it sure looked like him, Lan. I can't be 100 percent positive, but I sat next to him for over seven hours. All that time, he appeared nervous and agitated. I remember we had somewhat of a conversation about the civil unrest taking place in Thailand. He didn't seem to be interested in the conflict even though the news initially had his death pinned to the uprising. Sure, he was unfriendly, but it's still a struggle for me to process that someone murdered him."

Yen sighed. "So you don't think the civil conflict had anything to do with his death?"

Allison took a sip of her green tea. "The TV mentioned that possibility last night; but this morning, BBC reported the police have associated him with that brooch taken from the jewelry store in Tokyo. I guess his image was spotted on the store's surveillance camera."

Yen asked, "Did they actually show his picture?"

"Yes, but understand how syndicated journalism works. Whatever you see is continuously broadcasted all day, if not into the following week. His image may be blurred, but it definitely looked like he was the thief. To think all this happened hours before he got on the plane. I get the creeps whenever I think of how he sat next to me."

Lan shrugged her shoulders as she took the last bite of watermelon. "That's frightening. We never know who we might run into."

Allison smiled. "Perhaps, but not as frightening as what you girls endured at the hands of Mr. Banh and Madam Kolab. We haven't talked too much about it, but your experiences can't be erased by sweeping them under a rug. They'll always be there–hiding."

"Lan nodded her head. "I know, we need to sweep them outside the door, right?"

"My experiences were not as harsh as Lan's," Yen said. "Sure, they held me prisoner at the silk factory, but with Lan? Well, major healing had to take place."

Lan reached across the table and grabbed Yen's hand. "After recuperating at my grandmother's, Uncle Trung suggested I go to a Safe House in Ho Chi Minh for counseling. I resisted at first, but he insisted. That turned out to be a wise decision. I guess I needed that time away more than I realized. Actually, that is how I discovered the field of study I wanted to pursue—you know, work with other trafficked victims."

"Your personal conflicts can result in compassion for what the girls at the Thai Safe House went through," said Allison."

Yen squeezed Lan's hand. "Yes, she's very supportive and the girls love her. They kept inquiring where she's been this past week."

"See how much you're loved, Lan? Well, as much as I hate to do this, I need to call an end to this wonderful evening. My flight to Chiang Rai leaves early in the morning. Can you take me back to the hotel now, Lan?"

Once outside, the girls heard a loud commotion taking place one block away. "Come on, let's see what that's about," said Allison.

"It's best to stay away," said Lan.

Allison appreciated the insecure feelings that must stir inside this young girl. No longer was she that free-spirited, naïve teenager. Lon had changed—how could she not?

"You know, girls, you run along and I'll take a taxi back."

"No, we will drive you to your hotel," said Lan.

"I'll be fine, Lan, but as long as I'm here I need to find out what's happening. You do remember I'm one of those meddling reporters, right? It's in my blood to do that."

Lan hesitated but realized how futile it was to talk her determined friend out of heading towards any disturbance. Instead the two hugged tightly as tears appeared.

"You are very special, Lan. I'm so proud of you and what you've overcome."

"Thank you for helping me," Lan said, wiping her eyes with her sleeve.

"Look, I plan to stop by and see you at the Safe House when I return to Bangkok. You know, I'll have a day before returning to America." After one last hug, the girls separated. Allison stood at the corner and waved as Lan and Yen drove down the road. With mixed emotions, she turned around and headed towards the angry crowd.

Unlike the peaceful, half-empty street she left behind, this one was jam-packed with people. So many in number that only an isolated scooter, marked with the letters BBC, succeeded to find a spot to park. The red, white and blue flags of Thailand waved everywhere. People of all ages marched, blew whistles, and chanted as they pushed their way through the throng of police. In the center of this mob sat a large, white van with a sophisticated speaker system secured on its roof. Two men stood on top and stirred the crowd while the constant shrill of whistles replicated the sounds of a swarm of passing cicadas. It didn't take Allison long to realize she was amongst the Yellow Shirts she so wanted to interview.

Allison wasted little time and took note of a small family group sitting on a blanket at the side of the road. She could not help but think how much this resembled an American town watching the 4th of July parade. Although cheers and loud music were present, the marching bands and floats were not. The cheers may have been passionate but unquestionably not joyful. Regardless of the roar of people chanting *GET OUT,* Allison approached the family.

"Sawatdee *(hello),* could you explain what is happening here?"

The older woman gave Allison a blank stare making it clear she didn't understand English, but the young fellow sitting next to her jumped in with an answer.

"Chai, we are protesting against the current government. Our plan is to paralyze the government so they can't operate with efficiency. They will not step down, but instead act unconcerned and indifferent. They think by behaving this way, all will calm down and we will go away. But we will not. We will push the government to force them to act."

"What is it about the current government that the Yellow Shirts dislike?" asked Allison.

"It started with Thaksin Shinawatra whose family became wealthy through the telecom industry. Elected as the Prime Minister, he used his power to gain further wealth for his family and his friends."

Allison nodded. "Do you feel the Prime Minister's government was corrupt?"

"It's not what we feel; it's what we know. The court tried and found him guilty of this crime."

Allison said, "I understand he's now living in Dubai."

"Yes, he fled to escape prison."

Overhearing their conversation, a young woman shook her fist in the air and yelled, "This is not a recent problem because it's been going on for several years. We got rid of Shinawatra in 2006 and scheduled another election, but then the Red Shirts managed to get his sister into office. She is now the Prime Minister—her brother's puppet."

The more Allison listened, the more the family wanted to share. "Are you from America?"

Allison nodded. "I understand Thaksin Shinawatra's sister is claiming she's not a puppet and makes her own decisions on how the government should be run based on her own experiences."

When the young woman heard that, she yelled, "That is not true. She's from the same family and does what the brother tells her to do. That's how it's been for the past two years. We want her out!"

The young man nodded. "The government wants to grant amnesty to Shinawatra and all of his cronies, resulting in the anger you are witnessing today."

"What is the solution?" asked Allison.

"The solution is simple," the young man said. "We must find an opposing candidate willing to be mutual. This person must get the support of both sides in order for the Thai people to believe and trust him. If not, the cycle will continue."

Chapter 13

SNATCHED

THE EVENINGS IN Chiang Rai were normally cooler than mid-afternoon, but today it was different. The number on the thermometer had not budged since recording 95 degrees Fahrenheit. It was hot, and the streets were empty due to this intense heat. Most of its population stayed home and sat in their front yards hydrating with cold drinks.

A sole individual walked out of Pracha Nukhro Hospital. He received a call earlier that morning that his mother had a stroke, and so he rushed to her side where he remained most of the day. He had to leave the following morning for a work assignment and was trying to decide if he should call and cancel. His employer would understand his situation and a replacement could easily be found. Work opportunities had been slim in recent months because of the civil unrest in Thailand. He needed the money and felt guilty taking off for several weeks while his mother recovered.

Around the corner parked a beat-up, black sedan with two men slouched in the front seat. They sat there for several hours with nothing to do but wait. The hours dragged on until the man sitting on the passenger's side got out and ran into a restaurant on nearby Satharn Payabarn Road. He knew that would be frowned upon, but no one ever considered they would be on this stake-out for most of the day. He returned with two orders of pudthai *(stir fried noodle)* and somtum *(papaya salad)*.

While eating, the men chatted about their favorite sport, circle takraw, where a ball is passed from player to player while points are given for style and retrieval of ball. They debated and argued which team excelled at this sport until the driver of the sedan noticed a man walking towards them.

"There he is!" he said in a hushed voice.

Both men stashed their food cartons on the floor. The driver of the vehicle yelled out to the man, "Khum chuai haai phorn?" *(Can you help me?)*

The man sauntered over to the car and asked, "What is it?"

"My friend here is sick, and I need to get him to the hospital. He is quite heavy. Do you have the time to help me take him across the street?" The man nodded and agreed to help.

While the driver got out of the car, the man started to open the door next to the ill passenger. The guy slumped over in his seat suddenly sprang into action, swung the door wide open, and wrestled the unsuspecting victim to the ground. The driver grabbed a heavy rope and tied the man's hands behind his back. He pulled him up from the ground and shoved him into the backseat of the car. In a matter of a few minutes, the Good Samaritan found himself gagged, bound, and laying on the floor in the back of a car.

The black sedan sped off heading out of Chiang Rai. Laying in the back with a blindfold covering his eyes, the man was unable to figure out where they were taking him. He listened to sounds, hoping that would give a clue. Nothing stood out until the car stopped, and he heard the intermittent roar of airplanes placing his location near the airport. An immediate silence followed the thud of two doors opening and shutting. He tried to wiggle out of the rope that bound his wrists together; but as he tried, the rope tightened and nearly cut off his blood supply.

The backdoor opened without warning, and an arm reached in and dragged him out of the car and into a building that smelled of mold and mildew. Their voices echoed, leading him to believe he was in a vacant building. The two men talked—nonstop—about how much money they could make from this job.

"Yeah, if we do this right, there could be some sweet change for us," said the driver.

They shoved the man into a small room with no furnishings except for a torn chaise cushion. They removed the blindfold from his eyes, but kept the rope tied around his wrists and the bandana around his mouth. Exhausted and barely able to breath, the only sounds the captive man was capable of making were suppressed moans.

He caught a glimpse of the two men before they left his cell. One was stocky with the tattoo of a reddish-orange phoenix in flight. This tattoo stretched from the man's wrist straight up his left arm, and its wings spread out around his shoulder. Across his nose was a nasty scar which indicated a possible involvement in a recent fight.

The second man reeked of urine. He had deep-set, angry eyes that burned an imaginary hole with every look. Although he walked with a limp, his upper-body strength compensated for any disabilities.

After his captors left, the man lay there in this dank room and felt the sweat drip down his forehead, his cheek, and onto his neck. He could not fathom why he was imprisoned. They took no money or gave any explanation. Was this a random kidnapping or was he targeted? Surely, someone would inquire when he didn't show up for work in the morning.

Chapter 14

CHIANG RAI

IT'S NOT ONLY the geography that separates the north from the rest of Thailand. The history, traditions, and millions of rice fields all paint a different picture. Allison noticed this as soon as she landed in Chiang Rai. After climbing into a taxi, she asked the driver to take her to the Bodesta Lodge. The driver was chatty and eager to show off his ability to speak a little English. Even though it wasn't always easy to understand him, Allison enjoyed her interaction with this amusing fellow.

"So where you from?"

"I'm from New York," Allison answered.

"Ah yes, New York—tall buildings, crazy like Bangkok."

Allison chuckled. "I have to agree with you on that. Do you get many people in your taxi from America?"

"Not so much lately—many people from America stopped coming to Thailand."

"So the tourists' number has slipped?"

"What you mean . . . slip?" the driver asked, confused.

"You know, got smaller," Allison said.

"Oh . . . slip . . . got smaller. Doesn't slip mean someone falls down?"

"Yes, it can mean that, too. We have many words that can mean different things."

The driver shook his head. "Very confusing sometimes. To answer your question, many people from Australia and England come here, but Americans—like you say—slipped. So, how did you like Bangkok? Was there any protesting?"

"I saw several demonstrations but most of the time things were fine."

The driver looked at her in his rear view mirror and said, "You go home and tell Americans that. We need their visits to help change our people's lives. It is good you come to Chiang Rai, too. We are different from the people you meet in Bangkok."

"How's that?"

The driver steered his cab around a farmer's truck and then pointed to a far-off place. "See those rolling hills over there? That makes us different. We are proud of our culture. We want to hang onto our values—work hard, save money, be with family. Will you be going to Chiang Mai, too? Many Americans like to go there."

"Possibly, depends on how much time I have," said Allison.

The driver laughed. "Do you know Chiang Rai is older than Chiang Mai? Yes, we are thirty-four years older."

Allison smiled after hearing this revelation. For a place founded in the mid-13th century, thirty-four years seemed rather insignificant.

"Chiang Mai might be a fancier place, but we are more traditional and have a simpler way of life," the driver continued.

Allison noticed this looking out the window as they made their way to the hotel. Not much was there—a few houses separated by fields and fields of rice.

"Do you have any suggestions of places to go while I'm here?" she asked.

"Sure—most people like to visit the hill tribe village. They are called the 'Long Neck' people because they wear these gold rings to stretch their necks."

Allison said, "I heard about those villages. Do they have a problem with farangs coming?"

"No, no—they like visitors because that is how they earn their money. They sell their handicrafts to the tourists," the driver said, pulling into the hotel's circular driveway.

"Then I will be sure to visit their village. Khob khun kha *(Thank you)*. I enjoyed talking to you," she said, placing her palms together and bowing her head in the traditional *wai* greeting.

The Bodesta Lodge proved to be posh with a long, wooden walkway that cut through the center of a koi pond. The high-ceiling lobby appeared intimidating with its chic sofas and chairs scattered throughout, but Allison knew she would like it here. To get to her room, she needed to leave the main building and walk along a sculptured tile pathway that ran past a huge pool. Her room turned out to be a wooden cottage with a cozy front porch. The spacious interior not only had the predictable bed, but also a large sitting area. Outside each cabin, a hedge encircled a well-manicured lawn and a growth of shade trees giving this area a woodsy feel. Bordered exclusively by rice paddies and pineapple fields, Bodesta Lodge could accurately be described as a retreat. No town, no traffic, nothing—only this one resort shrouded in its own serenity.

Allison kicked off her shoes, put on her bathing suit, and headed for the pool. It was too appealing to pass up in this Thai heat. The mountainous regions of northern Thailand were cooler than Bangkok, but still the hot air could not be ignored. After a swim, she ordered a strawberry daiquiri and then laid back to rest on the chaise. Just as she drifted off, a voice startled her out of her daydream.

"Sa-wat-dee-krub, are you Allison Wagner?"

Allison took off her sunglasses and looked at the fellow standing over her—tall, well-built, and sporting a wide smile. She found his bright yellow shirt attractively contrasted with his olive skin and jet-black hair. "I am. Are you Ashwin?"

"Yes, Ashwin Willapana." Following the Tai custom, he placed his palms together and bowed his head in the wai greeting. Allison promptly returned the respectful gesture.

"Please sit down, Ashwin," Allison said, pointing to the adjacent chaise. She could not help but instantaneously like this fellow. While he talked, his smile never disappeared. Allison enjoyed people who were genuine—Ashwin was one of those.

"Did you receive my letter with the suggested itinerary?" he asked.

"I did. The itinerary looks exciting especially since I want to get a feel for Thailand's rural culture and the life-style of the people in this part of your country—not as an observer but a participant."

Ashwin nodded his head. "No problem. That can be arranged."

Allison stared at his teeth, so white and flawless; perfect teeth for the perfect smile.

"Did I say something wrong?" Ashwin asked.

Embarrassed, Allison said, "Oh no! I'm sorry; I was thinking what a nice smile you have."

"Thank you. I think it's better to smile than be grumpy all the time, right?"

"Yes, of course—anyway, I didn't mean to stare at you." Her hand trembled as she lifted her glass to finish the last swallow of her daiquiri. "Would you like something to quench your thirst in this heat?"

"No thanks, I'm used to it. Not like New York, huh?"

"Last week when I left, it was snowing."

"Snow—never saw snow except on television. Tell me, how was your week in Bangkok?"

"I found it to be a fascinating city—so much energy, but I'm ready to discover what this part of Thailand has to offer."

"That we can do," Ashwin said. "I received a report from Bangkok this morning that the city is having problems with not just the demonstrations but also the recent murder."

Allison looked at her guide. "Murder? Oh, the person who robbed the Tokyo jewelry store." Allison sat up and swung her legs around to the side of the chaise. "Ashwin, I was right there when they pulled the body out of the water, and I can't get that image out of my mind. It shocked me to learn he was the same person who sat next to me on the plane leaving Tokyo."

"You sat next to him?"

"I'm sure it was the same guy. Did they ever find the brooch?"

Ashwin shook his head no. "I believe they're still look-ing for it. Maybe whoever killed him has the brooch."

Allison thought about that for a while. "That's possible, Ashwin. I'd hate to think it was at the bottom of that river."

Ashwin nodded. "Yeah, that brooch was one of Thailand's treasured heirlooms that was missing for many years until it showed up in Tokyo. Very puzzling how something that valuable could simply disappear."

Allison shrugged her shoulders. "If they didn't find it on that guy's body, I'm sure somebody has it. Unless it fell in the water—you know, that's a possibility." She looked at her watch. "I better go and get myself organized. I pretty much dropped everything as soon as I arrived and hurried out to enjoy the pool. Do you plan to leave at a special time tomorrow?"

"How about right after breakfast—around 8:30? Will that work for you?"

"Perfect—I'm an early morning person," Allison said, slipping her sandals back on her feet.

"Okay, I'll pick you up then."

Chapter 15

HILL TRIBE PEOPLE

"HOW DO YOU like your hotel, Allison?"

"Very nice, Ashwin. Tonight was one of the few nights I slept well since arriving in Thailand."

Ashwin started up his beige Toyota and made his way out of the Bodesta Lodge onto a road that cut through acres of pineapples. "Why? Have you been ill?"

"No, more like worried because someone broke into my hotel room in Bangkok. Nothing was taken, but that's because anything of value was either on me or in the room's safe. The hotel reset the key card, but I still felt uncomfortable. Here I feel rather protected."

"I'm sorry that happened to you. Thailand isn't typically a place to worry about such things."

"That's what everyone tells me. Whoever broke into my room, also rummaged through my purse . . . probably looking for money."

Ashwin nodded in agreement. "There's also a problem with stolen passports."

"Really? I kept that in the room safe, but I will be careful. Hey, tell me a little about these hill tribes we're off to visit."

"I can do that. There are four tribes here in Chiang Rai— the Akha, the Palong, the Lisu, and the Karen. Each one has their own culture, dress, and language. What's interesting is that their languages are only spoken and not written."

"Are we going to all four?"

"No, we're going to the Karen tribe. You asked about the long-necks? That's where we're heading."

"I read something about their involvement with the opium trade," said Allison.

"Yeah, they're located right in the area known as the Golden Triangle. They were heavily into the opium trade until our king developed a plan to educate the hill tribes on better farming techniques. He wanted to improve their lives and not have them be dependent upon opium cultivation."

Allison looked out the side window and saw several areas of smoke rising from the jungle.

"Are they using slash and burn here?"

Ashwin glanced over to where she pointed. "Yes, cutting down the trees in the forest and then burning them is how they prepare for their planting. Not always good, right?"

"Hmm . . . not good for the air quality and not good for the forest."

"I understand. For us, everything is baby steps."

Allison looked over at the man behind the wheel. Although she didn't know him long, she was already impressed. Ashwin was a gentle, sensitive person who knew a lot about his country and the people living in it. Yes, she was going to enjoy these next three weeks.

"Ashwin, what should I know about the Karen people?"

"Well, they are the largest of the hill tribes, and something people don't always know is they're not Thai people."

"Really? You're right; I didn't know that."

"Yeah, they originated from Burma—you probably say Myanmar."

Allison pulled out her pad to jot down a few notes. "I hope you don't mind me writing down a few things as we speak."

Ashwin shook his head. "Not at all. Just tell me if you don't understand my English."

"Actually, you speak very well, Ashwin. I'm curious to know why the Karen tribe continues to hang onto their old ways, especially after being exposed to modern life."

"Yes, but you see—most of the Karen people are illegal immigrants. With few opportunities, they are forced to stay in their small village."

"As I drove from the airport yesterday, the cab driver mentioned that going to their village is good because it gave them a source of income."

Ashwin said, "That's true. Not only is there a fee to enter the village, but the women display their handmade crafts which can be purchased. It's a nice gesture to find a few souvenirs you might enjoy and buy from them."

"I would rather buy right from the people who've crafted the item than the mass-produced pieces found in every store in town."

They drove down a hard-packed road that led into the jungle until a young man flagged them down to collect the entrance fee. The couple got out of their parked car and followed the path that led to a dirt road with wooden stilt houses on both sides. Allison noticed that the stilted homes solved several problems by providing a place for storage and a spot for livestock to escape from the intense sun. Ashwin also explained being raised off the ground not only kept the houses from flooding during the rainy season, but air could circulate underneath the floor boards.

"Years of figuring it out," he said, leading her through the village.

They passed several men constructing a new house made from bamboo and banana leaves. It interested Allison to see how the materials all came from the environment surrounding the building site. No fancy power tools or large teams of people. Instead, a small community coming out to help a neighbor, much like the barn raisings of early America.

The porch of each home transformed into a small shop where a woman or child sat in anticipation of a sale. Even though they viewed her as a potential buyer, not one person called to Allison or rushed over with merchandise. No one followed and taunted her with a price that was continuously lowered. Quite the opposite—each person sat like a statue showing no movement, no expression, no joy.

That was when Allison saw her first long-neck woman wearing a colorful scarf wrapped around her head. She had to be in her mid-twenties and on her neck were at least twenty-five brass rings. Even though the cab driver assured her presence would be welcomed, she remained uncomfortable and awkward over this whole situation.

"Ashwin, it's like I'm at a museum or worse yet—a human zoo. Why do these women do this to their necks?"

As they continued to walk down the dirt path, Ashwin explained, "Although it seems that their necks are being stretched, what's happening is the brass rings are smashing their shoulders and rib cages down making their necks appear longer."

Allison reached into the depths of her soul to remind herself of what she learned whenever encountering a lifestyle far different from her own. *Things that seem strange should not be judged, but valued as part of a person's culture.*

"But why do they sit there like they're part of a display?" she asked. "This seems inhumane and so wrong."

Ashwin said, "It's tradition that they wear these rings to hold onto their heritage. Some women do it so they can make money. Often this is the only way they can provide for their family. Many of the young Karen women are breaking with tradition and it's been said that in a few generations this practice will be non-existent."

"So a young girl can decide not to go along with this practice?"

"Yes, except . . ."

Allison looked at Ashwin and asked, "Except what?"

"Except if born on a Wednesday during a full moon. Then she's expected to wear the rings."

"All right, now what's the rationale behind that?"

"If a child is born on that auspicious day, she is considered to be the daughter of the swan and so must wear the rings."

"Okay . . . that . . . explains it," she said with a hint of sarcasm in her voice. "What age would they start to wear the rings?"

"Girls begin to wear them when they are around five-years-old. A ring is then added every year until she's twenty-five."

"They have to be terribly uncomfortable. Are they ever removed?"

"Rarely, for a medical examination or to replace the ring with a longer one. What happens is the neck muscles become weak and unable to support the head so the rings become a supportive brace."

"With all that brass around their neck, isn't it difficult moving their heads from side-to-side? How do they ever sleep?"

Ashwin explained, "They sleep on their side. You will not like this, Allison, but they use a small, wooden plank as a pillow to keep their neck straight."

Allison shook her head in disbelief. "Do you know how all this started?"

The two passed by two pigs that laid alongside the dirt road. Ashwin pointed to them and said, "They certainly look comfortable, don't they?" Allison pulled out her camera and took several photos of the pigs and the tribal homes.

"So you want to know why wearing neck rings started?" asked Ashwin. "From what I understand, in the early days the practice of the brass rings started not just for beauty, but to protect the girls from tigers because when a tiger kills, he bites his victim's neck. Another reason was to protect the women from warring tribes who, upon finding these rings unattractive, might have otherwise turn the women into slaves."

"I see. So this practice was originally a solution to a problematic situation?"

Ashwin stopped to greet a little boy who ran up to him. He took a piece of candy out of his pocket and handed it to him. The child smiled and ran off to show his young mother who remained motionless on the porch.

"Yes, a solution at first," said Ashwin, "and then like other situations, it transformed into something else and became part of their culture."

A young woman with many bands on her neck stood by her display of brightly painted, hand-carved long neck figurines. Allison walked over to her and they both smiled at each other. She inquired on the cost of three of the figurines, and the woman placed the amount of bahts onto a calculator. Allison handed over money for all three of them. The woman searched but was unable to come up with the few bahts of change. Allison told her that was fine—no need. What happened next was amazing. The woman pulled Allison down next to her, loosely placed several rows of brass rings around her neck, and wrapped a headdress around her head. Not knowing what she was doing, Allison looked over at Ashwin with a puzzled look.

He said, "Hand me your camera. I believe she wants me to take a photo of you sitting next to her. This is her way of thanking you for your generosity."

After several photos and many shared giggles, Allison removed the rings, handed them over to her new friend, and the two smiled at each other. Allison stood up and gave the sign of respect with palms together and the bow of her head. The woman returned the wai.

Back at the car, Ashwin said, "Most tourists get their customary photo shoot, buy a few items, and then leave. Never do they have a personal interaction with the people. What happened with you and that woman was special, Allison. Do you realize that?"

"Yes, it was like the ice broke and we connected. I no longer thought of her as some kind of spectacle that people gawk at, but instead we were like two silly school girls sharing a fun moment."

As he backed the car out of its parking spot, Ashwin looked over at Allison. "You look a little disturbed."

"I am—actually, I'm bothered by all of this."

"Let's put it this way, the standards here are different. The women lack education which means if they leave their community and go to the city, they most likely will get caught up working in the sex trade."

Allison sighed. "Yeah, I guess when you put it that way, putting yourself out as a tourist attraction is a far better option."

"You'll be happy to know that today many of the hill tribe

people recognize the importance of their children attending school. Education will definitely change things."

As they drove away, Allison turned around and glanced back at the village she knew she'd never visit again. A place that will be a lasting memory only because she dared break through her self-conscious barrier to connect with another human being.

"You made that woman's day by treating her with respect and kindness."

"Thanks, but it was she who showed me how to act." Allison pulled out her camera and looked at the picture of the two of them sitting together. "I'll always treasure this photo."

Ashwin leaned over to look at the picture. "I know I took that picture, but I have to say that's one fantastic shot of the two of you sitting there like old friends enjoying a sunny morning."

Allison put her camera away and said, "It's pretty special when you recognize that an experience you're having will become a forever memory. It doesn't happen often; but when it does, you don't ever want the moment to end."

Ashwin smiled. "You actually look pretty good with brass rings around your neck. I think you ought to give it a try."

She laughed and said, "You think so, huh?"

The two drove for a few miles in silence until Ashwin said, "So tell me . . . what's going through your mind now?"

"I never did find out that girl's name."

"What girl?"

"You know, the girl in the picture."

Ashwin steered the car from the dirt road onto the paved highway. "There are some things that are unnecessary. Knowing her name may be one of them."

Chapter 16

KEERATI

ALTHOUGH THE DAY in Bangkok was hot, the atmosphere was free of its typical haze letting the blue sky show through. People carried on as usual, but rumors spread that the lady Prime Minister would soon be forced to step down from her office. This was not setting well with the Red Shirts. No one had any certainty of their future, and every day the news had something fresh to report. The daily newspaper amended their earlier account that the man found in the river was another civil unrest casualty. After the police identified the body as the person found on the security camera at the Tokyo jewelry store, Japan's law enforcers rushed to Bangkok to combine their investigative efforts with the detectives from Bangkok already on the scene.

The brooch needed to be found. There was always the possibility that it was at the bottom of the river, but the marubo-dekka *(Japanese detective)* believed that was unlikely. Whoever dumped this man into the river had to be connected to the brooch. Most likely, someone removed the brooch from Sarut's body between the time of his death and his water burial. All of this was speculation, but that is all the investigators had to go on. That and a waterproofed pouch containing a boarding pass from Tokyo, a scribbled address written on a wrinkled piece of paper, and a barely readable name found on a dampened napkin.

Naai Montri was a successful businessman who made his fortune dabbling in exports. Although his ethics were questionable, his cleverness barred any accusations from ever sticking. Naai Montri made sure of that. That particular afternoon Montri had guests—two men escorted into his study by his bodyguard.

"I tell you, Montri, the store owner doesn't suspect a thing. I concocted a story about a family emergency back home and requested a leave from work to take care of things," said Keerati.

"Not a good move," said Montri. "Not now—so soon after the robbery. What were you thinking?"

"What was I thinking? How about getting the hell out of there? If they caught on that I had anything to do with the stolen brooch, I'd be stuck in Tokyo's prison forever."

"Do you feel the store owner connected you with Sarut?" asked Montri.

"No, but every day the police asked questions and kept re-examining my every move on the security camera. I couldn't take the stress anymore. By the way, why did you give the order for me to kill Sarut?"

"We had to get rid of him, Keerati. He was starting to act crazy, isn't that right, Deng?"

Deng nodded his head. "He became paralyzed with fear that someone would recognize him after having his picture plastered all over the TV. His concerns matched ours, and Montri worried he would blab in exchange for a lighter sentence."

Montri said, "And then it would be only a matter of time before the three of us would go down."

Keerati reached for a match and lit his cigarette as he paced the room. "Deng, you instructed me to meet you at the river and be prepared to shoot the guy that accompanied you. I never received any information about the identity of this person and blindly followed your orders. I upset my life, moved to Tokyo to work in a damn store, and successfully handed the brooch over to Sarut. All this only to discover that the pin is nowhere to be found. Then you have the nerve to say you're not happy with me because I left Tokyo—really now?"

Hearing where this conversation was headed, Deng nervously finished his beer and placed the bottle on the table. "Hey, I got the instructions. I do whatever Montri tells me, right boss?"

"Deng, I left it up to you to decide who would kill Sarut. Why you had Keerati do this still confuses me as I would have selected someone else."

Montri picked up Princess and placed her on the couch next to him. He maintained his silence, stroking Princess until she started to purr. Keerati watched as the cat's long, rusty hair coasted to the wooden floor only to drift like tumbleweed to the four corners of the room.

"Geez, that hair is everywhere," Keerati complained, brushing off his pants.

"Keerati, there's something that's been bothering me. Why did you leave the surveillance cameras on in the store that day?"

"I forgot about them," Keerati said.

Montri pounded his fist into the couch causing the cat to jump. "Doesn't anyone around here think?"

"Look," said Keerati, "it's a damn good thing the cameras were on because they were suspecting me as the one who made off with the brooch."

"Why you?" Montri asked.

"I don't know—easy target, I guess. Think about it, I had access to the jewelry, new employee, not a Japanese citizen. Hell, I'd consider me, as well."

Montri laughed. "When are you returning to Tokyo?"

"Not sure if I will. I'm considering it might not be a good idea to go back."

"Won't the store owner be questioning that?" asked Deng.

"Nah, I'll make up a damn story about how things got worse with my father, and I must stay to help the family."

"Be cool about it," Montri said, putting the agitated Princess on the floor. "Now Deng, you know the whereabouts of the girl and what she looks like, right?"

"Yeah, she's staying at the Bodesta Lodge in Chiang Rai."

"You're to be on the first plane tomorrow morning. I want that girl followed—everywhere she goes, you go. Keerati, you better go with him. It's clear Deng will need help with this."

The room filled with tension as both Deng and Keerati realized the importance of not failing in this mission. To do so would be a straight road to an early death. As they got up to leave, Deng's phone rang. He looked and saw the caller's name and excused himself from the room to take the call. Meanwhile, Montri asked Keerati to take Princess upstairs to her room. Keerati muttered something under his breath about the absurdity of a cat having her own room.

Outside the study, Deng answered his phone. "Yeah, what's up?"

The voice on the phone said, "So far things are good at this end."

"Keep the situation under control, Anthony. I'm arriving in Chiang Rai tomorrow morning with this other guy. From now on, it's important we don't acknowledge each other, okay?"

"Not a problem," Anthony said.

Deng returned to the study. "That was the guy I told you about. This Anthony said he's got everything under control."

Montri asked, "So what about you? Are you ready to act on the plan?"

"No worries; I got it from here on in. With Anthony's help, we'll soon be back in business with that damn brooch," boasted Deng.

"Hey, let's be quiet about this Anthony fellow," said Montri. "The fewer people who know about him, the better; that includes Keerati."

"It will be difficult keeping Keerati out of the loop, Boss."

"So life is difficult. Keerati is to know as little as possible. Shh . . . here he comes."

Keerati walked into the room and asked, "Did I hear my name?"

"Yeah," Montri said, "From now on when talking on the phone, we will refer to you as 'Big K'. Those damn police have everyone bugged. We don't need to arouse suspicion that the clerk in the jewelry store may have been in on the theft. Know what I mean? Get that brooch as soon as you can. I got a guy ready to buy it for over 30 million bahts. Right now, I'm stalling and making up excuses about why this is not a good time to hand over the piece."

Montri took out his handkerchief and wiped the cat hair off his hands. He put the hanky back in his pocket and said, "Now get out of here. You have work to do."

Chapter 17

WAT RONG KHUN

"ALLISON, EARLIER YOU mentioned you were interested in learning how Thailand was transitioning from the old to the new, right? Well, I have the perfect place for you—Wat Rong Khun."

"Hmm . . . the word wat tells me we're going to a Buddhist temple," Allison said to her guide as they walked through the parking area of the lodge.

"Not just any temple, but one built by Chalermchai Kositpipat who actually comes from Chiang Rai," Ashwin said, handing her a helmet.

Allison looked at the helmet. "What's this?"

"That's for safety," Ashwin answered with a wink. "I thought you should become familiar with Thailand's adventurous side so we're going by motorcycle. Have you ever been on one?"

Allison laughed. "I have, several years ago. Well, not a motorcycle but more like a motorbike. It's crazy but my guide in Vietnam introduced me to this mode of travel. How bizarre is that? What is it with you guys and these motorbikes?"

"Did you enjoy the experience?"

"I thought I was going to die. Can you imagine sitting on the back of a small motor scooter zipping in and out of Ho Chi Minh traffic? Did I enjoy it? It was awesome!"

Ashwin waved his hand towards the road. "No crazy

traffic out here. You'll see only the occasional yak pulling a wagon of harvested pineapple."

"How far away is this temple?"

"The temple is 13 km from Chiang Rai—probably a 15 minute ride. So tell me, are you game for traveling by motorcycle?"

Allison put the helmet on and said, "Sure, why not? Let's go!" With her approval, the two got on the bike and took off down the road. Allison hung onto Ashwin as they maneuvered their way along the 13 km of road that most likely resulted from the efforts of former Prime Minister, Thaksin Shinawatra. Allison thought about the Thai civil unrest and understood the concerns of the people from Bangkok because of the way the government instituted their improvements. On the other hand, she connected with the Red Shirts of northern Thailand and appreciated the accessibility to miles of paved roads.

Wat Rong Khun turned out to be a brilliant white temple decorated with thousands of pieces of mirrored glass that sparkled in the sun. Spires—too many to count—with dragon-looking creatures encasing the roof, hinted at its fairy tale theme. Intricate sculptures of demons and Garudas surrounded the temple. From the trees hung severed heads sporting snarly-looking beards, bulging eyes, and elf-like ears. One tree in particular had the likeness of Jimmy Durante wearing his signature hat. Another head was unrecognizable, but what stood out were the countless nails piercing the face and back of the skull. As if that wasn't disturbing enough, Allison grimaced as she spotted one particular cranium with a snake's head coming from its brow, and its tail extending out of an eye socket.

"How does anyone come up with this kind of stuff, Ashwin?"

"Gruesome, right?"

"This place would be a wonderland for many 10-year-old boys back in the states."

A ramp spanned across a moat leading to the entrance of the main temple. In this moat, amongst so many symbols of fear and death, swam large goldfish representing peace and life. As the two reached this bridge, Allison stopped in horror. On each side of a stone walkway was a fairly deep hole jam-packed with arms stretching upward from an unimaginable hell below. The fingers were grasping, reaching out of desperation to be pulled out of their dismal and regrettable situation. Several hands held heads with closed eyes while a few others held up empty bowls begging for nourishment. No torsos, only the reaching hands resembling a massive bed of worms ascending from the interior of the earth.

"Ashwin, I'm at a loss for words. This place is totally bizarre."

"Bizarre is a good word, Allison. This temple is a merger of traditional Thai and science fiction."

"The guy who built this temple? Is he alive?"

"Sure, Kositpipat is one of Thailand's most distinguished neo-traditionalist artists. Actually, this temple is a work in progress. There will eventually be about nine buildings on the grounds, including the chapel, a pagoda, a crematorium, a preaching hall, and even a museum."

Allison took several photos of the unbelievable creation in front of her. "In some weird way this temple looks like the blending of Disney World's castle with the witch's cottage in Hansel and Gretel; but instead of gingerbread, he used demons for trim."

With a smirk, Ashwin said, "Wait until you go inside."

He was not exaggerating as the interior of Wat Rong

Khun was just as captivating if not intriguing. Signs of good and evil were apparent everywhere. On the good side, there were murals of superheroes such as Batman and Superman; while on the evil side, wall paintings showing the annihilation of planet earth as well as a plane crashing into the Twin Towers loomed over them. Amongst these interpretations of destruction and chaos sat a peaceful, white Buddha with angelic deities blissfully floating within a heavenly kingdom.

Ashwin said, "The artist built this as an offering to Lord Buddha with the hope it will give him immortal life."

"Who pays for this—the government or the people?" Allison inquired.

"Kositpipat funded all of this through the sale of his paintings. The white you see symbolizes Buddha's purity. It's beautiful during the day, but when you view it in the moonlight—well, it can be quite ghostly."

"Yeah, I see your point. I hate to say it, but this place would be one fabulous backdrop for Halloween. Are you familiar with Halloween?"

Ashwin asked, "Is that when you wear costumes and try to scare people?"

"Exactly, I guess you're thinking we do strange things, too."

The two made their way back over the ramp when Allison noticed the temple's reflection in the moat. She stopped to take a few more photos and then reflected on what she just experienced. "It's crazy but when I look at this temple, a tiered cake with crusty white frosting comes to mind. This Kositpitap fellow definitely walks to a different beat."

Ashwin laughed. "I read in a magazine that what he wanted to do was come up with a temple never done before."

"I dare say he achieved that. Hey, I need a little time-out

before moving onward. Are you interested in grabbing a cup of tea? Looks like a small café over there."

"Keerati, look inside the café. There's the girl, and she has the backpack with her."

"Who's the guy?"

"He must be the guide taking her around Chiang Rai. How about if I go inside and sit at the table next to them. I'll get a cup of coffee and listen in on their conversation to find out where they're headed next."

"Don't you have the itinerary you found in her hotel room?"

"Yeah, but we can't be sure they'll follow it. Look, while I'm there, you get your phone and take a picture of the backpack. It looks typical. We should be able to pick up a similar one."

"Okay, I can do that," said Keerati, "but why?"

"I've come up with this idea. What do you think of us getting a similar bag and swapping them, huh?"

"I like that idea," said Keerati. "If she spots us doing that, we can say it was a mix-up . . . an accident. You go ahead, and I'll sit on this bench in the shade and wait for you."

"Be sure to get a close-up shot of the bag. Right now would be good while it's hanging off the back of her chair."

"You know, Deng, I'm thinking. Why don't you just go and grab it? Shit . . . save us a lot of trouble."

"Surveillance cameras, Keerati. You forget so soon, don't you? If I follow your suggestion, I'll become a TV star like Sarut. And you? You'll be sitting here out of everyone's sight."

"This Thai ice tea is the best I've ever tasted, Ashwin. Are you sure you don't want any?"

"My bottled water is all I need," he said. "So what's in the package?"

Allison pulled out a silver heart-shaped piece of metal with scalloped edges. From the bottom hung a white cord with several silver beads and one rusty-colored, crystal lotus flower. At the top of the ornament was another cord with similar silver beads.

"What's the story behind this?" she asked.

Ashwin explained, "Oh, that's what is known as a good wish ornament. You're to write down a wish and hang it on the stucco tree over there."

"I already did, but this one I'm taking home with me. I wondered what was hanging from that tree-like structure, and when I checked it out, I saw thousands of these hanging ornaments. I can't believe how something so simple, when grouped together, can take on such a magical look. Back home when it snows, everything becomes icy—the roofs, tree branches, telephone wires. We say it looks like a Winter Wonderland. That's how this temple looks but without the snow and freezing ice."

"The one here doesn't melt, right?" Ashwin winked as he flashed one of his teasing grins.

"Well, you'll just have to come to the states during the winter and I'll show you snow."

"Tell me, Allison, what do you plan on doing with this memento from Wat Rong Khun?"

"I'm not sure yet. Maybe I'll treat it as a sun catcher and hang it in my window." Allison opened her backpack and slipped her souvenir into the small compartment. As she did this, she noticed a man sitting at the table next to them smoking a cigarette and drinking a cup of coffee. He appeared to be focused on her backpack; but when she looked at him, he quickly looked away.

"Ashwin, what do we have planned for tomorrow? Anything real exciting?"

"As a matter-of-fact, I do have an idea. It's not as amazing as Wat Rong Khun, but it's another example of old behaviors making way for new."

"Really? Where?"

"How would you like to visit the Golden Triangle?"

"That's the place you mentioned yesterday as once being the center of the opium trade, right?"

"Yes, the Opium Museum is there, plus it's the spot where the river actually butts up to the tips of three countries."

"I'm guessing Thailand and Laos, but what's the third?"

"Myanmar, interested in checking that place out?" asked Ashwin.

"Definitely," Allison said, getting up to leave. After walking a short distance, Allison touched Ashwin's arm and leaned into him. "Did you notice that man sitting next to us?"

Ashwin shook his head and said, "You mean in the café? No, not really. Why?"

"I felt uncomfortable. I'm pretty sure he was listening in on our conversation, and he kept giving me sideway glances? You know, like this." She looked straight ahead and then shifted her eyes to the right. "And I noticed when we got up to leave, so did he."

Ashwin reached for the helmets locked inside his motorcycle compartment, and handed one to her. "No, I didn't pay attention. Who knows? Maybe he was bored and, like me, found you to be interesting and amusing."

Chapter 18

THE INVESTIGATION

"THIS IS WHAT we found in Sarut's waterproofed money pouch—a boarding pass from Tokyo to Bangkok, the name Ashwin Willapana written on a napkin, and an address scribbled on a scrap piece of paper. We checked out the address and it's of a hotel near Silom Road," the police chief explained to the marubo-dekka *(detective)* from Tokyo. "We're still trying to locate this Ashwin fellow."

"Mind if I keep a copy of everything here? I would like to check and see if this information is connected in some way."

"Sure, I'll do that for you right now." The chief put everything in the copier and handed the duplicates to the marubo-dekka.

"So what can you tell me about the guy?"

The chief walked over to his desk and pulled out a folder. He handed it over to the marubo-dekka. "As you will read in the report, his body washed up on the Chao Phraya River bank several days ago. We've identified him as Sarut Wongsawat. It appears he died from a gunshot to the head."

"Not suicide?" the marubo-dekka asked.

"Not possible—we found one gunshot to the skull and two to the chest. The one to his head killed him. We don't believe this was a random shooting because we found a cable tying both wrists to his waist. Someone definitely had a beef

with this fellow. After reviewing the jewelry store surveillance tape, we concluded that this was the same person."

"No brooch?"

"No, we stripped his apartment and found nothing of interest except for a woman's name written on a notepad near
the phone—Allison W. No surname, only the letter W."

"Any idea who that is?" the marubo-dekka asked as he
looked through the folder.

"We hadn't gotten that far, but the name Allison—isn't
that a Western name?"

The marubo-dekka took out his handkerchief and wiped
his forehead. "Geez, it's hot here. I certainly don't need this
coat," he said, throwing his jacket on the chair.

"What? You don't get hot in Tokyo?" the chief asked,
annoyed.

"Not in January—Tokyo was in the low 60's when I left.
Okay, the first thing I will do is contact the airline and get
a copy of the passenger manifesto to check if he was with
anyone on the plane."

"I suspect he wasn't," the chief said.

"Oh, do you have the list of names?"

"No, but it appeared he traveled alone."

The detective picked up his jacket and sat in the chair.
Despite his small frame, his beady eyes and powerful voice
intimidated anyone around him. He stared at the chief as
though weighing what he planned to say. "This is something
that will need to be checked out. I never go on appearances
because speculation works only so far."

Disliking the arrogance of this Japanese detective, the
chief was on the verge of making a sarcastic comment, but
decided to remain quiet. A peeve of his was when the law
agency of another country arrived bent on controlling the

investigation. Finally, the chief spoke. "Once you get the manifesto, how will you use it?"

"Take the list of names to the hotel and compare it to their guest list for that time frame. Who knows? Maybe there will be a match."

"It's like finding a needle in a haystack," the chief said.

"And that needle you are referring to is valued over 200 million yens. We need to start somewhere." He grabbed his coat and started for the door.

"Oh, one more thing," the chief said, holding up a zip-lock bag. This may be nothing, but we found this hair on Sarut's pants. It was wet from the river, but we managed to brush it off and dry it out."

The marubo-dekka took the bag and opened it. "That's interesting, it's rather a rusty color." Carefully he pulled out some of the hair and smelled it. "I say from a dog or cat—definitely not human hair."

"Actually, we had it tested—it's from a long-hair cat."

"Did Sarut own a cat?"

"Not that we're aware. No sign of any animal at his apartment, and his neighbors claimed they never heard or saw any pet at his place."

"Mind if I hold onto this?" the marubo-dekka asked.

"Here, let me split the bag so we both have samples. This could be valuable evidence."

After the marubo-dekka left, a police officer entered the chief's office. "How did it go?"

The chief stood up and walked over to the window. He watched as the Japanese detective got into his car and drove off. "I'm betting he'll waste no time. The jerk most likely is heading straight for the airport." Then he turned around and walked over to his desk. "This marubo? What an arrogant ass! We'll see how fast he finds the damn brooch."

After obtaining the manifesto from the airlines, the marubo-dekka left for the hotel named on the paper. He walked into the lobby, headed straight to the front desk, and asked to speak to the person in charge.

"Is there something I can help you with?" the clerk asked.

"No, I prefer to speak with the general manager."

"Chai, I will get him for you."

After a few minutes, the hotel manager came out and asked the Japanese customer what he could do for him. The marubo showed his badge and requested to see the hotel guest list from the past ten days. The manager invited him into his office and questioned why he was there.

"We have reason to believe that one of your guests may have had contact with the person recently murdered and thrown into the river."

"The same guy reported to have made off with the Thai brooch?"

"Yeah, the same, but stolen from Japan."

"I can assure you that he never was a guest in this hotel," the hotel manager said in a defensive voice.

After ignoring his statement, the marubo once again asked, "So could you make a copy of the list of guests who stayed here during that time span? You do have such a list, right?"

"Of course, I will ask my assistant to print a copy. Please excuse me."

Five minutes later the hotel manager came in with several sheets in his hand. "This is what we have for you."

The marubo examined the list and just as he was about to treat it as a dead-end, he spotted the name *Allison Wagner*. "Do you remember this guest—an Allison Wagner?"

"We have so many people in and out of here. To be honest, I rarely make contact with the guests but let me call in Karn, our front desk clerk, and see if he recalls anything about her."

Karn entered the office and the hotel manager explained that the Japanese detective was investigating a crime committed in Japan but had ties with Bangkok. "Please answer any of his questions to the best of your recollection. I mentioned we service many guests so it may be impossible."

The marubo asked, "Karn, do you remember a Western woman who stayed at the hotel last week? Her name was Allison Wagner."

Karn thought for a second and then said, "As a matter-of-fact, I do remember Ms. Wagner. She was an American who stayed five days on the fifth floor. We re-keyed all the cards on that floor because of a situation where someone removed the master key card from the wall power socket while the housekeeper cleaned her room."

Interested in what he heard, the detective asked, "Did someone later break into her room?"

"We presumed that happened and asked Ms. Wagner if anything was taken. She didn't seem to think so, but later called back and said a purse she put in the drawer inside the closet had been removed and thrown on the floor. She felt confident nothing was taken."

The marubo-dekka jotted down whatever the clerk said and then turned to the manager.

"Do you mind if I keep this guest list? I'm particularly interested in the names of the people who were on the same floor as Ms. Wagner. I noticed to activate the elevator in your hotel, guests first need to swipe their key card. It's possible that whoever stole the master card could have been a guest staying on the fifth floor."

The manager nodded his head. "Let us know if we can be of any further help."

The detective picked up the copies and shoved them into his folder. He started towards the door, turned around and asked Karn, "Has Ms. Wagner left Thailand?"

"No," the clerk said. "She left Bangkok for Chiang Rai."

The detective wrote that down in his notebook and asked, "Any contact names or numbers?"

Karn said, "We have a copy of her passport. Do you want that?"

"Yes," said the detective, "that could be useful."

Karn left the room to make a copy of Allison Wagner's passport. Upon his return he said, "I remembered she used a business charge card to pay her bill. I made a copy of that, too."

The marubo-dekka looked at the copy of the bill. "It says here *New York Documentary News* paid her bill. Was she here as a journalist?"

The desk clerk nervously shifted from one foot to the other. "I have no idea why she came to Bangkok. That would be infringing on her privacy."

Chapter 19

ASHWIN

UNQUESTIONABLY, WAT RONG Khun proved to be another missing piece of the puzzle for Allison's report on how the Siam of old had changed. After spending a free morning at the lodge, Ashwin picked her up to head out for the Golden Triangle. She hung tightly onto Ashwin as their motorcycle left the paved highway and rumbled along a packed dirt road surrounded by sugarcane and bamboo. No doubt about it—the jungles of Thailand surrounded them, and Allison questioned where they were headed.

"First, I thought we'd stop for lunch so I'm taking you to a restaurant known only to the local people."

"Ashwin, how could anyone find a place out here unless they knew about it? Are you certain we aren't lost?"

"It's right around the next bend—you'll see."

Ashwin parked the cycle, and the two made their way to a rattan fence that separated the dirt road from the lush vegetation. Six children sat on mats across from the entrance gate. Curious, Allison walked over to see what they had spread in front of them. As it turned out, they were peddling their art work. The younger children displayed cartoon pictures they colored while the older kids had actual drawings they created. None of the children rushed over to them or even tried to grab their attention by calling out. Instead, like the long-neck children from the hill tribe, they patiently sat and waited to be approached. Ashwin described them as children of the neighborhood selling to visitors to earn some money.

Allison wanted to encourage free enterprise and discourage begging, so she walked over to one particular girl who had a somber expression on her face. She offered an assortment of neatly drawn elephant pictures. Although she realistically drew several of the elephants, most of them were depicted as whimsical animals chasing butterflies or lifting flowers with their trunks while happy birds glided above their heads.

The girl's name was Natalee. Dressed in blue warm-up pants, she wore a flowered tunic top that fell to her knees. In addition to the jet-black hair cropped above her shoulders, her red framed glasses distinguished her from the other Thai girls. All the children were barefoot, but unlike Allison's own barefoot days when she and her friends spent all summer running through a fresh cut lawn, no grass grew here. Tough, calloused soles resulted from running on the packed dirt, sharp rocks, stalks, large-leaf foliage, and coarse grass that only a machete could control. Still, she had to smile because it reminded her of those carefree summer days when the only items on the day's agenda included catching butterflies, riding bikes and selling lemonade. After receiving their permission to take their photo, Allison showed the children their image on her camera. It warmed Allison's heart to see this serious girl with the red glasses break into a smile.

"I can't decide which one I like the best," Allison said, looking at everyone's drawings. "How about if I buy one drawing from each of you? Would that work?" The older girl with the red glasses nodded her approval and gave Allison a clear bag to store the six purchases.

As she and Ashwin continued on through the gate, he

said, "That was nice of you to do that. I come here whenever I'm in the area. When school is not in session, I find these kids sitting on their mats drawing and hoping someone will pass by."

"How could I not?" asked Allison. "For a few bahts, they felt valued and I received some pretty nice but primitive art work! Hey, are you sure there's a restaurant in the middle of this jungle?"

After walking a short distance, the path took them to an outdoor eating area shielded from the sun by a tightly-woven straw roof. All around the perimeter of the crudely-constructed pavilion, bamboo shoots were strategically planted. Inside they joined six other people who sat on hand-crafted benches and ate at plank tables. Ashwin suggested the restaurant's barbeque fish which was a favorite of the local people. Upon his recommendation, Allison ordered the fish dinner which turned out to be the right decision. The owner of the restaurant brought out a plate containing steam rice inside a bamboo leaf bowl, stir-fry young bamboo shoots, a lime, and a whole fish, complete with opened eyes. In short, the meal was as Ashwin described—one of the best.

As she sat amongst the bamboo trees, Allison decided this environment could not be artificially duplicated. The lianas, creepers, and vines stretched across the open area and attached themselves to other trees creating a magical setting for two people to dine. Only nature could pull this off.

While eating their dessert of tapioca pudding, Ashwin asked Allison if she had any questions.

"I do," she said with an impish grin. "I've spent the past several days learning about Thailand, but absolutely nothing about you. Where do you live, how big is your family, how did you get started in this line of work—that kind of stuff!"

"I'm not interesting," Ashwin said, appearing a little frazzled.

"I believe I've caught you off-guard, haven't I? I'm not letting you off the hook. Spill the beans."

Ashwin looked puzzled. "Spill the beans, what's that?"

Allison finished her last bite of pudding and then said, "It means tell me everything," she teased.

"Okay, spill the beans," he said, laughing. "Let me see . . . growing up, I lived in a rural area outside of Bangkok along Highway 35 in Samut Sakhorn. I am the youngest of seven children and my parents expected all of us to work on the brine salt farms when we were not in school."

"Salt farms? Tell me about that."

"Imagine trapped ocean water standing in large square fields that resemble rice paddies."

"How did you trap the ocean water?"

"We built these low walls composed of large stones and pebbles. Then we'd either hose the water inside or just let the water overflow into the warming pens. Ditches resembling small canals connected all of these inner pens where the water sat until it evaporated leaving behind the salt."

"Really?" asked Allison. "How long did it take for the water to evaporate?"

"Oh, about five to seven days. Once the salt crystalized into flakes, a wooden broom swept the salt into small mounds. That was my first job when I was maybe eight or nine. The sun scorched my body and the salt worked its way through the pores of my hands. I had to be careful not to touch my eyes or they would burn."

Allison sipped her tea while Ashwin continued with his

story. "My older brothers raked and rolled the salt until it was ready to be shoveled into wheelbarrows and dumped into larger pyramid mounds."

"How long did that whole process take?"

"About two months—then we'd refill the warming pens with the ocean's water and start over again."

"I find that fascinating, Ashwin. Did this go on for the whole year?"

"No, from November thru April," Ashwin said, tapping his fingers on the table. Then we cleaned the salt, shoveled it into large bags, and finally sorted it. Although my older sisters did the grading, they also helped in the warming pens by raking and sweeping."

"How was the salt graded?" asked Allison.

"The salt was separated into groups according to how it would be used—for cooking, medicines, industrial use or cosmetics. The highest grade of salt was always set aside for cosmetics."

"Salt is used in cosmetics?" Allison asked.

"Yeah, products like body scrubs or bath salts. We'd package the salt into small plastic bags to sell."

"Is your family still involved in the salt production?"

"They are—my brothers and sisters took over the family business since both my parents passed away."

"So you managed to escape that hard labor?" Allison asked.

"Yeah, quite a while ago. With me being the youngest, my father didn't insist on me working the farm. He probably sensed my lack of interest, so I was lucky because I was the only one who went thru school and later attended the University for business. I believe my brothers resented that favoritism. Regardless, there was no way I could continue to do that kind of hard, manual labor. Years of running a salt farm aged my parents, and they both died too young."

"How long ago was that, Ashwin?"

"It's been awhile—my father died about six-years ago, and my mother passed away one year later."

Allison noticed that Ashwin lost his huge smile when he talked about his family. She never saw him look this serious.

"Hey, I didn't mean to bore you with the ins and outs of running a salt farm."

"Bore me? No way, I find it fascinating. Is this process still being used?"

"Yeah, total manual labor. Crazy, huh?"

"I imagine that could change once people start to equip themselves with machinery."

"That would be nice, but it all requires large sums of money to acquire that equipment. Until then, it's all done with brooms, rakes, and wheelbarrows. So, are you ready to go?"

Allison filled her cup with the tea remaining in her small pot. "Not yet, I have one more question to ask."

"Will do, providing I know the answer."

"Oh, you should know this one. Are you married?"

Ashwin smiled. "I was for four years."

"Was?" Allison asked.

"Narissa and I met at the University. We both worked as teachers in the same school in Bangkok. I taught English in the high school and she worked with small children."

"Ah, so that's why you have such a good command of the English language—you taught it. What happened?"

"We were doing well; saving our money to move out of our apartment and someday into our own home. Once we did that, our plan was to start a family."

Allison noticed how painful this subject was for

Ashwin and said, "You don't need to say anymore if it's too troubling."

"No, I will tell you. One morning Narissa woke up not feeling well, so she stayed home from work. By the time I returned home, she had a stiff neck and a fever. She stayed in bed all day, but woke up in the middle of the night vomiting. I took her to the hospital and after several tests, she was diagnosed as having meningitis. They placed both of us in quarantine. I never came down with it, and Narissa never recovered."

"Ashwin, how awful!"

"It took quite a while to get over her death. I completed the school year, but then quit my job. I spent the next two years drifting throughout Asia— picked up construction jobs, taught English for six months in Vietnam, tutored. Eventually, I realized all I was doing was running away from my problems instead of facing them. After two years, nothing was different except I was out of money, lost my apartment and job, and was now two years older. I returned to my family's home for a while, but I knew I didn't want to be stuck working on the salt farm."

"What brought you to Chiang Rai?"

"I heard about an opening to teach English to children in a private school. I applied and did that for two years until money became scarce for the community. There were two of us teaching English, but the other person was there longer so they let me go. Now I pick up jobs here and there."

"You mean with the tour guiding company?" Allison asked.

"Ah . . . yeah, right. I work any jobs sent my way."

"Are things better for you?" she asked.

"It's taken a few years, but I've learned to adjust and

accept what I can't control. What about you, Allison? Do you work for a newspaper in New York City?"

"It's not actually a newspaper, rather a news magazine. The last seven years we've expanded the business and formed a branch that produces documentary films. We've had much success with this one documentary focused on human trafficking in Vietnam and Cambodia. It was nominated for an Oscar which is a prestigious award given by our peers in the industry."

"Congratulations! That is an honor."

"Well, we haven't won it yet, but we've been nominated which is still exciting."

"Is that why you're in Thailand—working on another documentary?" asked Ashwin.

"Yes, that's why I'm interested in finding examples of where the old ways of doing things are being replaced by the new. Ashwin, do you mind if I use your story? I'm fascinated over the idea that Bangkok is moving into the next century with communication, transportation, and technical employment; but less than two hours away, people are still harvesting salt using their own hands, brooms, and wheelbarrows."

"No, not at all, as long as you don't use my name. I tend to be a private person. Somehow you got me to spill the beans, right?"

Allison laughed. "I did, didn't I? No worries, Ashwin, I'll respect your privacy."

"Hey, let's say we stop talking and head on over to the Golden Triangle area. Mae Sai is a nice town located on the river. There are lots of shops, restaurants, and that nice museum. You want to learn more about the changes in Thailand? Well, there's plenty of changes going on there."

⚜

"Just follow that motorcycle, Keerati. Only hell knows where they're going," said Deng, riding on the passenger side of their black Toyota.

"I can't get too close or they'll notice us," warned Keerati.

"They're pulling off onto a dirt road. You better stay a little behind and allow some space between us. Looks like we're the only ones on this road."

After another ten minutes of driving, the motorcycle made a sudden left turn and stopped at the edge of the road.

"They're stopping, Keerati. You better pull over. I have no idea where they're heading."

"I saw a sign with the name of a restaurant close to where we turned off. That's probably where they're going," said Keerati.

"Let's wait a few minutes and then get out," said Deng. "No one seems to be around except for a bunch of kids."

The two watched as the American lady walked over to each child looking at some kind of craft they had displayed on their mats.

"Alright already, what's she doing now?" asked Deng.

Keerati shook his head. "This is crazy. Let's just knock the two off and grab the bag."

"Sure, do it your way and not Montri's—that'll get you to the bottom of the river. You need to be patient and wait until the time is right."

"Did I tell you that guy at the jewelry store called me last night?"

"The store owner? What about?"

"He asked when I would be returning to Tokyo."

"What did you tell him?"

"I said I wasn't sure. Things weren't good in Bangkok with my father and all."

"Do you think he bought that?" asked Deng.

"Can't say for sure. He hesitated before answering which made me feel a little uneasy."

"Are you planning on going back?" asked Deng.

"Are you crazy? What for? I'm close to telling him I need to quit the job."

Deng lit a cigarette and stared at the girl buying something from the kids. "Timing is everything, Keerati."

Ten minutes later, Deng and Keerati got out of the car and made their way along the road. They veered off towards a slightly worn path that led to the rattan fence. Keerati pulled out his field glasses and scanned the area.

"I see them and I was right. There's a restaurant inside and they're ordering food." Keerati handed the field glasses over to Deng and walked over to where the kids sat. He glanced at the stuff displayed on the mats and asked the girl with red glasses what the two people wanted. She stared at the guy but didn't say anything. A boy sitting across from her explained how they bought drawings from them. "Do you want to buy any?"

Keerati laughed. "What? Pay money for this crap? Go get yourself some postcards to sell."

Deng motioned for Keerati to come over to him. "Are you crazy? Don't get involved with these ground rats."

"Just trying to pass the time, that's all."

An hour later, Keerati noticed the guy signal the waiter. "Hey, I think they're getting ready to leave. We better get back to the car. Where do you think they're going?"

Deng said, "The other day I overheard them talking about

the Golden Triangle so if I had to make a guess, I would say Mae Sai. Let's get out of here before they spot us."

The girl with the red glasses watched the two men take turns looking through the field glasses at the nice lady having lunch with the man with a friendly smile. They were kind but these men were different. She didn't like them. Maybe because the one guy described their drawings as crap, and the other man referred to them as ground rats. They were not like the people living in Chiang Rai province. These were Bangkok men—the kind that were unfriendly. And so she ignored them and refused to answer any questions. Having overheard their conversation, she was unsure what the two men wanted, but one thing she did know was that most likely they were looking for trouble. So when Allison and Ashwin returned to their bike, she forced herself to break through her shyness and leave the safety of her mat.

"Sa-wat-dee-kay, I wish to tell you something. While you were inside the restaurant eating, two men followed and watched."

They were watching us?" Allison asked.

"Yes, the one man asked me about you, but I did not answer. I think you should know this. They were not nice people."

"Where are they now?" asked Allison.

"Their car is hiding in the bushes down the road. You can't see it well, but it is there."

Allison glanced over without trying to make it look obvious. "Yes, I can see a black car. Ashwin, do you think someone is following us?"

"It's a possibility. Look kids, why don't all of you pick up your things and go home. It may not be safe for you to be here right now."

After the children picked up their mats and took off toward their houses, Ashwin and Allison got on their motorcycle and sped down the road. A few minutes later, the black car started up and followed. Ashwin glanced in his rear view mirror and saw the dust kicked up by this vehicle, but said nothing.

Chapter 20

NAAI MONTRI

"COME IN MY friend," Naai Montri said, leading the way to his study. "Please sit down. Care for a drink?"

An impeccably dressed Asian man approached the study with an arrogance peppered with obvious irritation. "This is not a social visit, Montri. What's this I'm hearing about the brooch coming up missing?"

"Only a slight detour in our plans—nothing to be concerned over. I will get that brooch to you within the week."

"We've already given you half the money. Maybe you should return that money, and we'll renegotiate after the brooch is recovered."

Montri stammered, "Ah . . . yes, but obtaining the brooch did not come without many expenses. I've spent much of that money putting the plan into play. I assure you, you'll get your brooch. These things take time."

Montri bent over to pick up Princess and placed her on the couch next to him. Stroking her fur worked like magic not just with relieving anxiety, but also giving him the time needed before responding to further questions.

"Naai Montri, I am a man of little patience."

"Yes, I understand. I'm working on getting the brooch, but I need to be discreet. So much is in the news about it now."

The man glared at Montri. "Are you telling me the brooch is not available because you want to be discreet?"

"Why is it so important for you to have that particular piece of jewelry? Perhaps you would be interested in something much nicer?"

The man stood up and walked over to the photo of an older woman that hung on the wall.

"Who is this?"

Montri said, "My grandmother—why do you ask?"

"Is she dead?"

"Yes, many years ago. Why?"

"You hang a picture of her on the wall to show respect for her life. Sunandha Kumariratana was the first wife of King Chulalongkorn—Rama V. Before the wedding, her mother presented her with the Royal Barge brooch as a wedding gift. Sunandha always wore this brooch as she did the day of that fatal boating accident."

For the first time, Montri appeared interested in the history of the brooch instead of viewing it as an opportunity. "What happened?" he asked.

"She was making her way up the river to the summer palace when her boat capsized."

"Didn't anyone try to save her?" asked Montri.

"No, in the 19th Century it was the law in Siam that no one could touch the Queen. If they did, they faced a death sentence. Queen Sunandha drowned along with her young daughter and unborn son."

"What happened to the brooch?" asked Montri.

"When they removed her from the water, the brooch was missing. King Rama had his men search the bottom of the river, but they never found it. No one knew of its existence until four years ago when it surfaced at that auction in Japan."

The man pulled a cigar from his front pocket and took

his time to light it before he continued with his story. "Our people put a generous bid on the brooch, but a jewelry store outbid us. That store didn't care about its history. Instead, they saw it as a gimmick."

Montri's demeanor changed as his narcissist personality became apparent. "I don't get it. Why be so obsessed over this one piece of jewelry?"

"Queen Sunandha was a distant cousin of my wife who is proud of her royal blood connection, no matter how extended. She could have any piece of jewelry she'd want, but no—it was always this damn brooch. She has an aged photo of the queen that was taken two years before her death. It shows her wearing the brooch. All the time my wife grumbled she should have this pin. I sent one of my men to approach the store owner, but he would not sell. We offered to pay him well, but this store owner—very stubborn man. It is difficult doing business in another country. That is why, out of frustration, I contacted you. Obtain the pin without getting my name muddied up, and you'll receive the balance from the deal we made. The brooch should be with my wife where it belongs. Maybe then she will stop complaining."

Montri stood up and walked to the bar to pour himself a half-glass of whiskey. "We had the brooch until my guy freaked out and made a stupid decision."

"Look Montri, I'm not interested in how you got the pin or how you lost it, but there will be many problems if it's not handed over? Do you understand? I take a deal agreed upon as a serious contract that should not be broken."

"You will have your brooch. As I said, right now the situation is a little complicated, but we know where it is."

The man stood up to leave. "Hey, what's the story I'm seeing in the paper that the police identified the man recently found at the bottom of the river as the thief who made off with the brooch? What's that all about?"

"Like I told you, it's complicated," Montri said as he escorted the gentleman to the door.

After the man left, Montri broke out in a sweat. He wondered how long he could stall this guy. He reached for the phone and called Keerati.

"Hey Big K, not to say too much on the phone, but the guy requesting the item we've talked about just left. He's not happy about what has happened. I managed to stall the transfer, but it's going to get tougher the next time we meet if I don't have the item on me."

"Who is this guy?" asked Keerati.

"He's a member of the Chao Pho. You don't mess with Thailand's mafia. What is it you two are doing and why is this taking so long?"

"What are we doing? Right now we're following their motorcycle to hell-knows-where. Here, talk to Deng. He'll fill you in." Keerati handed the phone over to Deng and grumbled, "Explain what it is we're doing."

Frustrated, Deng shook his head. "Keerati . . . I mean . . . Big K and I have been trailing them for several days. We've been to temples and restaurants and now I think we're heading toward Mae Sai. It would be much easier, boss, if I just ran up to her and grabbed the damn bag."

"No, that's the last thing you do. She's not to be aware that anyone took anything from her. That will only heighten her suspicions and get the police further involved. I don't need that."

Deng said, "That's what I told Big K you would say. I have an idea. Later tonight I'm going into town to find a backpack like the girl's. I'm planning on doing the accidental switch. You know, take the wrong bag, remove the item, and then realize I have the wrong backpack."

"Whatever works, Deng. Just get the damn job done, will you?"

"One other thing, Montri, Big K plans to tell his boss he can't return to work because of his father being ill. He doesn't want to go back to Tokyo."

"What? Put him back on the phone."

Deng returned the phone to Keerati and smiled. "Your turn."

Keerati asked, "What's up?"

"Hey, we won't discuss this over the phone right now, but not returning to work is stupid. You realize that, don't you?"

"Montri, I'm not going back. I don't see the rationale behind that so I plan to call and tell him. Don't worry about it—he won't suspect anything."

Chapter 21

THE INVESTIGATION DEEPENS

THE DETECTIVE FROM Tokyo removed the contents of the folder and organized it on the desk in his hotel room. Through a little exploration of his own, he connected some of the dots. For instance, he knew the man found shot and thrown in the river sat next to this Allison Wagner on the plane. There clearly was a tie here, but what? *Were these two traveling together? Did this Allison have anything to do with the theft?* The detective studied the slip of paper having Allison W written on it. *If this guy had a close relationship with her, would he write the first initial of her last name?* The investigator shook his head and muttered, "No, not really."

He also checked and discovered that Allison Wagner started her travel in New York, not Tokyo. The only time she was in Tokyo was at the airport for her connecting flight to Bangkok. His head raced with thoughts—so much so that even he recognized how much he needed a rest from work.

He walked over to the window and looked down at the early evening traffic. It rained hard that afternoon leaving the roads filled with puddles of water that reflected lights coming from both the vehicles and the surrounding hotels and office buildings. He observed that the shopkeepers started the process of locking their doors and pulling down the metal cages that secured their storefronts. Dressed in their yellow robes, two monks walked amongst the vendors still cooking and dishing out chicken swimming in coconut milk.

Hasn't anyone missed Sarut—the poor, dead soul who had the misfortune of becoming involved with a plan bigger than he could handle?

The marubo-dekka closed the curtain and walked back to the desk. He picked up the slip of paper with the girl's name and speculated perhaps the two were not traveling together. Perhaps they became acquainted while sitting next to each other on the plane for seven hours. Maybe they made plans to meet, and so he copied down her name. *Then why would he not write her last name and phone number?* The idea that someone wrote the hotel address on a separate slip of paper but didn't include her name was curious, too. The boarding pass and hotel address were actually found on Sarut's body, but the paper with Allison's name was discovered in his apartment.

The detective set the paper down on his desk and picked up the zip-lock bag containing cat hair. *What's the story behind this cat hair?* Sarut didn't own a cat, so he had to associate with someone who did. The detective knew cats shed from visiting his sister. Whenever he returned home, he always had cat hair all over his clothes, but the color of this cat was unique to Bangkok—rusty-orange. There were so many questions left unanswered. As he deliberated his next step, his cell phone rang. It was the owner of the jewelry store in Tokyo.

"Yeah, what's up?"

"I wanted to share something with you. It's probably nothing, but I have an uneasy feeling about Keerati, my employee who waited on the customer who stole the brooch."

"You have my attention. What about him?"

"Not long after you left, Keerati received a call from his family in Bangkok about his father being terminally ill. I gave the okay for him to visit his father, but today he emailed and said he decided to quit the job and not return. I found it coincidental that all this happened two weeks after the most expensive piece of jewelry was taken from the store."

"It could be just that—a coincidence."

"Well, the story gets more complicated. I wanted to talk to him about his situation and not through an informal email so I called him, but he never picked up. I got ahold of his family's number and, to my surprise, it was his father who answered the phone. When I asked to speak to Keerati, his father said they hadn't spoken to him in over four months."

The detective recorded all of this in his notebook. "I realize what you're saying. This does sound strange."

"I called your office, and they told me you're in Bangkok," the owner said.

"Yeah, doing some follow-up work. Someone murdered the suspect on your surveillance tape and dumped his body in the Chao Phraya River."

"I heard about that. Did you find the brooch?" the store owner asked.

"No, still working on it. It's of the utmost importance we don't let the trail get cold especially seeing this guy is now dead. I believe when we find who murdered him, we'll have the answers to many of our questions—including the whereabouts of the brooch."

Chapter 22

TROUBLE LOOMS IN BANGKOK

THE TIME WAS 3 AM when Thailand's military chief appeared on TV to declare martial law with the intention of preserving order and bringing peace to the country. Earlier the court had removed the prime minister, Yingluck Shinawatra, from office as well as nine cabinet members, but they refused to step down. Soldiers arrived to shut down all TV studios under the premise that any broadcasted news of the coup would be distorted. This could lead to further misunderstandings with a possible escalation of the crisis. The situation on the streets in Bangkok intensified. Soldiers remained stationed at intersections and soon the overpowering presence of tanks appeared. Traffic was a mess, and the Royal Thai Army failed to convince protesters to go home. An all-out effort to prevent any further rallies and strikes by both the Red and Yellow Shirt encampments met with resistance.

Yen prepared to leave for the market as she often had done to purchase vegetables, chicken, and fish for the Safe House. The head nun stopped her as she was about to leave the house.

"Yen, maybe today would not be a good time to go out. There's much unrest in the streets."

"I'll be fine. All I plan to do is shop for food supplies and then return home," she said, picking up her brown, bamboo shopping bag.

Using the public bus, Yen got off at the Khlong Toey Market where the stalls were set up inside a large, open pavilion. Unlike the floating markets, this marketplace was not a tourist spot, but a place where the locals came to shop despite its location in Bangkok's biggest slum neighborhood. Khlong Toey Market was known for its fresh food—meat, seafood, and produce. No one seemed to mind that the market sat beside a putrid river smelling from the continuous disposal of unwanted garbage.

Khlong Toey was a wet market with stall after stall of meat—geese, ducks, and chickens—in the process of being butchered. Not a place for the faint-hearted, so the wearing of boots to avoid the spilled blood on the floor proved to be a wise decision.

That morning the place bustled with activity; unlike other markets, no vendors pressured shoppers into buying their produce. Men in orange jackets carted food around in large-wheeled, wicker baskets avoiding the people gathered amongst the display of live fish, flapping their tails until one ended up on the grimy floor. Another vendor walking by noticed the displaced fish, scooped it up, and returned it to its tin tray.

Yen used the pedestrian bridge that led to the market's entrance to avoid crossing the busy road. As she approached the entrance, a truck whizzed by carrying a load of pigs ready for slaughter. She made a mental note that perhaps a nice treat for the girls would be bacon. Yen lingered beside the stall loaded with fresh apples and oranges and purchased a bag of each. After placing the fruit in her bag, she wandered over to the stacked rows of shrimp. It didn't matter if the only available refrigeration were large plastic coolers filled with ice, or that she flinched upon seeing flies hovering over the produce. To the Western world, these unsanitary conditions would be unacceptable, but not to the Thai.

After selecting the shrimp, Yen stopped to talk with a vendor she met several months ago. This woman sold fresh chicken which she raised at her house next to the riverbank. Free-ranged, the chickens foraged as they worked for their own supper and scratched around the barnyard looking for bugs and seeds. What resulted was a slow-growing chicken, tender with no added hormones. Yen's friend was not always at the market, but today she had a crate of matured chickens ready for the slaughter. After a little chit chat, Yen pointed to two chickens. The vendor reached into the cage and pulled the first one out. As she did this, the hens clucked wildly as if they knew their fate. She slit its throat, and waited as the blood drained into a large cup. She wrapped the chicken in a brown sack and handed it to Yen who then placed it in her bamboo shopping bag. Just as the woman reached for the second chicken, a loud blast was heard from the far side of the market. This was followed by screams and people crazily running through the narrow aisles between the stalls.

"What's going on?" Yen asked one man, rushing past her.

"Someone threw a grenade into the crowd," he yelled. Seconds later, another loud blast occurred. This time a small explosive device placed in a rubbish bin detonated. The scene was chaotic as no one knew where to go in fear that more explosives were set to go off.

Far-away sounds of sirens grew louder as police cars and ambulances approached. The stale blood of slaughtered animals slowly mixed with the fresh blood of humans. No one could determine who required help as the blast overturned kiosks, shredded opened umbrellas, and caused portions of the corrugated roof to collapse.

No need to speculate who caused this bedlam. Without saying a word, everyone assumed this directly resulted from the military coup that took place earlier that morning. It had to be the Red Shirts' retaliation.

People scrambled to transport both dead and injured bodies into the ambulances waiting a few feet away. One woman screamed as a man lifted her young child's lifeless body onto a stretcher. Another man could be heard moaning as the medics picked up part of a hand that laid beside him. From under the cages of screeching chickens, crawled a woman grateful for no injuries. She lifted a crate and stood it upright onto the floor. As she picked up the second crate, she noticed an arm reaching towards her. She yelled out for help and several men rushed over to lift the heavy stall. Under it was a young woman dressed in a blood-soaked, white robe clutching a bamboo shopping bag.

Chapter 23

THE GOLDEN TRIANGLE

THE BORDERS OF Laos, Myanmar, and Thailand come together in a place called Sop Ruak. Looking out at the confluence of the Mekong and Ruak Rivers, Ashwin pointed out to Allison Thailand's two neighboring countries. "Across the river you have Laos and over here you see Myanmar."

"Myanmar? I remember you said that the country was originally named Burma."

Ashwin nodded as he pointed to the large colorful sign with a diagram showing the location of the three countries and the joining of the two rivers. "Yeah, the military junta renamed the country in 1989, a year after thousands were killed during a popular uprising."

"How well have the people accepted the name change," asked Allison.

"It depends on who you ask."

Confused, Allison asked, "What do you mean?"

Ashwin picked up a stick laying on the ground and flung it into the murky river. "Well, it's like this. The United Nations and countries like France and Japan recognize the new name, but the United States and UK still refer to the country as Burma."

"Why's that?"

"Your government and the UK do not recognize the military regime since they were never elected."

"That can be confusing."

"Not to the people living there. Whether a person refers to his country as Burma or Myanmar can give a clue as to his political position. What's more important is the abuse of human rights."

Allison walked over and sat on the bench overlooking the river. The current was swift and for a few quiet moments she watched the water rush past her. There's something therapeutic about water—often leaving her mesmerized. The past couple of weeks had been intense as she struggled to understand the conflict Thailand currently faced between the Red and Yellow Shirts. Ashwin was right when he said what's more important is the abuse of human rights. This didn't just apply to Myanmar, but also to the Long Neck women. Her visit to the hill tribe proved to be enlightening, but also disturbing. She understood this cultural thing, but that didn't ease the desire to improve the life of those women.

"What are you thinking about?" Ashwin asked, breaking the silence.

"Just processing everything you've said. When the government changed the name of the country, is that when they also decided that Rangoon should be renamed Yagon?"

"Yeah," Ashwin replied, "most people are more familiar with the names Rangoon and Burma. If the Burmese people are writing a publication or making a formal statement, they will use Myanmar. Otherwise, in informal conversation? They say Burma."

"That I understand. It would be difficult for me to refer to my country by some other name. It's so embedded in my mind."

Allison stood up and looked over at a vendor cart with a small, glass refrigerated chest loaded up with bananas, strawberries and blueberries. Allison considered buying a strawberry smoothie until she noticed the vendor asleep with her head rested upon the metal counter.

"Could she be taking a power nap?" she asked, pointing towards the young girl.

"Hmm . . . I don't see too many smoothies being sold," Ashwin joked. "Okay, maybe not for her, but rest time is over for us. Shall we make our way over to the Opium Museum?"

The twosome walked past a park that exemplified a true glimpse of the old Siam. Two large elephant statues, complete with a decorated howdah on each back, stood adjacent to each other. They stopped and watched the tourists climb up a set of stairs onto these stone elephants to have their photos taken. "It's good to see they're using statues, Ashwin, instead of live elephants."

"Yeah, the country's experienced controversies over the elephant trekking companies."

"I read about that. I'd be interested in going to one of those tourist camps to see for myself. Can that be arranged?"

"Sure, there's one not too far from here. How about tomorrow?"

"Great!" Allison said. "I've been wanting to investigate this whole elephant debate. You know, how they're pulled from the wild and used in tourism."

Ashwin stopped in front of a building and pointed to a sign that said *House of Opium Museum*. "Elephants are a whole new topic we can explore tomorrow, Allison, but right now—we're onto heroin." It wasn't a large building—small, but crammed with products and exhibits associated with the opium trade that was once a major commodity in this part of Thailand.

"Look, Ashwin, they thought of everything." An array of colored poppies grew alongside the museum between a concrete wall and the tiled sidewalk.

"Yeah, poppies are the source of opium," said Ashwin.

"You mentioned it was illegal for the hill tribes to be involved in the production of opium."

"That's correct—thanks to the efforts of the royal family."

"So what kinds of crops do they grow?"

"Well, they make a living growing coffee, macadamia nuts, and vegetables. So you go inside and take a look, and I'll wait for you out here."

Allison wandered through the museum as she read the captions next to each display. After spending practically an hour in the semi-dark rooms, she walked out into the bright sunshine where she found Ashwin sitting on a concrete wall talking on his phone. Allison decided to sneak up on him but as she got closer, she overheard part of his conversation. She wasn't sure if it was what he said or the tone of voice he used that bothered her more.

"Look, damn it, these things take time," he said in an agitated voice.

"Is something wrong?" whispered Allison.

Ashwin looked up and stammered, "No, uh . . . just give me a second," and then distanced himself from her to finish his conversation. Shortly after, he returned to where she now sat on a bench reviewing the material she purchased from the museum.

Allison looked up and asked, "Is there a problem?"

"Problem? Oh, no . . . just my brother."

"It sounded as though you two were in a bit of a spat."

Ashwin sat down next to her and said, "Just some family

stuff. What can I say? He's always asking for money, you know? So tell me, what did you think of the museum?"

"I found it interesting," said Allison. "Do you know the largest producer of poppies today is Afghanistan?"

"Yeah, I heard that."

Allison continued, "I also learned the production of synthetic drugs has increased along the Golden Triangle."

"That's true," Ashwin said. "Meth tablets are produced in Burma along the Thai border. It seems heroin traffickers have found that meth is much easier to hide from authorities."

"So one illicit drug has replaced another. When will it ever end?"

"Not until people stop making money from it," said Ashwin. "It's disturbing what people have to do to provide for their needs—even if they feel it is wrong."

Chapter 24

THE BACKPACK

BACK AT THE Bodesta Lodge, the walk from the lobby to Cottage 107 was pleasant. The rows of detached bungalows abutted acres of rice paddies and were surrounded by hedges of pink flowers and long-leaf palms. As in previous days, attendants weeded, raked, and tended the well-manicured lawns that edged the concrete paths. As Allison approached her front porch, she stopped and looked through the space provided between Cottages 105 and 107. The setting sun created a bright hazy background behind the trees in front of her. She pulled out the camera from her backpack to digitally capture the moment.

Unbeknownst to her, two men hid amongst the thick bushes between Cottages 106 and 108. Careful not to move and call attention to their presence, they waited until she picked up her bag and walked inside her bungalow.

"So what do we do now?" asked Keerati.

"We wait until the right moment and then spring into action. Montri doesn't want us to stir up anything. Right now the police probably surmise the brooch is at the bottom of the river. Let them think that as they continue to send divers down to search for it."

"So when she leaves, we'll break in and swap the bags?" asked Keerati, holding onto an almost identical backpack they purchased earlier that day.

"We should have time to look for the pin while in the cottage. If we find it, we'll take it and be off."

"So why did we go through the trouble of finding an identical backpack?" Keerati asked.

"That's our Plan B, Keerati. You'll find that it's always good to have a Plan B. I'm sure she'll be going to dinner soon. I doubt she'll take the backpack with her."

"How do we get inside?"

"I noticed the upper window on the side of the bungalow is open. Once she's gone, we remove the screen and we're in."

Before too long, the sun had set on the horizon and night arrived. The two men continued to wait but as time elapsed, Keerati grew impatient.

"My legs can't take this any longer, Deng. I need to stand up."

"Keerati, don't be a jerk. Be patient. It shouldn't be much longer."

Another half hour passed and Keerati's legs could no longer tolerate the crouched position. He stood up at the same time as the door to Cottage 108 opened and a middle-aged man and his wife stepped out.

"Sheila, I'm taking the umbrella. They're predicting rain tonight."

Keerati fell to the ground as the man turned to lock the door. Out of the corner of his eye, he spotted what looked like the dark image of someone falling.

"What's the matter?" his wife asked.

"Say nothing," he whispered, "but there's someone hiding in the bushes. Let's get back inside." He reopened the door, and the two went back into the cottage.

Once inside, the couple turned off the desk light and the

man slowly pulled the drape a little to the left. "There they are—there's two of them!"

"What are they up to?" whispered his wife.

"Not sure, but if I had to make a guess, I would say mugging. Be quiet or they'll break into our room."

Back outside, Deng and Keerati watched as the couple no sooner stepped out of their cottage, but then disappeared back inside. "Did you notice that couple, Keerati? I think they saw you."

"Nah, too dark."

"So why did they immediately go back inside?"

"Maybe they forgot something—I don't know, Deng. Stop looking into things—you're making me crazy."

"Shh . . . quiet, the girl's coming out and she's without her backpack."

They spent a few anxious moments watching Allison walk towards the hotel lobby. Nerves were on overdrive—so much so they forgot about the couple in Cottage 108. Deng was the first one to step out of the shadows and head towards Cottage 107. "She's gone, Kerrati, come on out."

Both men preceded to walk around the bungalow until Deng pointed out the open window in the bathroom. Deng gave Keerati a boost and supported him while he pulled out his knife and sliced around the frame of the screen. Once done, Keerati pulled it apart.

From inside Cottage 108, the man whispered, "Just as I thought, Sheila. They're breaking into that other cottage. Call security."

Sheila hurried to the phone and dialed the hotel lobby. "Send someone! There's a break-in taking place right now in Cottage 107. Two men are crawling into an opened window.

My husband and I are watching them from our room. Oh, we're in 108. Okay . . . we will."

"Is someone coming?" the man asked.

"Yeah, he's alerting security. He also said to stay inside and keep our door locked. Are they still there?"

"Yes, they're both inside now."

Once inside Cottage 107, Keerati and Deng used flashlights to survey the room. They looked inside the closet but no backpack. "Shit! Keep looking, Keerati."

Keerati flashed his light on the bed, table, and chairs but found nothing.

"Where is that damn bag?" Deng said, sitting down on the bed. "I'm sure she didn't have it with her. What do we do now? Damn that Sarut and his stupid ideas!"

Keerati continued to cast light from floor to ceiling, letting it fall onto every inch of space until the light focused on three wall hooks. On the far left hook hung the backpack. "There it is, Deng!"

Both men ran over to the bag and opened it. "Shit, she has so much stuff in here. Screw looking for the pin. Grab the bag and let's get out of here," said Keerati.

Deng agreed but just as they were about to leave, a bright light flashed over the whole front entrance of the bungalow.

"Someone's unlocking the front door," said Keerati, "it must be the girl. Quick! Go through the window!"

Deng pulled a chair over to the window and lifted himself up. He crawled through the ripped screen and fell to the ground. "Keerati, throw out the bag."

Keerati mounted the chair and attempted to pull himself up to the window as the door to the room flew open.

"Keerati, throw me the damn bag, will you?" Deng whispered with a frantic voice.

The security man with his dog rushed in and turned on the room's light in time to see Keerati's legs hanging from the ledge. Keerati was about to toss the bag out the window when the dog jumped up, reached for his leg, and dragged him down to the floor—backpack and all. Hearing the commotion, Deng took off behind the cottage, into the rice paddies, and disappeared into the darkness.

Inside Cottage 107, Keerati struggled to free himself from the dog while the security officer grabbed his arms and cuffed him. "What are you up to?" the guard asked.

"Get that dog off me! There's a mistake," Keerati yelled. "I'm trying to find my cousin. Isn't this his room?"

"Do you always enter a building through a ripped out screen window?"

"The screen was like that, and I decided to crawl through because my cousin forgot to give me the key."

"That's bullshit," the man from Cottage 108 said, now standing in the doorway.

"Who are *you*?" asked the guard.

"We're the people who made the call. This guy had a partner who took off into the fields. We spotted both these men hiding in the bushes which raised our suspicion. They most likely were waiting for this place to empty out so they could break-in."

"Thanks for the call," the security guard said, pulling Keerati to the door as Allison approached the front of the bungalow.

"What's going on? Why are you in my room?"

"Are you staying in this unit?" asked the guard.

"Yes, what's wrong?"

"Can you identify this person?" he asked, pulling up Keerati's head.

"No, never saw him before."

"You mean he's not your cousin?" the guard asked in a sarcastic tone.

Keerati yelled, "I told you I thought this was my cousin's room. I went to the wrong cottage."

"Oh yeah, so who is this cousin? We'll check to find in which room he's registered."

Keerati said nothing. "Look guys, this is all a big misunderstanding. No hard feelings and I'll be on my way."

"You're going nowhere," the security officer said.

Allison looked from Keerati to the couple standing by the door. "Who are all you people? Why is this guy in my room?"

"That's what we'd like to know," said the security guard. Pointing to the couple from Cottage 108, "These people alerted us to suspicious behavior around your place. I arrived to find him ready to climb out the bathroom window. The guy with him had already escaped by the time I approached the scene. Looks like they were attempting to steal your backpack."

Allison stood in the doorway and watched as the guard pulled the man along the path. She thanked the couple for intervening, went inside and locked the bathroom window. On the floor next to the sink was the backpack.

"Why would anyone want this?" she thought. An overwhelming fear came over her when she realized the guy's accomplice was still out there. She picked up the phone and called Ashwin.

"What's the matter? You don't sound like yourself."

"I'm scared. Two men broke into my room while I was at dinner; and when I returned, the security guard was hauling one of the guys away. The second guy got away by crawling out the window. Ashwin, he's out there somewhere and I'm scared to be here by myself."

An hour later, Ashwin tapped on her door. "Allison, open the door. It's me."

For the next half-hour, Allison explained all that happened that night. "Don't you see there may be a connection between this situation and the car that followed us?"

"Or it could be a coincidence, Allison. Did you mention any of what you told me to security?"

"No, everything happened so fast, but there's something else. Remember how I told you someone broke into my room in Bangkok? I mean, twice in two different cities within weeks of each other? Something crazy is going on." After Ashwin listened to everything Allison told him, he asked her to get the backpack.

"Why?"

"Just get it. I want to take a look at it. You mentioned the guy was about to toss it out the window."

Allison walked over to the table and brought the bag over to Ashwin. "Just a bunch of things I had with me today –a jacket, notebook, pens, water bottle."

Ashwin opened the bag, pulled everything out, and laid it on the bed. "Is there anything missing?"

"No, not that I'm aware. Back in Bangkok the only thing disturbed in my room was my purse. Everyone must be after money."

Ashwin drew out her wallet. "Perhaps, but here's your wallet. Wouldn't it be easier for them to just pull this out and go?"

Allison nodded. "Maybe there wasn't any time."

Ashwin felt along the interior pocket and said, "There seems to be something else inside here—something small and bumpy."

"I don't know what that could be. Let me see." Allison looked inside the bag but all interior pockets were empty. She rubbed her hand across the lining until she touched the small, bumpy object. "Yeah, I feel it. There's a rip in the lining. Do you think something slid inside?" She maneuvered the bumpy object through the slit in the material and pulled out a glitzy pin.

"What in the world? What is this?" she asked.

"It's not yours?" Ashwin asked, looking inside the bag at the ripped lining.

"No, I never saw it before. It's beautiful but I wonder how it got in my bag." Looking at the pin more closely, she said, "Ashwin, could these be sapphires and diamonds? It looks quite expensive."

She handed over the pin for Ashwin to check out. "Sapphires? No, most likely rhinestones. What looks like diamonds are probably glass crystals. I know little about jewelry, but I'd guess this pin is probably some cheap costume stuff. How did the pin get inside your bag?"

"I have no idea."

"Do you think it's been there from before arriving in Thailand?"

"I doubt it. The lining ripped as I was going through security in New York. I remember pulling out my bag of liquids when the zipper snagged the material."

Ashwin took another look at the brooch and said, "This pin looks like some kind of barge—it's actually pretty gaudy. Hey, if you don't want it, I'll take it off your hands. I have a great-aunt who is into this kind of thing. She would love it. I don't think there are too many women who favor wearing brooches anymore."

Allison took the pin from Ashwin and held it under the

desk light. "I'm not sure. Looks like something more than rhinestones." She walked to the nightstand and put it inside her zipped cosmetic bag. "No, better not. Someone back home may recognize it."

Ashwin pulled out his phone and dialed the lobby. "I'm requesting that you be moved to another room." After some deliberation with the desk clerk, Ashwin reported a room would not be available until tomorrow. "Look, I'm not comfortable having you stay by yourself tonight. They can move you tomorrow, but how about if I crash on your couch to make sure nothing else crazy happens?"

Allison's face lit up. "Do you mind? I mean, I would appreciate that so much. Thank you, Ashwin."

Chapter 25

REVELATION IN THE NIGHT

SLEEP DID NOT come easy that night. So many things weighed on Allison's mind. Was she being followed or was it pure coincidence that someone broke into the only two hotel rooms she occupied while in Thailand? If so, why? Did it have to do with Thailand's civil war conflict? She had difficulty making any sense out of why her arrival in Bangkok and now Chiang Rai would raise a red flag to anyone. She needed to stop fantasizing and force herself to find the peace that would allow sleep.

That luxury lasted a few hours before, once again, she woke up. She sat up in bed and glanced at the alarm clock—5:13. Across the room on the couch lay Ashwin all bundled up in the spare blanket pulled from the closet. Allison experienced a little guilt realizing couches were never comfortable places to sleep, but she had to admit it was a relief knowing he was there. She smiled and rested her head on the pillow. It had been over a week since he first accompanied her throughout Chiang Rai. All kinds of thoughts flooded her mind—some she understood while others confused her. She stared up at the ceiling witnessing the first bit of light entering the room.

Hard to believe I've known this guy for such a short time. You can find out so much about a person when you spend this quality of time with him. Ashwin is different from the men

I've met back home. I always take control and when I let my guard down, I'm hit with disappointment. Well, perhaps not disappointment—more like disillusionment. Yeah, that's the word. Disillusion over what I thought existed, didn't. How many times can a person suffer through that? So what if I'm focused on my career. But Ashwin? Hmm . . . he's different. He's sweet but still takes the lead. And that smile? Lord, that smile makes me melt like a slab of butter. Could I be in some sort of dream? I never need to ask for anything because he figures it out ahead-of-time.

"Like last night," Allison whispered to herself. "I would never have asked him to stay here, but he knew how frightened I was and had the insight . . ."

"Who are you talking to, Allison?" Ashwin said from across the room. "Are you talking to me?"

Allison jolted up in surprise, but then giggled with embarrassment. "Oh, I'm sorry. I hope I didn't wake you. It seems I have this habit of talking to myself, and I don't always realize I'm doing it. Are you concerned I might be a crazy woman?"

"Nah, I've seen worse," Ashwin joked. "I've been awake for almost an hour now. How are you doing?"

"I'm okay but I have to tell you, I'm thankful you stayed last night. Every noise, every creak, every gust of wind—I heard it all and thought the worse."

"That's normal . . . the front desk will move you to a different room this morning. I suggested a room inside the hotel proper instead of a bungalow. Hope that's fine by you."

Allison smiled to herself realizing how once again he took over on her behalf. It comforted her to know someone was looking out for her. She could grow to like this.

"That's a good idea. I've enjoyed this little cottage; but after what happened last night, I'd feel more secure inside a hotel room."

From a nearby farm, a rooster crowed his *good morning.* "Did you catch that? I guess it's permissible to get up now," said Ashwin.

Allison didn't respond but instead entered into a bit of a trance. "Are you okay?" Ashwin asked.

Allison sat up and reached over to turn on the bedside lamp. She pulled the blanket up to her neck and wrapped her arms around her folded legs. "Yeah, I was thinking that the room I had in Bangkok was inside a hotel and someone still broke in."

"You know, don't have those thoughts—that happened almost two weeks ago, and we are many miles from Bangkok. As for last night? They nabbed one of the guys so maybe we'll find out more after they interrogate him. Hey, it could be fodder for your story! It's certain to make your account of Thailand more interesting, huh?"

Allison laughed. "How would you feel if I take the day off and just hang around the hotel? We've been going non-stop, and I could use a little respite. Besides, I need to spend time organizing my notes."

"Whatever you say—sounds good to me. I'll use the day to get a few things done, too."

"Good . . . it's settled. We'll check out the demise of the elephants tomorrow. I also need to call my friend, Lan. She left a message to call her but with everything going on, I never got to it. I'm not sure what she wants, but her voice didn't sound right."

"Lan? Is she the Vietnamese girl you told me about?"

"Yeah, I have plans to meet up with her before heading back to New York. I'm sure it's nothing—probably some sort of conflict. I'll give her a call later on."

After Allison climbed out of bed, she headed towards the bathroom. "I'm jumping into the shower—won't be long. Why don't you turn on the TV and see what's going on in the world? I've been so out of touch."

As Ashwin approached the TV, he spotted the cosmetic case sitting on the end table next to the bed. He waited until he heard the shower running, and then walked over to it. He opened the case and pulled out the brooch. As he examined it, the door from the bathroom opened.

"I forgot my shower cap . . . oh . . . what are you doing, Ashwin?"

Startled, Ashwin dropped the brooch back into the bag. "Nothing—just taking another look at the pin."

Allison grabbed her shower cap and headed back towards the bathroom. She turned around and said, "How about meeting me around the pool for lunch?"

Ashwin picked up his jacket and said, "Sure, how does 12:30 sound?"

Chapter 26

CRAZY BECOMES CRAZIER

AFTER DENG JUMPED out of the window, he waited for Keerati to toss the backpack to him, but that never happened.

"Keerati, come on—let's get out of here."

"I'm trying," he gasped, "but I'm having trouble raising myself up to the ledge."

"Quick! Give me the backpack!" As Deng waited for the bag to be tossed out the window, he heard the barking of a dog and the shouts of a man. Keerati wasn't climbing out, not with the dog there, so Deng turned and ran into the rice paddies. Not going far, he hid in the shadows. That was when Deng caught sight of the couple from the other cottage standing at the edge of the walkway.

"Shit, they did see us," he said to himself.

Then the American girl showed up. Unclear about what took place inside, he realized they now had a major problem when he saw Keerati led away in handcuffs. How would Montri react to this tidbit of news? Deng planned to wait until things quieted down, and then he'd make a return visit impersonating a hotel employee checking up on her to make sure she was okay. He spent part of the night amongst the shadows creating this whole scenario in his head. When she'd open the door, he'd burst into the room, grab the bag, and be out of there before she realized what happened.

And so he waited for over an hour dodging the rice rats busily making their meal from the unharvested rice kernels. He'd wait until the time was right, but what he didn't count on was someone else arriving at the cottage. The night was too dark to make out the figure, so he chose to take off after the cottage lights went out.

Telling this to Montri the following morning wasn't easy. "Hey, the people from the other cottage called security on us. I tell you, Montri, I had the bag in my hands."

"This is going from bad to worse. Where's the bag now?"

"Big K was about to toss it out the window when a damn dog attacked him. Between the dog's piercing bark and Big K's screams—it was ear-splitting."

"They caught Big K? Tell me this is all a joke, right?"

Deng said nothing. What could he say? That he screwed up again? Instead he remained quiet like an insubordinate schoolboy while Montri shouted threats over the phone.

The next morning the lodge employees remained attentive to Allison's needs. As soon as a room became available inside the hotel, they helped her move into it. Someone breaking into one of their rooms is not what they wished to see reported in an online trip review.

Allison and Ashwin decided to eat their lunch on the outdoor patio where tables were set up for guests. "This is beautiful out here. So peaceful—hard to imagine last night even took place. Tell me it was all a dream," said Allison. Ashwin shook his head and flashed that smile. *God, what amazing teeth he has.*

Ashwin gave his order to the waitress and said, "I wouldn't call it a dream, Allison—more like a nightmare. Have you received any information about either of the two guys?"

After waiting for the server to pour the coffee she answered, "No, but that's one of my action items for today. I told the desk clerk I wanted to speak to the manager." She poured a little crème in her coffee, took a sip, and touched the white orchid placed in the center of their table. "Ashwin, what do you know about flowers?"

Ashwin looked up and said, "Not much, but this orchid here can't be found growing in the wild. It's called the White Orchid."

Allison laughed. "Now there's an original name for you."

"It gets better," he teased. "We also have the Brick Red and the Bright Yellow Orchids. What use to grow wild in the jungle are now found in nurseries where special greenhouses are built to preserve these flowers and create new hybrids."

"These are expensive back in the states and here they grow everywhere," said Allison.

"Well, lucky you to be here during orchid blooming season. For an orchid to bloom it needs to retain enough moisture, or it's not going to . . . ah . . . what's so funny?" he asked.

"You . . . you're funny. You tell me you have little knowledge about flowers, and then begin this whole dissertation on how orchids are grown. Is there anything you don't know?"

"Sure, there's a lot," he said, watching Allison pull the flower out of the vase and smell it.

Allison put the orchid back and said, "Okay, here's the test. Name something you know little about and I mean very little."

Ashwin's eyes looked upward mimicking a contestant at a quiz show probing his brain for the answer. "Hmm . . . biochemistry. Can't say too much about that."

Allison laughed. "Whew, that's good. What else? I bet you can't come up with anything else."

Ashwin gave her a sheepish look. "Yes, I can but are you sure you want me to tell you?"

Puzzled, Allison waited while the server set their salad platters down in front of them and asked, "Sure, why not? Come on, one more thing."

"You—I know little about you."

Caught off guard, Allison felt the blood rush to her face. For once she couldn't respond—no sarcastic or quirky follow up, no clever retort.

Ashwin picked up his fork and pointed it at her. "The American journalist is at a loss for words, huh?"

"Well, no . . . er . . . I mean, what's there to tell that I haven't already said?"

"Other than you live in New York City and work for a place that produces short films, I would say a lot."

"Okay Ashwin, throw me some questions."

"You're not married, right? At least you've never spoken of anyone."

"No, I'm not married, but I once was."

Ashwin looked down at his untouched salad and said, "Does that mean you're divorced or is he deceased?"

"I'm divorced—have been for several years now."

Ashwin waited for her to finish, but she said nothing more. Silence can be either a welcomed break or an uncomfortable lifetime. In this conversation, the silence was quite painful. So painful he wished he never brought the subject up.

"I'm sorry if I've taken you to a place in time you'd rather not speak of," he said.

Allison smiled. "No, please—you've done nothing wrong. I asked about your personal situation; it's only fair that I share with you about mine. His name was David and we married while still in college. It seemed right at the time but looking back, such an insane thing to do."

"Why's that? You were in love, right?"

"Yes, but we both missed so much of the college life. It forced us to take grown-up roles way too soon. I sacrificed the experience of living with friends in a dorm or apartment, and going out for pizza and beer. Instead, we were home acting more settled than we should have been at the ripe age of twenty. Does that makes any sense to you? Kids today don't get married that young, not in America."

"So what happened—you and David?"

"Well, within a few years we started drifting apart. Our goals changed for what we wanted in life. He wanted an immediate family and I wanted a career. So much tension and neither of us would compromise. The fissure widened until life together became impossible."

"Do you ever see him?"

"At first we'd run into each other and sometimes go out to dinner, but it's been eight years since the divorce. No, we haven't had any contact for several years; not since he moved to Boston. From what I've been told, he's engaged to a lovely girl so I'm happy for him."

Ashwin said, "I sense there are regrets."

"No, if I stayed in that situation I'd be a miserable person right now. I needed the space and time to grow up and discover who I could be. Actually, we both did. Neither of us was at fault. The mistake was in marrying too young. It was a bad decision."

"So how do you view things now, Allison?"

"What do you mean?"

"Are you content living alone or does it ever get to you?"

Allison looked up at the patio roof trying to push back the tears. "Yeah, I have my moments when it gets to me. It would be nice to share successes and failures with someone. The problem is many of the great guys are taken. I'm like a chaperone at the club scene, and I don't have the grit needed to do the online dating thing. Cutting through the crap to find a nice guy requires time, and I don't have too much of that."

"Are you still dead set against having a family? I'm sure that could be a deal breaker."

"Ashwin, I never was against it. I just wanted to wait and get established in my career. I spent so many years working towards that degree and wanted to spread my wings and fly a little. It's difficult doing that with children because once they come along, it's mostly about them. I guess I needed to be a little selfish for a few years."

"It's all about timing," Ashwin said.

"You're exactly right."

At that moment, Allison caught sight of a man dressed in a security uniform heading towards their table. "Excuse me, but are you Ms. Wagner?"

"Yes, is this about the break-in?"

He nodded. "Please take your time with your lunch; but when you are finished, could I speak to you for a moment?"

"Sure, I can come now. Do you mind, Ashwin?"

"Of course not, go ahead. I'll have my second cup of coffee."

Allison got up and followed the officer into the hotel

manager's office. Although anxious to hear what information they had, he was grateful for the time to sit and think
about the conversation that took place between them.

*How crazy is this? You've known this woman a short
time. How is it possible to develop such a strong attraction?
I can't let it happen. We're from two different worlds having grown up in different cultures, and in a couple of weeks
she'll be returning to New York. Crazy! I need to check these
emotions because they're affecting my job. It would not be
good if she catches onto how I feel about her.*

"Ashwin, are you okay?"

Ashwin looked up and saw Allison standing over him.
"Oh, sure . . . just deep in thought, that's all. How did things
go in there? Did you find out anything?"

Allison sat down and said, "This is unbelievable.
Remember how I told you the man who sat next to me on the
flight to Bangkok was the same person who stole the brooch
from that Tokyo jewelry store?"

"Yeah, but isn't he dead now?"

"He's dead alright, but are you ready for this? The guy
they caught breaking into my cottage was the clerk who
waited on him at the store. He's supposedly on a work leave-
of-absence so he can take care of some personal family
business, but the police have been keeping their eye on him.
Evidently, he's under suspicion for involvement in the conspiracy to steal the brooch."

Ashwin's face grew serious. "That's unbelievable!"

Allison nodded. "Are you thinking the same thing as me?
I believe I know why he was in my room. That pin we found
in my backpack? It's got to be the missing brooch."

"Did you tell that to the officer?"

"No, he's only part of the hotel security. It's the Thai

police I would need to speak to about it. I'm not sure how to handle this. I mean—how does this all look?"

"Are you worried the police might believe you're part of the conspiracy?"

Allison placed both hands to her temple and shook her head. "Yes, of course. This could all become a huge mess for me if I don't handle things correctly."

Chapter 27

THE BROOCH

ASHWIN WAITED FOR Allison in the hotel lobby to take her to the Elephant Camp. When she didn't show up he called her room. She answered the phone and told him that she couldn't make it that day.

"Something's come up. I can't talk right now, but I'll call you later. I'm sorry about this." With no further explanation, she ended the call.

Ashwin thought this was not at all like her and grew concerned. What he was unaware of was, earlier that morning, the hotel security guard had accompanied the Bangkok police chief and the Tokyo marubo-dekka (*detective*) to Allison's room. Upon hearing of Keerati's arrest, the marubo-dekka immediately made plans to fly to Chiang Rai. Worried that Japan would permanently acquire the brooch that rightfully belonged to Thailand, the Bangkok police chief also tagged along.

The police chief showed Allison the scrap of paper with *Allison W.* written on it. "Do you recognize this?"

"No, not at all."

The chief showed her the paper with the Bangkok hotel and a copy of her bill. "Is this your signature?"

"Yes, but why do you have it?"

"Can you confirm this trip itinerary?"

Allison looked at the dates listed and nodded. "What's going on? How did you get all of this?"

"Let's put it this way, we've been looking for you," the marubo-deeka said.

With a growing lump in her throat, Allison sensed that no matter what she'd say these men would not buy it. The more she'd try to defend herself, the deeper the hole she'd dig.

"Here's my employer's phone number. His name is James McGregor, and he's the editor-in-chief of a company that produces short subject films. Call him and he'll verify why I'm in Thailand."

"So what's your connection with Sarut?"

"The only contact I had with this Sarut was on the plane when he sat in the seat next to me. That's it."

"So why was he interested in you? So much so that he wrote down your name and the hotel you stayed in?"

"I have no idea. The seating on the plane was random and not arranged. Jim will back that up. I was not the person who made the travel arrangements as we have staff that does that for us."

The police chief copied the phone number and the marubo-deeka jotted down some notes.

The detective asked, "How did you become acquainted with Keerati?"

"I never did. I never laid eyes on him until the night he broke into my room. But if I try to connect the dots, perhaps it was those two guys who followed Ashwin and me while we've traveled around Chiang Rai."

"Who is Ashwin?" asked the chief.

"Oh, sorry—he's the guide my employer hired to take me around northern Thailand."

"So you never saw these men up close?" asked the marubo-deeka.

"No, but I think I can give a description of the guy who

ran off. I didn't see his face that night, but I may have seen him in the Wat Ron Khun cafe. Ashwin and I were having tea, and this guy sat at the table next to us. All during that time, I felt he was listening to our conversation. When we got up to leave, so did he. I'm not sure if it was the same man, but I did receive bad vibes from him."

"Can you describe this guy?" asked the marubo-deeka.

Allison closed her eyes to recall his description and then replied, "I remember he was rather stocky, black hair, and had a stubby beard. He didn't look friendly—more agitated."

"So what's the reason these people would be interested in you?" asked the chief.

Allison pondered. *Should she tell them about the brooch she found in her backpack? Would they stack that against her?*

"I have something to show you. I'm nervous about showing this to you because of what you might assume, but I'll take my chances." The chief and marubo-deeka looked at each other.

Allison walked over to her cosmetic bag and took out a small white envelope. "After the hotel security removed Keerati from my room that night, Ashwin and I discussed at length about everything that appeared suspicious or coincidental. We decided there seemed to be an interest in my backpack since they left behind a nearly identical one. So we took all the bag's contents out and carefully laid each item on the bed. That was when we noticed it."

"Noticed what?" asked both the marubo-dekka and the police chief.

"This bumpy thing inside the lining." Allison retrieved the backpack to show them. "See this? The lining is ripped and inside we felt a small, bumpy item. This is what we found after Ashwin fished it out." Allison handed the envelope over to the chief who gently shook the inside item into the palm of his hand.

"Kee (*shit*), I'll be damn!" What fell out was a brooch in the shape of the emperor's barge. "This is it! This is the Royal Barge brooch. How did you get it?"

Allison shrugged her shoulders. "I realize how this must appear, but I was unaware it was in my backpack. The one person who had access to my bag would be that guy sitting next to me on the plane. Now that I know he's the one who stole the brooch, I'm surmising he put it inside my bag. I can only surmise that it happened when I was asleep, but I have no idea why."

"Why didn't you say something sooner?" asked the marubo-dekka.

"I discovered this pin two days ago. I didn't know what it was or from where it came. Believe me, it was a mystery. Why would I even assume that this pin was the stolen Thai brooch, huh? It wasn't until I learned the guy who broke into my room had a connection with the jewelry store that I started putting the pieces together. I mean, even Ashwin regarded the pin as a piece of cheap costume jewelry."

The chief stared at Allison. "So when you first spotted the brooch you didn't realize it was the one talked about on TV? How could that be? It's all over the news."

"Hey, TV hasn't been at the top of my agenda. I've been rather busy. I knew someone stole a valuable pin from a Tokyo store, but I never saw any photos of it or even heard of any description other than some Thai queen once owned it."

The police chief from Bangkok stood up and said, "Yes, and it rightfully belongs to the people of Thailand."

The marubo-dekka disregarded his remark and said, "With all the information out there about this brooch, you didn't think this might be the missing one?"

"As I just got through saying, I've been busy. Look, I'm here for work. I leave the hotel early in the morning and I'm gone all day. When I get back to the hotel, I eat dinner, organize my notes, and go to bed. Most of the TV channels in Chiang Rai are in Thai, so I rarely turn it on. Once I realized that this could be the stolen brooch, I planned on taking it down to the police headquarters. Then you guys showed up here before I could."

Annoyed over the police chief's earlier claim that the brooch belonged to Thailand, he confronted the chief. "Let me remind you, that brooch was stolen from Japan."

"That's true, sir, but rightfully it's the property of the people of Thailand," answered the chief.

The detective argued, "Let me be clear about this. I've come here to bring that brooch back to its rightful owners, and I don't plan on leaving without it."

The chief placed the envelope holding the brooch inside his breast pocket. "Not anymore. This is part of our history and it should be displayed in Thailand's National Museum. Your time here is finished. Consider returning to Tokyo. We will complete the investigation ourselves." The chief turned to two of his men and said, "Please accompany the detective to his hotel so he can gather his belongings, and then you can escort him to the airport."

Upon hearing the orders, the two burly men each took one of the marubo-dekka's arms and led him out the door. The detective protested loudly and resisted their grasp, but he was no match for these two beefy Thai men.

After the detective was removed from the room, the chief

said, "I'll take the brooch with me to have its identity validated. We need to make sure it's not a copy."

Allison nodded her head in agreement. "I understand."

The chief continued, "In the meantime, you are not to discuss any of this with anyone."

Allison asked, "Why's that?"

"We need to find Keerati's partner. He's still on the loose and most likely will try to contact you if he believes you have the brooch."

"Well, hearing that doesn't sit well with me," said Allison. "I'll need to tell Ashwin. He's been involved throughout this whole mess."

"Ashwin, the guide?" the chief asked.

Allison nodded her head. "Yeah, he'll be asking questions."

The chief shook his head. "No, tell no one. As for this Ashwin, make up something. Do not discuss what happened in this room and tell no one I have the brooch—not even this Ashwin. You let one person know and the probability of others hearing about it increases."

Allison followed the chief as he walked to the door. He turned and said, "As for you, there will be no leaving Chiang Rai."

"For how long? I planned on traveling to Chiang Mai in a couple of days."

The chief stared at Allison. "I repeat—there's no leaving Chiang Rai."

Chapter 28

LAN

"I'VE TRIED CONTACTING her several times with little luck," said Lan. "She finally returned my call, but my phone was turned off. That might have been while I sat with Yen in the critical care unit at the hospital."

"So she doesn't know yet?" asked Mae Chi.

"No, I didn't want to leave that kind of message on her phone. I figured there wasn't much Allison could do being in northern Thailand."

Mae Chi nodded and said, "But it's important we let her know, Lan, before she finds out from someone else."

Lan agreed. "Something must be going on with her, Mae Chi. It's not like Allison to ignore my calls. I hope she's okay." Lan grabbed her sweater and said, "I'm going out for a short walk. I'll be back soon."

Located on a street off the beaten path, the Safe House stood amongst a few shops and several apartment buildings. Lan enjoyed living close to the small park across the street. Bangkok had only a few green spaces, so Lan felt fortunate to have one so close to where she lived. As often was the case after dinner and before meditation, she walked around the block and then sat on one of the park benches. Sometimes she'd watch the people coming from work. Often they'd stop and pick up food for their dinner and take it home to eat. Many young, hard-working people lived in these apartments.

Several rode motorcycles, some took the sky train, and a few drove their own vehicles. The tricky part of owning a car in Bangkok was finding a parking place. Seeing the same car circling the block waiting for a spot to open proved to be entertaining for her. Not much was needed to amuse Lan.

She wouldn't trade this simple life because her work of counseling oppressed women partially filled the hole that existed in her own heart. She knew she wouldn't be doing this line of work forever. After all, she was young and someday hoped to have a family of her own. Besides, she missed her home in Vietnam as well as her grandparents and Uncle Trung. Someday she'd return, but not yet.

As she sat on the bench, she permitted her mind to wander to that horrific day last week when the call came that Yen was in the market when a device exploded. Lan rushed to the hospital and arrived in time to spend several hours with her. They spoke about the progress of their work at the Safe House, and what more could be done to help the girls—so important to both of them.

When it became apparent that Yen would not recover, Lan repeated one of the names of Buddha, Phra Arahant, over and over again in Yen's ear. In Thailand it was the custom for the dying person's mind to be fixed upon the scriptures of Buddha so that good would transpire in this new existence.

At the moment of death, the girls at the Safe House stood by Yen's bed along with several monks chanting sutras. The teachings of Buddhism described existence as suffering. Chanting aided any person crossing over to the next life where there was the expectation of rebirth. Sadness existed, but they believed in the idea that any acts of merit performed in this world would benefit them in the next. Yen qualified as a candidate for a better life.

After Yen's departure from this world, the girls performed a bathing ceremony in which they poured water over her hand and then placed her in a coffin. They laid wreaths and candles as well as sticks of incense all around her body. A picture of Yen hung by the coffin as people approached and honored her by paying their respects. The room filled with the continuous chants of monks as they held onto a ribbon attached to the coffin. The ribbon, or bhusa, symbolized the connection Yen still had with the living.

After three days, the ceremony ended with a funeral procession to the crematorium where they placed her body on a pyre made of brick. Then one-by-one, each of the mourners approached with lighted torches of candles, incense, and fragrant wood and tossed them beneath the coffin. The ribbon, no longer attached to the coffin, signified that Yen's body was now cut off from the world. Her ashes were collected and stored in an urn.

Lan thought back to that day several years ago when her abductor sold her to the owner of the silk factory. Several girls lived together in that cold, depressing room, but it was Yen who stood out. Yen, with her beautiful braided hair twisted around her head. Although that night proved terrifying for Lan, Yen's quiet voice settled her. It was also Yen who discovered the bracelet that slipped off Lan's wrist during that early morning struggle minutes after the other girls left for the factory. Yen picked it up and kept it on her wrist with the anticipation that one day it could be returned to its owner. All her life, Yen endured one struggle after another until she turned the corner of her own suffering. And now this—how senseless! What a waste. Not fair—not fair at all.

Chapter 29

THAI ELEPHANTS

"SO WHAT DID the police chief have to say?" asked Ashwin, as they made their way to the elephant camp.

"He had questions, you know, about my relationship with this Keerati. I told him I never met him before, but the way he looked at me was scary. I don't think he believed me."

"So how did it all end?" asked Ashwin, putting his windshield wipers on.

"I have no idea. They asked me a bunch of questions, I answered them, and they left."

Ashwin gave a short, shrill whistle between his teeth. "Whew, that's insane. So you have no idea what they'll do next?"

"Not at this point." With that, Allison turned her attention to the change of weather. "Tell me, how is this rain going to affect our time at the elephant camp?"

"Oh, it's a temporary shower—we get these off-and-on. You're in the jungle," Ashwin said. "It shouldn't last long."

"I'm a little anxious over where we're going. I didn't tell you this, but when I was in Bangkok I saw this mahout guiding his elephant through the city begging money from the tourists. The people laughed and took photos as they handed over their bahts to the elephant who quickly sucked them up with his trunk and handed the money over to his driver."

"This bothered you? It's part of our culture to use elephants as work animals."

"But they should be in the wild—not domesticated," insisted Allison.

"And so . . . you feel the same about the horse?" asked Ashwin.

"What do you mean?"

"At one time the horse was a wild animal happy to graze and roam in the open fields with no one taking care of it. Isn't that true?"

"What are you getting at, Ashwin?"

"What I'm saying is humans hunted down the horse, broke its wild spirit, and used this animal for farm work, transportation, sport—am I not right? So how is that different?"

This was a new side to Ashwin that Allison had never before seen. She looked over at him and said, "So you're okay with capturing elephants out of the wild?"

"Of course not. Laws exist against poaching and killing the elephant for its ivory. As of now, it's even illegal to bring ivory from African elephants into Thailand."

"But from what I'm hearing, it's legal to sell ivory from domestic Thai elephants resulting in vast amounts of African ivory laundered through Thai shops."

"I agree with you on that, and reforms are being passed to make it illegal to buy or sell ivory no matter where they originated."

"Well, that would go a long way in checking the poaching problem where tens of thousands of elephants are slaughtered each year."

"Allison, I'm taking you to a well-respected elephant

conservation camp so you can witness the work they are doing in regards to protecting the elephant. It would be wonderful if every elephant could be set free, but then what?"

Allison looked over at her companion and decided she struck a nerve with this otherwise cool and collected fellow who had been showing her around his country. "I don't know what you mean."

"The problems are not only with poaching for ivory. Consider this—the forest in Thailand is not what it used to be. Matter-of-fact, it reduced from 80 percent to 20 in twenty-five years due to logging, cultivation, road construction, pipelines, and even the building of resorts like the one you're currently enjoying. So tell me, where should the wild elephant live and feed now that his natural habitat has been severely diminished?"

Allison remained quiet as she sorted out what Ashwin said. "We have similar problems with our wildlife, Ashwin. Communities developed in areas that formerly had been dense woods or fields. This resulted in the residents getting upset because of the property damage brought on by deer and bear."

"And so . . . the same is happening here with the elephants, Allison. Conflict between plantation owners and foraging elephants often results in the elephant killed or poisoned."

"People need to be educated," Allison said.

"I agree, but try to explain that to a farmer whose livelihood depends on that field of sugar cane destroyed by a herd of elephants. That's where part of the problem lies."

"Is there any talk about protecting what forest remains?"

"Sure, any further development of the forest needs to be prevented in order to preserve the ecosystem."

"Well, I understand all this, but how do you justify the transporting of elephants into the city to beg for money?"

"Many elephant owners can't afford to feed their animals so they bring their elephants to the city to beg. Did you know the average adult elephant consumes about 200 kg of food each day?"

Allison shook her head. "No, I had no idea. Two hundred kilograms of food—that amounts to over 440 pounds. I can see how that could be a problem."

Ashwin said, "After the government banned logging, most elephants became unemployed. Sure, some patrol the jungles with forest rangers and others are used in the tourism industry, but few are adapted for this type of employment."

"I have another question for you. Does the elephant camp give rides?"

"They do but don't view elephant rides as something new."

"But it borders on abuse," Allison argued.

Ashwin shook his head. "Perhaps to the Western world, but places like Africa, Myanmar, India and Thailand? It's natural. The Asian and African countries have used elephants to carry goods and people for thousands of years. Giving a ride to a tourist is nothing to an elephant compared to the hard work they've endured in the past. But there is a restriction."

"What's that?"

"The camp I'm taking you to offers elephant rides, but strictly on the elephant's bare back. You don't sit on any howdah."

"I'm not comfortable riding bareback," Allison said, laughing.

Ashwin raised his eyebrows. "Really, now? I thought you were a little bit of an adventure girl. Where's that 'try it all' spirit of yours?"

"I believe a little disappears around each birthday. There's this phobia I have about breaking a leg, arm, or head. You're not going to shame me into it, are you?"

"No one will make you ride bareback, Allison. It requires a little practice, but you'll see many people at the center doing just that."

The two drove the rest of the way in silence as Allison anticipated the visit. She understood the fine line drawn in regards to the treatment of elephants, but how should she handle this in her report? Ashwin had a point. The use of elephants as work animals has been part of the Asian culture for many years. Do we try to push our values onto them? Are the elephants truly better off? She needed to think about that.

Their car passed a roadside sign announcing the approach of the Elephant Conservation Center. Located in a quiet valley surrounded by dense forest, they passed by the typical information kiosk and several gift shops that offered everything Thai. With a quick stop inside the visitors' center, they viewed an interesting short movie on Thai elephants. They also received information as to how the center has helped with conservation, and its attempts to reverse the depleted numbers.

"Allison, most camps have their elephants performing circus acts like playing soccer or balancing on one foot. This is not good for the welfare of the elephant because it can cause bone disorders. That won't happen here. You'll also find the mahouts not using bull hooks to control the animals, but instead use voice commands."

"What about after the visitors leave? Are the elephants confined by a short chain?"

"Absolutely not. Have you ever seen an elephant continuously swaying its head from side to side?"

"Yes, I believe I have."

"That's a neurotic behavior that often results from being chained."

"I never knew that. What about the trainers? Does each elephant have their own?"

"Yes, here they do. Elephants are sentimental animals with a need to bond. This can't be done if they are always having someone different take care of them. They aren't that much different from young children."

"Does a mahout take care of more than one animal?"

"No, here at this center each mahout is responsible for one elephant. These mahouts do not regard their assignment as a job, but consider their elephant as part of their family and will often sleep with them."

"They actually sleep with the elephant? That seems a little extreme."

"You might find it interesting to know the mahouts you'll see today come from the same tribe we visited early last week."

"You mean the Karen Hill Tribe?"

"The same—these mahouts are so dedicated that taking care of their elephant is considered an everyday commitment."

"So Ashwin, it appears our elephant philosophy is not too far apart."

Ashwin grinned. "I had you going there for a spell, didn't I? Come on, let's hurry down to the river. You don't want to miss seeing the elephants taking their bath, do you?"

Allison hurried to catch up to her companion. "Okay, remember—I don't ride bareback."

Ashwin smiled. "Ah . . . you'll love it."

"I'm serious, Ashwin."

Chapter 30

A TURN OF EVENTS

"MS. WAGNER, YOU need to come with me," said the police officer.

"But why? Where are we going?"

"Down to the station—we need to ask you a few questions."

"But what do you want to know? You can ask me here."

"No, not here—you need to come with me now." The officer gently wrapped his hand under her elbow and led her out of the hotel lobby to his car.

"Once inside the car, Allison asked, "Can I call a friend to meet me there?"

The officer shook his head and refused to respond to any of the questions Allison asked. She wondered what faced her. Thoughts drifted to earlier news reports of how journalists disappear. Could that happen to her? Vanish from Thailand and all because of a brooch. She had no tie to this piece of jewelry. Could they be making a case against her? Just a few days before, everything seemed okay. So what has happened?

The distance to the station was short, but the ride seemed endless before they pulled in front of the three-level white building. On the roof were two flagpoles that hoisted the red, white and blue striped flag of Thailand and the yellow flag representing the royal family. A large pendant with the portrait of a much younger King Bhumibol Adulyadej hung off a pole across the street.

A second officer greeted their car and escorted Allison into the building. They walked the length of a long hall before entering a conference room. The door opened and a detective motioned for Allison to sit in the chair opposite his desk.

"Please tell me why I am here?"

"Can I get you some coffee?" asked the detective.

"No, just tell me what this is all about."

The detective picked up his pen and pointed it at her. "I'm Detective Chaidee of the Chiang Rai police department. You're aware we're investigating the theft of one of Thailand's most valued heirlooms. As a matter-of-fact, if it wasn't for you and your friends, the Thai people would not have it in their possession. So we want to thank you for that."

In disbelief, Allison stared at the detective. "You don't understand, I had nothing to do with the brooch. I haven't had any kind of relationship with any of these people."

The detective, now tapping his pen on his desk, smiled and said, "But the pin was in your bag."

"That doesn't mean I put it there."

"Okay, let me ask you this . . . what is your tie with Sarut Wongsawat?"

"He sat next to me on a plane, that's all. Didn't Bangkok's police chief fill you in on everything?"

The detective dropped his pen, stood up, and leaned over his desk staring right at Allison.

"Take a look and explain your way out of this." He shoved a black and white photograph in front of her.

Allison studied the photo which showed her standing in

the center of a group of people. In the background was Sarut with an unidentified man.

"Oh, this was at the Red Shirt Encampment in Bangkok."

"We know. Their security camera caught it. Why were you there with Sarut?"

"But I wasn't. I remember spotting him in the crowd, and I even called out to him to say hello; but he never responded. He turned around and left. That's all I can tell you."

Detective Chaidee stared at her. Without saying a word, he picked up the photo, looked at it, and repositioned it in front of Allison. Pointing at the man standing next to Sarut, he asked, "So who is that?"

"No idea . . . I guess he must be with this guy you call Sarut." Allison picked up the photo and gave it a closer look. "Yes, I believe that is the same person who has been following Ashwin and me."

"Ashwin?"

"Yeah, the man that my office hired to take me around Thailand."

The detective asked, "So why are you here in Thailand, Ms. Wagner?"

"I'm a reporter doing research for a documentary."

"What kind of documentary?"

Allison glanced over at the two police officers who stood behind the detective. She noticed how one of them held a recorder. "Are you recording this?"

The detective said, "Does that bother you?"

"No, I have nothing to hide. I guess in Thailand you don't have to tell a person they're being recorded, huh?"

The detective ignored her comment and said, "This documentary . . . tell me about this documentary you're working on."

"Sure . . . it will focus on the blending of Old Siam with present day Thailand. It'll show how your country has maintained its cultural charm as it progresses into a modern society."

For only a moment, the detective's expression showed his approval; but like a stretched rubber band, he immediately rebounded back to his usual gruff style.

Allison pleaded, "I swear I was unaware of that brooch until the other day when I found it stuck inside my backpack. You see, I had this backpack with me on the plane. This Sarut must have dropped it in my bag either while I slept or when I went to the bathroom, but I'm totally baffled as to why."

The two officers said nothing but watched as she spoke— her eye movements, hand gestures, and even the way she tilted her head. This all could be used for or against her.

"Look, I gave Bangkok's chief of police my employer's phone number. I'll give it to you, too. Why don't you call my employer, Jim McGregor, and ask him about me?"

"I already did—talked to him this morning. Your story checks out with his."

"Okay, so why was I dragged in here and accused of being part of this mess?" asked Allison.

"We need your help in solving this case."

"But I'm not cut out for detective work."

Detective Chaidee said, "Come on, you're a journalist, right? I'm sure you've developed some of those skills along the way." The detective pointed to the photo of the guy standing next to Sarut. "We identified this person—he goes by the name of Deng. We're almost certain he was the guy with Kerrati the night they broke into your cottage. Turns out he's part of a Thai ring notorious for illegal dealings such as scams, blackmail, and other devious schemes. They love to relieve people of their money, and they're good at it. We believe he thinks you still have the brooch and may try to contact you."

"Is there anything else you can share?" Allison asked.

"Deng works for a wealthy man—a Mr. Montri. He's one of the big fish we want to catch, and we're hoping Deng can lead us to him."

"What is it you want me to do?"

"Just continue with your job assignment but keep your eyes open. I'm sure you won't have to go looking for him. He'll be looking for you."

"What about the guy you caught in my cottage?"

"Keerati? We have him locked up in his own private suite," said Detective Chaidee with a smirk. Allison decided that this was the closest this guy will ever come to smiling.

"Right now we've led him to believe that we know he was the clerk during the robbery," the detective continued. "Otherwise, we're playing dumb. The important thing is to keep him away from the others. Since he's aware we have the brooch, we don't want him to share that piece of information with any of his cronies. Are you in?"

"It doesn't appear I have much of a choice, Detective Chaidee, does it?"

The detective stood up and directed Allison to the door. "No, not really."

Chapter 31

DISTURBING NEWS

"HELLO, LAN? IS that you?"

"Allison, I've been trying to reach you all week."

"Lan, I returned your call twice but could not connect. Things have been crazy here."

"Why's that?" Lan asked.

"Well, I can't get into the details, but the authorities have me connected to the brooch that's been in the news. Somehow it got into my luggage—you might say, I've had lots of explaining to do."

"I don't understand, Allison. How did that happen?"

"Lan, that's a question I'd like answered, too."

"Are you alright?" Lan asked.

"Yeah, somewhat. Don't worry, I'm sure this situation will get straightened out."

"This doesn't sound like you. How bad is it?" Lan asked.

"Like I said, I'm unable to talk about it now, but when I return to Bangkok I'm sure it will make interesting conversation with you and Yen over dinner."

After a long pause, Allison asked, "Lan, are you still there?"

"Yes, but I have disturbing news to tell you about Yen."

Concerned, Allison sat at the edge of her bed. "What happened?"

"Oh Allison, I don't know how to tell you this, but there was an attack on Khlong Toey Market last week."

"Isn't that market located near you?"

"Yes."

"Okay, go on."

"Well, Yen went to the market that morning to get the food supplies we needed. While there, two bombs exploded. One detonated in a garbage can next to where Yen stood. Several people were injured and three died. One of those killed was Yen."

Upon hearing this news, Allison's body stiffened. Could she possibly be in the middle of another nightmare? After all, she experienced several lately. Maybe this was one more, and she'd wake up and realize this conversation never happened.

"Allison, I'm so sorry to have to tell you this news. Yen lived a short time with brief periods of consciousness, and during those times we had several conversations. She asked me to express her gratitude for all your efforts in uncovering the trafficking ring. She held Banh primarily responsible for the suffering of so many girls."

"Lan, I did nothing that any decent person would not have done. Once we figured out what was going on, we could not ignore it."

"But it's true, Allison. Had you not come along, we would still be leading miserable lives."

"Oh my God, Lan. I'm having difficulty wrapping my head around this. Did you have the funeral?"

"Yes, there are time restrictions for this in the Buddhist religion. I was unable to reach you, and I didn't want to leave such a dreadful message on your voice mail."

"I understand, Lan. Truth be known, I'm not allowed to

leave Chiang Rai just now because of this situation with the brooch. I had planned to go to Chiang Mai in a couple of days, but that looks bleak. How is everyone dealing with this at the Safe House?"

"It's been rough for Mae Chi. She was the last one to talk to Yen. Mae Chi warned her of the uprisings going on in the city and advised her not to go out, but you know Yen. She felt she'd be fine. Now Mae Chi is upset she didn't insist Yen stay home."

"Did she suffer much, Lan?"

"Yen experienced many complications, so the doctor gave her medication to numb her suffering. The medication made her sleepy and for the last two days of her life, she went in and out of consciousness. No one could help her. She suffered much internal damage standing so close to the explosion."

The girls talked for another twenty minutes and promised to stay in touch. Hanging up the phone left Allison alone which proved to be too difficult for her to handle. There was so much she needed to share with someone—anyone. She wanted so much to bag this whole trip and take the next flight back to New York. Never did she miss home as much as she did that moment.

Allison reached for the phone and called Ashwin. She let it ring, but he didn't pick up. *He's probably sick of me and all my problems.*

Allison laid down on the bed and turned on the TV where the only English speaking channel carried non-stop news. A week had passed since she listened to anything on television. After hearing more about the Red Shirt demonstrations that continued in Bangkok, there was a brief report about the brooch. Allison sprung off the bed when they posted a photo of the brooch.

Yeah, that's it alright. That's exactly how the brooch looked. I can't believe I carted it around in my backpack all those weeks, unaware I even had it.

The news reporter introduced an elderly historian who went into an explanation of the significance of this pin to Thailand and the Thai people. Nothing was mentioned about the discovery of the pin, so the chief's decision to not disclose that information remained intact. She wondered why the Japanese detective said nothing. He left Thailand steaming mad when the police chief ordered him off the case. Wouldn't he want to reveal that the Thai chief refused to hand the brooch over to him? After all, it was stolen from a Tokyo store. Instead, he remained quiet.

Chapter 32

AKHA HILL WATERFALLS

"WHAT? NO MOTORCYCLE?" asked Allison.

"Not today, it's a bit of a ride and not on easy roads."

"Where's this place again?"

Ashwin started the car and headed out of Chiang Rai. He smiled and said, "Actually, it's a little surprise."

"So why the hiking shoes, bathing suit and lunch?" Allison asked.

"Since you can't leave town and refuse to tell me why, we are hiking to a spot that is one of my favorite places."

"Ashwin, it's not that I have anything to keep from you; the police detective said he wanted me to stay in Chiang Rai."

"But why? Because someone broke into your room?"

"Yeah, I guess so . . . you know, they may need me to testify or something."

She knew Ashwin wasn't buying the story, but she remembered the detective's orders of not discussing the whereabouts of the brooch with anyone. *I hate lying, especially to Ashwin.*

Ashwin gave her a sideway glance and shook his head. "Makes little sense, Allison. You're not the suspect; you're the victim. There's no reason for them to keep you from leaving Chiang Rai. Did you tell the detective about the backpack?"

"Only that the guy was all set to take the bag when the hotel security officer caught him."

"Oh, so no mention about the pin?" Ashwin asked.

"Ah no, didn't see why. Like you said, the pin was costume jewelry. Who would want it? Kind of ugly at that."

God, lying is tough.

"Yeah, can't see you wearing it around anywhere," he laughed. "Like I told you, I have a great-aunt who would wear that kind of thing. She doesn't have too much and would love it—if you ever want to get rid of it."

"Well, perhaps . . . okay, enough about that pin. Tell me about where we're heading."

"It's called Akha Hill Waterfalls, and it's an hour outside of Chiang Rai which is why the early morning start. Hey, that won't get you into trouble with the police, will it?"

"No, shouldn't—we're coming back later today. So what's this place like?"

"The views are spectacular and it all ends with a swim in the neatest swimming hole that's replenished by a waterfalls. I've stayed at a nearby guest house several times, but I didn't think that would appeal to you."

"Why's that?"

"The individual cottages are kind of cool, but rustic. They're made of bamboo and have a balcony overlooking the valley and hills."

"Do they have indoor plumbing?"

"Yes, there's an attached bathroom with a small electric heater for the shower."

"That doesn't sound bad," Allison said.

"Wait, you haven't heard the best part yet. Because you're in the jungle, there's a lot of wildlife."

"Ashwin, I like wildlife."

"Sure, but I'm talking about things like giant spiders and oversized cockroaches—sometimes in your bed."

He looked over at her and laughed as Allison's face went from adventurous to a squinty frown.

"There's more. The last time I stayed there, I had a room with a bed but no mattress. So the owner dragged in an old mattress he found stored in the shed. I found my room dirty and the bathroom dirtier. Still feeling adventurous?"

"When you put it that way . . . uh, no!"

The rest of the hour they spent in silence as Allison wrote in her journal. "What do you write in that book?" Ashwin asked.

Allison smiled and closed the notebook. "Oh, just impressions and notes that will remind me of what I've seen and done."

"Ever write about me?"

Allison looked over at her driver as he pulled into a parking lot with four other cars.

"Sometimes, I do."

The two got out of the car, each grabbing a backpack. "So is the pin in your bag?"

A little annoyed they were back on that subject again, she said, "No, it's at the hotel."

After they applied bug spray, the two took off on the gravel road leading to the trail.

"This place is owned by the Akha people," Ashwin explained. "The accommodations I mentioned earlier may be stark because these people lead a simple lifestyle."

Once they reached the trailhead, the gravel road turned into a dirt path surrounded by thick bamboo. Steps were dug into the ground which made it a little easier for the trip down. An hour later, the two hikers heard the roar of cascading water.

"The sound is deafening but delicious," Allison said as she quickened her pace, eager to see what was up ahead.

There in front of them stood Akha Waterfalls. The large-leaf tropical trees were the brightest color of green imaginable. The sun, high in the sky, shone through allowing its rays to bounce on the water adding charm to the scenery. None of Chiang Rai's oppressive heat was apparent in this environment, but instead there was a natural form of air conditioning as the clear water cascaded onto the large boulders creating a cool, smoky mist.

"Ashwin, this is paradise."

"I thought you'd like it." They quickly disrobed revealing their bathing suits underneath and jumped into the water.

"Wow, this is refreshing!" yelled Allison, as she playfully threw water on Ashwin. He grabbed her foot and pulled her under the water. She surfaced gasping for breath and instantly went into the attack mode. The two ended up in a crazy water fight that perhaps only ten-year-old children might engage; but in that moment, that's what they were. The swimming hole, trees, boulders—it all chipped away at their defenses.

Ashwin climbed onto a large boulder, half-covered with green plant life. Allison swam over and he pulled her up next to him. The setting was perfect and the moment was right. The feelings both were secretly suppressing could no longer be ignored and before too long, they were in an embrace. With their emotions unleashed, neither held anything back as it all seemed so right and perfect. The passion they felt turned into giddiness while they acknowledged the line they crossed. There was no turning back since what was a short time ago, no longer could be.

Ashwin teased, "Hey, I shouldn't have done that. I'm on a job here."

"So you think of me as a job? I think we're past that now."

He touched her long blonde hair and kissed her. "I shouldn't tell you this, but I've had strong feelings for you from the time we first met. I can't explain it, but this rush came over me, Allison. I haven't been this happy in a long time."

Allison rested her head on his shoulder. "It's the same with me. It's crazy how quickly things happened, but there's this joy I experience whenever you're around. I don't want it to end."

"It doesn't have to end."

"Ashwin, there just seems to be too many obstacles. We live half-way around the world from each other. I've lived awhile in your world, but you haven't a clue about mine. I don't believe you'd like it."

"So how do you know I wouldn't?"

Allison sighed. "That gentle spirit of yours would be torn apart in New York City. You mentioned how you hated living in Bangkok—New York is far crazier."

Ashwin pointed to a hummingbird flitting through the spray of water. "See that bird—not a worry in the world. All his needs are taken care of by the natural environment. What's wrong with that?"

"Nothing," Allison said, "but eventually that bird might want more. They always do, and so would you."

"There's so much more about me that you really don't know."

"Well, then tell me."

Ashwin grinned and said, "Hey, let's not have reality ruin this moment." He slid back into the water and pulled her in after him. Holding hands, they floated over to the falls and allowed the water to topple over their bodies as they passionately kissed and re-entered their perfect world—a world with no obstacles.

Chapter 33

LOCKED AWAY

DAY AFTER DAY, it was the same. The imprisoned man woke up to the sound of heavy footsteps, the door opened, and the guy with the phoenix tattoo walked in carrying a container of food. Several weeks before, he removed the bindings that held his prisoner's hands behind his back, and pulled off the bandana that covered his mouth. Warned if he didn't maintain good behavior all of those entrapments would reappear making an unbearable day intolerable. And so the captive man co-operated. He tried to befriend the guy with the tattoo hoping to gain his confidence by showing his more personable side.

"Good morning," he said to his captor. "How are things out there today? I can't tell from inside this stuffy room. Is there any way I could get some fresh air?"

"That's not possible. This is not a resort," the tattoo man snarled. "Maybe in a few more days we let you go."

Acknowledging this first ray of hope since being pulled off the street and thrown into this hell, the man accepted the container of food and pointed for his captor to sit down across from him.

"Is it possible for you to tell me why I'm here? If it's ransom, my family doesn't have much money."

"No, no ransom—no more questions from you. Just eat your food."

At first, it didn't matter what the man tried, the tattoo guy never budged, softened or responded to his friendly gestures. Eventually, he convinced the tattoo guy to bring him a blanket, pillow, and something better than the lumpy chaise cushion to sleep on. At other times the tattoo man smuggled in books and magazines to help pass away the time. This situation could be worse, he reminded himself in an attempt to keep his spirits from becoming totally depleted.

Every so often the sound of a plane either taking off or landing supported his assessment that his location was close to the airport. The days were long and the nights even longer, but his captors intimidated him to such great lengths that the fear of the unknown resulted in compliancy. The need for survival outshone his need to save face. His ego would have to wait.

He worried about his hospitalized mother. Did she ask for him? He speculated no one in his family would be concerned. Why would they? Often his job took him out of Chiang Rai. He informed his sister several days before he went missing that he would be on an assignment for most of that month. The tattoo guy seized his cell phone despite the argument he needed to check on his mother's condition. The tattoo guy cared less.

After the tattoo man left, he knew he would be alone until supper. He received no lunch and the time span between the two meals seemed like eternity. He tried banging on the concrete wall, but no one heard him. So he sat and thought. He wondered how this situation would end and questioned why he was even there. The room had a bare bulb hanging from the center of the ceiling and on occasion a moth would flit around it. How interesting that something so basic became a source of entertainment.

Alone with little to do forced him to evaluate his life. After thirty years of marriage, Dara died of cancer. He took care of her for two years which often resulted in difficult days, but also allowed them the time to reflect on their marriage including their regret of not having children.

His mother helped during this time by assisting Dara so that he could work. In time, he needed to take a leave of absence due to her worsening condition. After Dara died, he experienced the loneliness that often follows.

Dara's name meant evening star in Thai, and most evenings the grieving widow sauntered outside, sat on a garden bench, and looked up at the sky until he found her star. He'd have a one-sided conversation relaying the events of the day—what went right or what went wrong. That was the routine for two years until the day two men overpowered and snatched him from the street. He wanted to view the sky from his cell but impossible—no windows. He talked to Dara anyways, asking for her help in freeing him from this situation. But how could that happen? She was no longer a person of the earth. She was a spirit of the heavens.

Chapter 34

THE PROPOSAL

"WHAT IS IT you want me to say?" the marubo-dekka barked at his supervisor. "Once they had the brooch, they took me by force and stuck me on the next plane to Tokyo."

The supervisor said, "The brooch belongs to the store, and it must be returned. You do understand the owner is a wealthy man and has always been financially supportive of our needs. You wait here while I put in a call to the police chief."

He reached for the phone and connected with the Bangkok office. At first the conversation started out civil, but deteriorated when the Bangkok police chief stubbornly insisted that he had no intentions of handing the brooch over to a foreign country.

"Look," Tokyo's officer said, "it's not as if Thailand doesn't have possession of heirlooms and artifacts belonging to other countries. Things happen—births, deaths, wars—treasures are sold, borrowed, and seized. That's the way it's been. So why should we fight the battles of our grandfathers?"

"I agree; maybe we could make a deal," the chief suggested.

"No deal," the Japanese officer said. "I understand there's been no public announcement about the discovery of the brooch, huh? Why is that?"

"No, not until we locate Keerati's accomplice. These two men were part of a conspiracy to obtain this brooch illegally and sell it. We need to sit tight until we have a handle on the identity of all these individuals."

"What about the girl? What's her role?"

"The best we've determined is that Sarut used her as a vehicle to get the brooch through security. We believe she had no knowledge of the plan and was simply another victim in a plot that went wrong."

"But that doesn't solve our problem over here. There's an investor from Tokyo who bought that brooch at an auction for a hefty sum of money and will remain unconcerned over your predicament."

The Thai chief said, "Hey, I understand your situation, but you need to understand ours which is why I've been having private talks with the curator of the Bangkok Museum. They have the personal calligraphy of Japan's Emperor Go-Nara which goes back to 1526 until 1557 when he died at the age of 62. The curator explained that Thailand has an extensive amount of his personal property because he needed to sell it."

The Japanese officer replied, "Yes, Go-Nara's Imperial Court was so impoverished that they even had to ask for contributions from different clans in order to hold a formal coronation. As it was, the coronation didn't take place for ten years."

"We hope your country will consider an offer we feel to be respectable. We'll trade this calligraphy and several samples of the emperor's poetry along with a bronze statue of Emperor Go-Nara which the museum purchased in auction from the previous owners. We believe this to be a fair trade. You would have heirlooms of your past, and we will have the brooch that belonged to King Rama V's first wife."

A pause in the conversation ensued as the police officer explained to the marubo-dekka what the Thai chief proposed. Then he got back on the line. "I can't make that decision. I need to talk to the owner of the jewelry store and get back to you. In the meantime, list each piece of artwork and calligraphy you agree to exchange so that offer is in writing."

The conversation between the two top men of both the Bangkok and Tokyo police agencies ended with optimism that a resolution could be reached while avoiding any international crisis.

Chapter 35

KITE FLYING FESTIVAL

TWO PEOPLE IN bed stirred as the morning sunshine streamed through the window. The man opened his eyes and looked at the sweet girl lying next to him. He groaned as he realized he violated a self-imposed rule—never to mix his personal life with work. The temptation, too strong to resist, resulted in pulling out all restraints as he and Allison made love most of the night. An attraction existed from the moment he first met her. As they spent each day traveling around Chiang Rai, the attraction grew into a pining he found difficult to control; but still he kept his distance and his feelings in check. That is, until yesterday afternoon when they sat together on the rock at Akha Hill Waterfalls. After pulling Allison out of the water, he recognized the same desire in her eyes. That was all he needed to see before tossing aside all logic. The pounding of the water over the rocks matched the pounding in his chest. They were one with nature; and what appeared wrong, now felt so right.

Allison opened her eyes and leaned over to kiss the handsome guy.

"Good morning, Ashwin. Must be yesterday wasn't a dream, huh?"

Ashwin snickered. "If it was, then I believe I have some explaining to do. Would you buy into the idea I sometimes sleepwalk?"

"No, but you are quite good at protecting me from the forces of evil," she said as she raised her head from the pillow. "I hate to bring this up, but with yesterday being a day of—er–rest and relaxation, we probably should put in a day's work."

"I plan on taking you to a kite festival that's happening at a nearby park. Interested?"

Allison smiled and said, "I'm always interested."

The two never made it to breakfast that morning, but instead lingered in bed and skipped right into lunch. The restaurant was a little hole-in-the-wall that only served lunch. Allison asked Ashwin to order something he thought she might enjoy. In a short time, the waiter brought out two dishes for them to share—lahp and som-dam.

"Okay, what do we have here?" Allison asked as he held her hand from across the table.

He gently removed his hand from hers and picked up the large spoon to serve the lahp. "This is a spicy minced-meat which is an Isan dish and a specialty of this restaurant." After placing a helping on both plates, he dished out the som-dam. "Can you guess what kind of salad this is?"

Allison took a bite and said, "Ah, green papaya salad but spicier than I'm used to eating."

"Right . . . and mixed amongst the noodles are peanuts, chopped chili, shrimp and grated sugar palm." Ashwin grinned. "Do you like it?"

"Well, it's different. You said it was an Isan dish? What's that mean?"

"Isan is what we call the northeastern region of Thailand bordering the Mekong River. It's actually the largest region of Thailand and was once the country's poorest area, but now is the site of Thailand's fastest growing economy."

"Really, how did that happen?" Allison asked.

"Private investors financing the start-up of many industries."

Allison made no comment when she realized Thailand's gain coincided with the closing of many American factories.

After lunch, Ashwin and Allison headed toward a park that had several cordoned-off areas centered around kite-making, live music, professional lessons on how to fly the kites, and an exhibition on the history of kite flying. After visiting each area, they walked toward a roped-off section where they watched people flying kites of various colors, shapes and designs.

Ashwin asked, "Did you know kite flying is a sport over here?"

"No, I didn't. Does it come with competition?"

"Of course, are you surprised?" Ashwin said, pulling gently on her long pony tail. "Do you know how many men over here look at your light-colored hair?"

"They do?"

"All the time—so pretty," said Ashwin.

Allison smiled and said, "Ashwin, I believe you are getting off-track. You were about to tell me about the kite competition."

"Ah yes, sorry but I'm a little distracted," Ashwin said, smiling from ear to ear. He pointed to one of the kites still on the ground. "Over here is a male kite called the Chula, and over there you see a female kite called a Pakpao."

Allison laughed. "Hmm . . . I think I'm figuring out what's to follow."

Ashwin grabbed her hand, kissed it and said, "So would you care to explain it to me?"

Allison wrapped her arm around Ashwin's waist and said, "I would say the Chula goes after the Pakpao. The Pakpao pays little attention at first until she can no longer ignore the Chula's persistence, charm, and attentiveness."

Ashwin said, "So the Pakpao gives up and falls for the Chula like . . . how do you say . . . head over heels, right?"

Allison looked at Ashwin with flirtatious eyes and answered, "Possibly."

Ashwin said, "Check out the strings on the kites. They have strands of glass used to cut the line of the opposing kite."

"Hmm . . . cutting a kite's line? That could hurt and be dangerous to the kite, right?"

"It could be risky if the victorious kite encircles the trailing line of the wounded kite and secures it. The person flying that kite can then fly both kites."

"And then, what?" asked Allison.

Ashwin pulled Allison over to the side of a food tent and kissed her. "And then the winner pulls in the prize.

Chapter 36

THE POT BOILS

"HEY MONTRI, THIS situation is difficult with Keerati locked up in jail. I have no one helping me here."

"What about this Anthony friend of yours? What's going on with him?"

"Hard to tell—unable to get ahold of him."

"It was upon your recommendation that I took him on, and now you're telling me you can't reach him?"

Unaware of who might tap the lines, Deng didn't want to disclose anything on the phone. He never used to be paranoid, but ever since Keerati's arrest, he felt sure the police were only days away from hauling him into jail, too. Keerati's reliability wavered during times of stress, and Deng predicted he'd break telling the police everything about him and Montri in an exchange for a deal.

"Deng, as time drags on, the guy interested in obtaining the brooch has become more edgy. I've given one excuse after another, and I'm not sure how long I can keep him hanging. Right now he's close to forgetting the whole deal which means I'd have to return his deposit. Well, that's impossible since I spent half of it."

"I'll see what I can do—maybe rev up the pressure on Anthony."

"Well, do it and do it now."

Deng put the phone in his pocket and paced from one end

THE STOLEN BROOCH

of the room to the other. He looked out the window at the rain wondering if he should venture out. Unsure of what his next move should be, he pulled his phone back out and dialed up Anthony. The phone rang several times until Anthony's voice mail switched on.

"Hey, Deng here. Where the hell are you? I got you this job, bragged about your ability to get things done, but as of now—nothing. The boss is getting very anxious and when he gets anxious, I get anxious. Call me—now!"

Deng grabbed his jacket and left the shabby hotel room Montri arranged while he stayed in Chiang Rai. Outside on the street, he pulled up his collar to keep from getting soaked, but that was useless. Finding himself being the sole person walking the streets, he hurried past the blue ATM machine, the few parked motorbikes, and the secured vendor kiosks. Deng quickly ducked into the town's 7-Eleven and purchased two snack bags, a can of soda, and a dried out sandwich that sat on the counter since early morning. His phone rang as he approached the check-out attendant. He looked at the number and saw it was Anthony.

"Yeah, Anthony . . . I've been trying to get ahold of you."

"Right, been busy."

"Busy doing what?" Deng asked.

"My job. Look Deng, I decided to back out of this assignment. It's not for me."

"Ah . . . not a chance. You're involved and the only way out is to finish the deal."

"Hey, no worries—no need to pay me any money for time spent. As it turned out, I have other stuff going on and no time to help you out. Sorry about that. "

"Perhaps our connection isn't good. I said there's no backing out."

193

Anthony stammered, "But . . . what's the point? I'm no longer interested in being involved in this mess of yours. I want out."

"Hey Anthony, what's changed here? You were happy to get the work, and now you want to quit?"

"Sorry Deng . . . I thought about it and decided I can't do this. I don't care about the money. Tell that to your boss."

"He won't like this one bit, Anthony. You know, I stuck my neck out for you. How's this going to look? You don't want to mess with Montri. He's arranged for people to disappear for as little a reason as disagreeing with him about the weather."

"Deng, I'll take my chances. Cut me loose." And with that, Anthony hung up the phone.

The head of the Chao Pho sat in his Bangkok office puffing on a cigar. He reached for the phone and personally called Naai Montri to see how things stood with the brooch. Montri explained the situation was close to being resolved, but all his alibies and promises no longer held value.

"Montri, I'm giving you two days. Either I have the brooch or you return my $500,000 deposit."

Montri said, "Hey, you gave me $400,000."

The head of the Chao Pho swiveled his chair around to watch the passing skytrain. He puffed on his cigar and said, "Interest, my friend. I pulled money from my investments to turn that sum over to you. I expect to recoup on the interest."

Montri said, "I don't have that kind of money. I told your guy to tell you I spent about $200,000 just on the logistics of putting this plan into place. Be patient and you'll get that brooch for your wife."

The Chao Pho's boss slammed the phone down and called in one of his guys. "Have our people take care of those thugs. I don't trust that double-crossing thief."

The ante was high as the two men sat inside the warehouse playing cards. One man drew a card, looked at his hand, and then laid his cards down on the table. "Done deal."

"Shit, Virote! You drew from the bottom of the deck."

"Like hell I did; I won," Virote said, stacking his winnings in neat little piles.

The man with the phoenix tattoo stood up, and flipped the table over spilling the cards and money. Virote pulled the table off of himself and grabbed the tattoo arm twisting it behind his challenger's back.

"Try that again and I'll detach your legendary phoenix and feed it to the vultures." Virote stood the table up and collected the scattered money. "I won . . . get over it."

On the other side of the door, the imprisoned man yelled through the wall. "Open the door. I need air. It's stifling hot in here."

Virote glared at his card-playing opponent as he unlocked the door and warned the frantic hostage to shut his face up.

"When do I leave? Why am I here? I demand to know what's going on."

Virote shoved the weakened man into the corner of the room and said, "You'll be out of here when we're done with you. So shut up!" Virote slammed the door, locked it, and left the building.

Chapter 37

BAFFLED

"JIM, THERE'S A man on the phone from the Thai Booking Agency," said Ellen, his secretary. "He wants to speak to you."

Jim looked up from his computer and said, "What's that about?"

"Not sure, but he appears to be anxious about something."

Jim looked at his watch and said, "Get his number and tell him I'll call back tomorrow."

"You might want to take this call now. He sounds uptight."

"Ellen, I should have been out of here two hours ago. I promised my wife I'd be home early and here it's after seven."

Ellen gave him a stern look. "What if something has happened to Allison—you know, like an accident or something."

Jim looked away from his computer and said, "Okay, I'll take the call. By the way, why are you still here?"

"I had some loose ends to finish, but I'm leaving now. Talk to you in the morning."

She put on her coat and walked out of the office as Jim picked up the phone. "McGregor here, what can I do for you?"

"Hello, Mr. Jim McGregor? This is the Thai agency you used to book a guide for this month."

"Yes, for our reporter, Ms. Wagner. What's up?"

"Have you heard from her?"

"Yes, she calls every few days to bring me up-to-date on what she's doing. The last time was three days ago. Why?"

"That's good to know. I feel better. We've been trying to get in touch with her guide, but he's not picking up his phone or responding to our messages."

"That's odd. I surmised things were going well since Allison had spoken highly of him." Jim laughed and added, "He even gave her the experience of riding on the back of a motorcycle."

There was a brief pause until the man on the other end of the phone said, "Motorcycle? Ashwin doesn't drive a cycle . . . not at his age."

"What do you mean?" asked Jim. "Isn't he in his mid-thirties?"

"No, Ashwin is in his late sixties. He might be older, but he's our top guide—very knowledgeable about Thai history and culture. We gave you the best of the best. He's been working for us for over thirty years."

"I see," Jim said, tapping his pen on his desk. "I'll give Ms. Wagner a call and tell her to have Ashwin get in touch with you."

"Thank you, Mr. McGregor. His family is wanting to contact him because his elderly mother passed away two days ago."

"I'm sorry about that. Okay, I'll see what I can do." Jim held the phone for a long minute attempting to process the implications of that disturbing conversation. He thought for sure Allison mentioned her guide was in his thirties . . . or then again . . . maybe he assumed that was the case. *But no, I also remember she said they were riding around Chiang Rai on a motorcycle.*

McGregor looked once more at his watch and noted the time was 7:15. He should have been home by now. He promised his wife he wouldn't work so late, but there were meetings all day and deadlines to meet. Although she worried about his health, he reassured her he was doing fine. It would be early morning in Thailand so he picked up the phone and dialed Allison's number.

The phone rang and Allison stretched her arm over to grab it. "Yeah, okay. Thank you."

Ashwin reached over to her and snuggled his head into her neck. "Who was that?"

"Hotel wake-up call. Can't believe it's morning already."

Ashwin smiled. "Morning comes early when you get little sleep during the night."

Allison sat up and tossed her pillow over his head. "Thanks to you." She got out of bed and went into the bathroom.

He pulled the pillow off his head and looked at the digital clock that showed 7:30. He yawned and yelled, "Hey, come back!" The phone rang again, but this time it was Allison's cell phone.

"Can you get that for me?" Allison yelled from the bathroom.

"Sure can. Hello?" Ashwin said.

"Uh, I think I have the wrong number."

"No, perhaps not. Are you trying to reach Allison?"

Ashwin asked. "She can't come to the phone right now and asked me to pick up."

"Oh, okay. Who is this?"

"I'm . . . uh . . . a friend."

"Could you tell her to call me as soon as possible? This is Jim McGregor, her employer. It's important I speak to her."

Concerned, Ashwin sat up in bed. "Is there a problem?"

"Oh . . . uh . . . no, not at all. Just something we need to discuss."

"Okay, I'll give her the message." He hung up the phone, laid it on the end table, and stared at it for a long moment.

Allison came out of the bathroom and asked, "Who called?"

"Just a wrong number," Ashwin said. "Now come and visit with me for a little while, huh? We have plenty of time before the school visit."

Chapter 38

DENG

DENG DECIDED TO ignore everything Montri told him. Keerati was right and acting cautious was nothing but a waste of time. He followed the couple into the breakfast room and hid behind a bamboo curtain waiting for the right moment. On the chair was the girl's backpack. No longer did he plan to swap the bags. He decided that would take too long and be too risky. Instead he would walk over to the table, pick up the bag when no one was looking, and get out of the hotel as soon as possible. Deng chose a pair of black framed glasses and a fake beard as part of a disguise. He selected clothes that made him appear heavier and finished the outfit off with a baseball cap. Not much of a plan, but with Keerati in jail and Anthony not willing to do anything, choices were few.

He watched as the two snuggled up to each other while drinking the coffee the waiter poured. *Well, will you look at that—if we aren't getting cozy?*

Not much time elapsed before the two stood up and walked over to the omelet station to put in their order. The girl filled up two glasses of orange juice, took them over to the table, and returned to the omelet station to watch the preparation of her eggs. Deng recognized this to be the right moment. Avoiding eye contact, he walked out from behind the screen and hurried over to the chair where the backpack remained unattended. He picked it up, tossed it over his shoulder, and left the hotel without attracting any attention. He rushed to his car and drove it off the hotel grounds, heading to his hotel located in the center of town. Once in his room, he threw the bag onto the unmade bed, unzipped the center compartment, and pulled out a pair of shoes, sunglasses and a notebook.

Sarut said the brooch was inside the ripped lining. He saw the rip and felt all around the area, but found no brooch. Frustrated, he opened the bag's smaller compartments only to find the same thing. Perspiration soaked through his shirt as he shook the bag.

He heard a knock at the door and froze with fear. *Who could that be? Did anyone follow him from the hotel?* He looked through the peep hole and saw the chambermaid standing in the hall next to her cart. "Not now, come back later," he yelled.

Deng found a pair of scissors and completely ripped the lining out of the bag, but still no brooch. With no more options available to him, he called Montri.

"Montri, I have the backpack."

Montri said, "You do?"

"Don't get excited. I have the bag, but there was nothing inside you'd be interested in; ya know what I mean? Just clothes, shoes—that kind of stuff."

"Did you look inside the lining?"

"Of course, I actually tore out the whole damn lining and found nothing there. The girl must have it."

"Shit! Deng, I have a few bahts riding on this."

"I know, boss, I know. I'll think of something."

After he hung up the phone, he walked into the bathroom and splashed cold water on his sweaty face. The morning was still young, but the temps were already in the high 80's.

He was in the process of changing his shirt when his phone rang.

"Yeah," he said, "it's about time I heard from you. What's going on?"

"Stop calling me. I told you, I'm not on the job anymore," said the voice on the other end.

Deng said, "Yeah? You're on the job, Anthony, until I tell you otherwise."

"You don't seem to understand that I changed my mind."

"No, it's you who's having problems understanding. It's impossible to change your mind. You're in this too deep. I have her bag, but there's no brooch inside. I'm counting on you to do something about that. Look, I have to hang up now. The damn maid is knocking on the door trying to get into the room. Remember, you're obligated to see this through. That was our agreement, and there's no backing out."

Deng hung up the phone and finished putting on his shirt. After several minutes, the knock on the door became louder and more rapid. "Alright already, I'm leaving. The room's all yours."

Deng opened the door expecting to see the maid but instead faced two men in black coats. One of the men had a deep scar on his face that went from the left side of his nose down to the corner of his mouth. The other guy wore a scarf around his neck that partially covered his face.

"Are you Deng?" the man with the scarf asked.

"Yeah, who are you? What do you want?" Deng asked, thinking someone from the Bodesta Lodge spotted him taking the backpack.

"We want to talk to you."

"Hey, if it's about the bag, I can explain. I thought it was mine. Just now realized it wasn't. I'll hand it over to you."

"We have a personal message to deliver from our friend. It appears he's interested in a certain brooch, and we understand you have it," said the man with the scarred face.

"No, it's missing, but I'm looking for it."

The men closed the door and stepped inside the room pushing Deng aside. "The story told to us was some clown hid the brooch inside an American girl's backpack."

Deng nodded his head and said, "That bag over there. I grabbed it this morning but found no brooch inside. Like I told you guys, I'm working on it."

"That's a bunch of shit," said the man with the scarf. He walked over to the backpack, looked inside, and noted that it was empty. "Nothing here. Our friend is tired of listening to excuses from you and Montri."

"They aren't excuses. Things got complicated along the way; that's all I can tell you."

The man pushed Deng up against the wall and said, "Our friend no longer cares about your damn pin, but instead wants his money back."

Breathing hard, Deng said, "You're asking the wrong person. It's Montri you need to ask about any money. Hey fellows, this is all a big misunderstanding. I take my orders from Montri. I tell you, he's the one you want to see."

Before Deng could say another word, the man with the scarred face pulled a large stiletto from his coat and jabbed it into Deng's chest. Deng stumbled to the table and fell onto the floor as blood poured out of his major artery.

Back in Bangkok, Montri stared out his window attempting to conceive another plan. The client from Bangkok lost all patience. The thought of selling his house and returning the money was a possibility but not one he favored. He looked down at the floor and saw Princess pushing the side of her body against his leg telling him she wanted to be fed. As Montri always did when stress overpowered him, he reached for his cat and pulled her onto his lap. Her soft fur and steady purr distracted him to such a degree he didn't notice the large sedan pull up to the side of the house. The front door opened and two thugs overpowered the bodyguard pushing through to the study where Montri sat petting Princess. Several shots rang out, a bloodied cat fell to the floor, and a man slumped over his desk.

Chapter 39

SCHOOL VISIT

"SAWATDEE-KAH, MR.CHOKDEE," SAID Allison, bowing with her hands together and her fingertips to her nose. "Thank you for allowing us to visit the students at your school." The headmaster returned the wai and indicated for Allison and Ashwin to accompany him to his office set up at the end of a narrow building. The office had few furnishings—a desk, several chairs, and a small table set up in the corner of the room.

"I welcome you to our school," said Mr. Chokdee. "Please sit down. I understand you want to learn about Thailand's educational system."

"Yes, in particular the structure you now have in place, and if there's been any recent changes."

Mr. Chokdee said, "Yes, we have many changes. Years ago Thailand educated only the boys, but today we recognize the importance of including girls, too."

Allison nodded her approval. "That's good to hear. It's taken many years for people to understand the value of doing that. Tell me about your teachers."

"That has been changing, too. Years ago, the Buddhist monks were the teachers, but now we hire lay teachers from Thailand and also from other countries. Many come from America, too, especially to help with teaching the children English."

Allison asked, "Is education compulsory?"

The headmaster said, "We have several levels. From ages three to five—school is optional, and from six thru eleven—children must attend. Those years are part of our primary school. Then at ages twelve thru eighteen, we have the secondary school. All children are required to attend the first three years of secondary, but the last three years are optional. To continue onto the university level, a national exam must be taken and passed."

"Allison looked up from her notebook. "So you're saying school is compulsory for children up to age fifteen?"

"Yes, but I must point out to you that there are children in remote rural areas or in urban slums who are unable to come to school. It is sometimes a difficult thing to make parents understand that just because they never attended school, that doesn't mean their children shouldn't. We are many times faced with that kind of thinking."

"I know . . . it's hard to get people to change their values. Tell me about your school."

"The school here is primary. We have a six year curriculum with forty weeks of instruction. The children attend school for twenty-four hours each week."

"Hmm . . . that's about five hours each day. Could you tell me how you set up the curriculum?"

"Yes, of course. In the primary school, we focus on Thai language, Math, life experiences, character development, and work orientated experiences." He looked up at the clock hanging on the wall and said, "Oh, it's almost 8:30. Please come outside and participate in the morning's opening ceremony."

The two visitors followed Headmaster Chokdee out of his office onto the center courtyard which was bordered by several rectangular, white buildings—each building housing a different grade level. Although most of the classrooms were attached, there was no center hall. Instead, each classroom had its own door that led out to this courtyard. The children stood in several lines with each line representing a different class. All remained quiet except for two girls who giggled and whispered to each other.

"Not too different from what you would see at an American school," Allison pointed out to Ashwin. In center front, a flagpole stood with the flag of Thailand about to be raised by a young boy. The Thai national anthem played over the loud speaker as the flag slowly advanced up the pole. Then, with their eyes focused on the flag, the children sang the anthem. Allison stood behind one such group of children, all of varied ages wearing identical uniforms—a pair of loose-fitting, blue-indigo denim pants topped with a matching tunic.

After the anthem, several children pulled out a variety of instruments—xylophones, drums, and melodicas—and blended their talents by playing a few national songs. The program ended with an older group of children carrying out a knife dance followed by the performance of a class of first graders demonstrating one of Thailand's folk dances. Allison couldn't help but notice how sweet these six-year-olds looked with their round faces, large dark eyes, and short cropped hair.

"Ashwin, I've often heard Thailand is the land of smiles. Looking at these children, I can understand the origin of that expression."

"So happy you're enjoying this," he said.

"Did your previous job as a teacher help with the arrangements for this visit?"

"No, I have no affiliation with this school. I gave the headmaster a call, and he seemed delighted to have a visitor from America come and see the children's progress. It's good for the children to interact with Westerners and be able to practice their English."

After the morning exercises, the children dispersed and went to their respective classrooms. Allison walked over to the headmaster and said, "I have to tell you how impressive your opening ceremony was. Do you do that every day?"

The headmaster nodded. "Every school in Thailand assembles each morning at the same time to sing the national anthem and read announcements. It is required. Ms. Wagner, our 6th grade teacher has invited you to his class to observe a Math lesson. Would you be interested in seeing that?"

"Of course, that would be wonderful. Thank you."

The Algebra lesson had the class of twenty figure out the significance behind a formula the teacher wrote on the chalkboard. Allison enjoyed the positive environment inside the classroom as the children—one by one—went up to the board and wrote down an answer. If correct, the class clapped twice and chanted 'Good Job' in English. No smart boards, textbooks, or other equipment could be spotted. The closest thing to technology was an outdated computer station located in the far corner of the small, congested room.

After Math, Allison participated in the children's English lesson as she went from student to student listening to them read from easy picture books. She finished up her visit by taking several photos during the playground break. It delighted her to see the excitement on their faces when they viewed themselves on her camera's monitor. In some ways they were like American children, but in other ways they were so different. Their naïvetés and lack of sophistication appealed to her and reminded her of the time when she, herself, was a child. As she waved good-by, she bowed her head towards the teacher and clasped the palms of her hands together in thanks for welcoming her into his room.

As she and Ashwin headed back to town, Allison chatted about everything she observed that morning. "Ashwin, where did you go when I was in the classroom?"

"Oh, nowhere in particular. You appeared to be well taken care of, and I had a few phone calls to make."

"You know, I forgot to tell you. I wasn't able to find out what happened to my backpack at breakfast the other morning. I shouldn't have left it on my chair like that when I went to the omelet station. I thought things would be safe in the hotel so I let my guard down."

Ashwin said, "I'm glad you had nothing of value in the bag."

"No, just a little money, an extra pair of shoes, and a spare notebook. So grateful my camera wasn't inside the bag."

"That's good. So much trouble over that backpack," he said as he looked over at Allison. He studied her face and saw this pensive look. "What are you thinking about?"

"Oh, that 6th grade class I visited. I loved how the teacher fostered this team-spirited attitude. You know, after each child succeeded in giving a right answer, the class did this awesome chant. He encouraged both group and individual participation. I found that to be interesting." Ashwin smiled but said nothing.

"Is there anything wrong?" Allison asked.

Ashwin looked over at her and said, "No, I'm fine. Why?"

"You seem quiet this afternoon. Not use to that. So where are we off to?"

"I need to contact my office and take care of some things. I can either drop you off in Chiang Rai to perhaps explore more of the town on your own, or take you back to the hotel."

"Okay . . . drop me off in town, and I'll take a taxi back when I'm done."

"Are you certain that's okay?" asked Ashwin. "I thought tonight we'd join in on the Sky Lantern ceremony that's taking place not far from here. How does that sound?"

"Fabulous, but what's this sky lantern thing about?" asked Allison, stepping out of the car.

"I'll never tell. Part of the magic comes from the element of surprise. I'll pick you up at the hotel around eight which will give you plenty of free time. You have my number if there's a problem, right?"

Chapter 40

THE HOSPITAL

"WHAT HAPPENED?" THE Bangkok detective asked.

The police officer looked at his notes. "A man, early sixties, wealthy businessman, arrived at the hospital with two gunshot wounds. Three shots were fired, but only two actually entered his body—one braised his head and the other came close to his heart."

The detective copied everything down in his book. "Anything else?"

The officer said, "Yeah, that third gunshot killed his cat. His bodyguard said two men burst through the door, fired the shots, and rushed out of the house. And that cat?"

"Yeah, what about it?" asked the detective.

"It sat on his lap during the ambush," said the officer. "Everything happened so quickly that this guy didn't have a chance to react. We believe the cat took the bullet that would have entered his heart, but we aren't certain where the bullet entered the cat."

"Why's that?"

The officer said, "Because the blood blended in with the cat's fur."

The detective looked up from his notes and asked, "What's that supposed to mean?"

"The cat's hair is this strange rusty color. Don't see much of that color on a cat."

"Where is the cat now?" the detective asked.

"Across the hall," said the officer, nodding towards the room.

The detective entered the room to find the animal on a table already stiff with rigamortis. He took a photo, and then grabbed a small plastic bag he found sitting on the counter. Using his pocket knife, he cut off a large chunk of fur and placed it in the bag.

The police officer walked into the room and asked, "What are you doing?"

"This cat's fur may be connected with the Thai brooch case I'm investigating. When we pulled Sarut's body out of the river, we found cat fur clinging to his pant legs. Even though he was in the water for several hours, the fur just clung to his clothing."

The officer asked, "What's that got to do with this cat?"

"Possibly a lot. As you said yourself, rarely do we see this color on a cat." He held up the bag of fur in front of the light. "I'm taking this in to be analyzed."

The officer shrugged his shoulders and asked, "The same cat? What would be the chance of that happening?"

The detective ignored the officer's sarcasm and asked, "Do we know the name of the man brought in?"

"His name is Montri."

"Montri?" the detective said. "Now I find that interesting. He's been the focus of our investigation with the brooch. We would have some mighty fine incriminating evidence if this cat's fur matched the fur found on Sarut. It would connect Sarut and Keerati with this Montri fellow. At the very least, it would show they've been in each other's company. What's Montri's room number?"

"Room 425—we have an officer at the door in case anyone decides to finish the job," said the police officer. "You should know, he's been asking about the cat, but we've avoided the question. His bodyguard says he's attached to the animal and will have trouble dealing with its death."

The detective put his notebook in his pocket and said, "I find it interesting how some people value an animal's life more than a human's."

"Someone call 9-1-1! Something has happened to Jim!"

Jim Gallagher's secretary had knocked on the door and when no one answered, she opened it and found the editor laying on the floor next to his desk. It wasn't long before the ambulance arrived and three men entered the office. Two men positioned Jim onto the stretcher, while the third hooked up a defibulator which sent an electrical shock to his heart in hopes of restarting its rhythmic beating. Within seconds of their arrival, Jim regained consciousness and found himself in an ambulance rushing towards Mount Sinai Hospital.

After a long sleep, Jim woke up in the hospital wanting to know what happened and why he was there. "I tell you, I'm okay now."

The nurse argued that he was in no condition to leave and would be going nowhere until his cardiologist said he could go.

"Cardiologist? When did I get a cardiologist?" he asked.

"You were assigned one upon your arrival in the emergency room. Now just relax. You've been through a lot. Be grateful you're still here."

"Where's my phone?" Jim asked.

"Your wife has it. She's out in the hall. Do you want me to get her?" Jim nodded.

A few minutes later, Jim's wife walked into the room with a worried look on her face. "You had us all concerned," she said, stooping over to give him a hug.

"What happened, Maggie?" he asked.

"You had a heart attack and if it wasn't for Ellen finding you when she did, well . . . I hate to think how this could have ended."

Jim laughed. "Remind me to give that girl a raise in salary. By the way, the nurse said you have my phone."

"I do, but you're not using it for a while. You're going to regain your strength, and then we'll see what the next step is."

"Next step? What's that mean? I need to get to the office tomorrow."

Maggie said, "The people in the office can handle whatever needs to be done. They're capable people. Right now, you are to take care of yourself—nothing else."

"Maggie, it's essential I get ahold of Allison. She's in Thailand and I'm thinking something isn't quite right."

Maggie shook her head. "Not today, save it for tomorrow."

"But you don't understand. I need to speak to her to make sure she's okay."

"You are one hopeless case, Jim. I'm not handing over the phone. You can call her tomorrow. I'm sure Allison is just fine. Now get some rest."

"Housekeeping," the maid announced as she opened the

door to Room 267. Pulling the vacuum cleaner behind her, she stepped inside the room and noticed blood stains on the carpet. She looked around the bed and saw a man laying against the wall. Although his eyes were opened, he didn't appear to be breathing. Blood soaked through his shirt and pooled next to the large knife lying beside him.

The maid raced out of the room and down the hall to use the housekeeping phone. She frantically dialed the front desk and screamed how someone slaughtered the man in Room 267. The hotel called the Chiang Rai police and several officers arrived on the scene in a matter of minutes. They roped off the room, took photos, and preceded to fingerprint the room. An investigator placed the knife in a sealed bag and marked it as evidence. The hotel manager identified the person in Room 267 as being a Mr. Deng from Bangkok. After several hours of careful investigation, the ambulance arrived and took Deng's body to the Kasemrad Sriburin Hospital for an autopsy.

Chapter 41

UNREST

AFTER SEVERAL WEEKS at the Bodesta Lodge, Allison felt comfortable there. It turned out to be a good move on Ashwin's part to switch her from a bungalow to a more secured room inside the main building. The housekeeping, wait staff, doormen, desk clerk—all seemed like family to her now. Each morning as she approached the breakfast room, she was greeted with the traditional wai; and when she returned from her day's activities, the doorman gave the same greeting. The wai, which appeared awkward and uncomfortable at first, now seemed natural. She found it interesting that a person could quickly adjust to another country's culture by simply living amongst its people for several weeks.

She put in a call to the office only to hear the news that Jim had a heart attack. Her first reaction was to return home, but his secretary assured her that his condition had improved. His body needed rest, so he couldn't take phone calls or have visitors except for the immediate family.

In Bangkok, Lan had finished her daily meditation and settled in for the night when she received a phone call from Allison.

"How are you, Lan? Hope you're doing well."

"Yes, we're doing the best we can. We miss Yen so much—such a bright star removed from our reach. How are you, Allison? Are you getting the information you need for the news documentary?"

"I am. This morning I was at a Thai primary school. Ashwin arranged for me to be a part of a sixth grade class for the morning. What fun!"

Lan laughed. "This Ashwin fellow appears to be a good fit for you, huh?"

"What do you mean?"

"You know, a good guide. Looks like he's taking you to see many interesting places."

"Oh, that . . . yes, he has."

After a slight lapse in conversation, Lan asked, "Is something wrong? You sound different."

"I need to talk to someone, Lan, because I'm about to go crazy. Even though I've known this guy for just a few weeks, I find myself strongly attracted to him."

"You mean Ashwin? You're attracted to the guide?"

"Yes, is that nuts or what?" Allison asked.

Lan said, "No, not really. Attraction is just that—often spontaneous, but will it last?"

Allison thought about what Lan said. "You're a wise girl for someone so young, Lan."

"I may be young, but I've experienced a lot. Tell me, have you expressed any of this to Ashwin?"

"No, well . . . sort of. I haven't said it in so many words, but you might say we've crossed the line. I've always felt it important to keep my personal life separate from my professional life. Unfortunately, our relationship is no longer purely professional which leaves me in a little bit of a mess. I mean, how can this play out? I leave Thailand at the end of the month. What happens then?"

"Do you know how he feels?"

"I think he's invested in our relationship, but I've noticed a subtle change in him."

Lan asked, "How's that?"

"Not sure—like something is on his mind. At times, he appears preoccupied."

"Maybe he's having the same thoughts as you, Allison. He might be in love with you, but realizes that soon you will return to America and that will be the end of that."

"I don't understand why I allowed this to happen. The attraction was there right from the first hello, but I kept those feelings in check until that afternoon at the swimming hole. That setting destroyed all barriers and put both of us in a vulnerable spot."

Lan said, "Swimming hole? Looks like you two were doing more than one kind of research, huh?"

Allison laughed. "I guess so. Hey, I'll let you go. Ashwin will be picking me up soon to go to this Sky Lantern event which is why I called you. I don't have any idea what that involves and wondered if you could fill in the blanks."

"You'll enjoy this. It's a custom especially found in northern Thailand. Perhaps by participating in this you might sort out some of your questions."

"What do you mean, Lan?"

"Well, I'll let Ashwin explain that to you, Allison, because that's not the real reason you called me. You wanted me to tell you it was okay to have a relationship with this fellow."

"Oh really, what brought you to that conclusion?"

"Intuition . . . I learned through counseling, I can't tell anyone what they should or should not do. It's not that simple. I can listen, but each person needs to figure out what's best."

"But I want you to tell me what to do," Allison said, laughing. "They trained you too well in those psych courses you took at school. Oh . . . speaking of the devil, there's a knock at the door and he's here. I'll talk to you later."

"Bye Allison and good luck."

Allison put her phone in her purse and opened the door to let Ashwin in. There he stood with that big smile he always wore on his face. A smile that seemed to welcome her into his heart. He walked into the room and she said she was ready to go.

Ashwin said, "Hmm . . . I'm not ready yet, but maybe in a few minutes." He wrapped his arms around her and the two ended up in a long, intimate embrace. Her concerns about the appropriateness of their relationship vanished as she allowed her heart to once more take control. Unable to explain why, she noticed her resistance melted every time Ashwin touched her. One thing led to another and just as Ashwin tugged at her sweater, she pulled away.

"Oh no, we have to stop or we'll miss the Sky Lantern ceremony," Allison said. "Doesn't it start in a half-hour?"

"Oh yeah, the ceremony. You know, we don't really have to go to it."

Allison reached for her purse. "Ah, yes we do. Come on."

"Okay, but this requires a rain check." Allison smiled and went to the mirror to brush her hair.

Ashwin came up from behind and wrapped his arms around her waist. "No need to do that. You look beautiful just the way you are."

He turned her around and kissed her forehead. "You know, I love that long pony tail you wear, but tonight I'd like to see your hair like this." He reached over and pulled the band out letting her hair fall down to her shoulders. "Do you mind?"

Allison shook her head and said, "Not at all." Then she grabbed his hand and directed him towards the door. "Come on, crazy guy. I can see we're getting a little distracted. Sky Lantern ceremony . . . remember?"

They left the room and walked toward the elevator. Ashwin pushed the button and the door opened. After they entered, Ashwin pulled her to him and the two kissed until they felt the elevator come to a stop. They had descended only a few floors when the door opened and a disheveled man joined them. Having been caught, they tried hard not to laugh. Instead, they occupied themselves by focusing their attention on the decreasing floor numbers. Like watching a pot of water come to a boil, it took forever for the elevator to reach the lobby. The door finally opened, and they waited for the other guy to walk out. Unable to contain themselves any longer, the couple broke into a fit of laughter. As they walked through the lobby, Ashwin caught sight of a police officer talking to the hotel manager. He steered Allison out the front door and they headed toward the car.

Chapter 42

SKY LANTERN CEREMONY

ASHWIN CARRIED A small package under his arm as he and Allison made their way through the crowd of people in a park located behind a hotel. He opened the package and unfolded a fairly large paper lantern.

"This is called a sky lantern. In Thai we say 'khom fai'. It's made from oiled rice paper which is fitted on a bamboo frame. See this? It's a small fuel cell made from this waxy material. Much like a hot air balloon, when we light the fuel, the lantern will inflate."

"Won't it catch on fire?"

"No, as you hold it, you will feel a pull or a tug. That is when we let the lantern rise into the sky."

"So the light won't go out?" Allison asked.

"Not until the fuel is burned up, and then the lantern will descend. Look, there's a full moon tonight. This is the best time to release a sky lantern."

"How often does this happen, Ashwin?"

"In my country there's a festival called Lanna Yi Peng when over a thousand launchings take place throughout northern Thailand, but you'll also find them launched at special events like weddings or birthdays. When a lantern is sent up, we believe all our problems and worries will float away."

Allison thought about what Lan said to her during their

phone conversation. 'I think by participating in something like this, you might sort out your questions.' *Could that be what she meant? That my problems and worries will float away. I certainly hope so.*

"That's a beautiful custom, Ashwin."

"Yes, we say upon releasing a lantern, you'll have good luck because it will take all misfortune with it." Ashwin straightened out the paper and handed one side to Allison.

Everyone around them were at different stages of their launch. Some of the lanterns had started their ascent while other couples were attempting to light their fuel cell. Allison stared in awe as the surrounding lights resembled millions of twinkling stars.

Ashwin said, "As we send the lantern to the sky, the light is said to offer both knowledge and the wisdom of following the right path in life."

Ashwin lit the candle and the lantern gradually filled with hot air. At first it tilted towards Ashwin, but as Allison became aware of this process, she held onto it with a stronger grip.

"Now, Allison, do you feel a tug?" Allison nodded her head. "Let the lantern start to take over. As it does, loosen your grip. Okay, there's the tug— let the lantern go."

They followed their lantern into the night sky as it mingled with hundreds of other lanterns floating wherever the wind directed. They watched until the flame became a small dot of light and eventually disappeared over the tree line.

Allison asked, "Is this an old tradition?"

"Uh huh, it dates back to ancient times when people made their own lanterns and offered them up at the temple. It was their wish to become a successful and clever person. Today, the color of the lantern reflects the wish."

"Really? Now that's interesting. What is the significance of the different colors?"

Ashwin said, "Red is normally for a special celebration, green is usually for growth, purple requests opportunity, and white is for good health."

"Our lantern was pink. What's that color mean?"

Ashwin pulled her close to him and whispered in her ear. "Love."

Allison smiled and said, "Ashwin, you are truly a romantic." Ashwin tossed a blanket on the cool grass, and the two sat and watched the light spectacle above them. Allison laid her head on Ashwin's shoulder as he wrapped his jacket around her shoulders. "I don't want this evening to end," she whispered to him.

They said little as they relished the moment. After all the sky lanterns vanished from the night sky, Ashwin suggested they return to the car. He folded the blanket and together they climbed up the hill to the car. Allison saw what looked like sadness on Ashwin's face. She wondered how such a perfect evening could be troubling to him.

"Is there a problem, Ashwin?"

"Why?"

"I don't know. All evening I've been receiving vibes something may be wrong. Is it something I said or did?"

"No, of course not," Ashwin said, throwing the blanket into the back seat of the car, "but there is something I need to talk to you about. I just don't know where to begin."

The blush in Allison's face drained leaving behind an ashen color. "What is it?" she asked.

"I'm terrified that what I have to say will change everything between us, but I can no longer keep this from you. You mean too much to me."

"You're worrying me. Are you married or something?"

Ashwin smiled. "No, that's not it."

"Well, go ahead and tell me. My stomach is beginning to turn."

He took both of her hands and said, "Allison, have no doubt that I love you. I realize there are obstacles, but I believe we can work through them. Even though our backgrounds are different, there are so many other ways we are alike. You're everything I've been looking for, and it's so hard for me to accept a life without you in it. So much has happened in such a short time."

Allison kissed him and said, "I know, it's crazy at how fast things progressed, but that's fine with me. I'm ready to see where this can go."

Ashwin looked into her eyes. "I'm not sure what I like best—your hair, your eyes, your energy . . . it's crazy."

"I have a secret, Ashwin. Do you remember when you came up to me at the pool and introduced yourself? Well, I took one look at your huge smile and found it difficult to talk. Me—having trouble talking! But I haven't seen too much of that smile lately. Why is that?"

"Allison, I want to be upfront about everything." Ashwin put his head into his hands.

"Just tell me. I'm sure it can be worked out."

He cradled her face with his hands almost as if this would be the last time he'd ever have that opportunity. Kissing her forehead, he said, "Allison, things are not what they appear. You see, I . . ."

A loud rumbling sound encircled them as the earth shook and then rolled from side-to-side. They both grabbed onto the dashboard as the car vibrated. Several trees uprooted and fell close to where they parked. Chaos resulted as people screamed and ran for cover.

"What's going on?" Allison cried.

"Quick, we need to get out of the car. We're having an earthquake."

Chapter 43

MOTHER EARTH RUMBLES

NEAR THE AIRPORT in Chiang Rai, stood a vacant ware-house. Inside sat an imprisoned man having little hope that his nightmare would ever end. He lost track over the num-ber of days of confinement in this damp, rodent infested, hell hole. The last time he experienced natural daylight was the evening he left Pracha Nukhro Hospital after being summoned that his mother experienced a heart attack. He worried about her condition and if the family wondered why he wasn't in touch with them. With nothing to occupy his mind, he imagined every possible scenario as to why these two guys snatched him off the street. He found it incredible that they would be interested in him; and no matter how of-ten he asked, neither would explain. He learned the guy with the phoenix tattoo was approachable, but the man known as Virote? He proved to be a nasty son-of-a-bitch.

Every day he'd overhear the two men pass the time by playing cards. The scene played out like the rerun of a classical movie—one accused the other of cheating, insults followed, and then the sounds of a scuffle. Eventually, he'd hear a door slam which left the other guy alone amongst a discarded pile of cards and tossed money. The following morning, both men would return as though nothing took place. They'd present him with his morning ration of food and resume the card game. Today proved to be no different.

There were no windows where he sat, and if not for the bare lightbulb that hung from the ceiling, he'd sit in total darkness. At first the stench in the room overpowered him; but as time dragged on, he became so accustomed to the smells that he grew unaware of them.

Nearby were two buckets—a wash bucket and a waste bucket. The latter needed to be emptied every day or the odor would overwhelm the room. Arguments erupted over whose turn it was to empty the bucket as well as heated discussions over the possible end of their miserable sentry duty. The imprisoned man tried to persuade them to set him free, but they complained about the time invested in this deal to give up on it now.

His captors were about to start another card game when the sounds of a distant rumble became louder and closer. "Shit, what's that?" asked Virote. The room shook causing the window glass to break. The force intensified with each successive tremor.

"It's an earthquake," the tattoo guy yelled. "We gotta get out of here." They got up to leave just as the building rolled back-and-forth. The tattoo guy ran to the door and escaped in time to watch the whole building collapse and bury the other two men. The tattoo guy waited by the side of the road until the tremors subsided, and then ran over to the destroyed building to look for Virote.

After the building collapsed, the imprisoned man crawled out of the rubble with only cuts and bruises. The full moon proved to be sufficient and allowed him to see his way into the black night. He heard Virote's moans, but ignored them. He was not concerned over Virote. *Let the tattoo guy dig him out.*

Weakened from several weeks of confinement,

undernourished with meals consisting solely of rice and beans, and sore from sleeping on a hard, damp floor with only a thin mattress, he stumbled down the road in search for help.

The earthquake not only took out all power but collapsed most of the buildings on both sides of the road. He crawled over the large slabs of concrete scraping his knees and hands, but he didn't care. He wanted to get to a safe place—safe from further aftershocks and safe from Virote and the tattoo man. Sirens interrupted the night's silence, but ambulances and other vehicles could not be functional until the roads were cleared. The only way out was for him to walk or crawl.

Ashwin put the handbrake on, opened the door, and pulled Allison out after him. The ground continued to roll as several trees around them snapped like toothpicks. "Here, lay on the ground next to the car. If anything falls near us, the car will take the impact."

He pulled Allison closer to the car and then covered her with his own body. "We need to get as close to the side of the car as we can without getting under it. How are you doing?"

"I'm okay."

After a minute of severe tremors, the earth stopped rolling and all became still. Ashwin stood up and helped Allison to her feet. They looked around the car and saw several fallen trees. The hotel behind the park seemed intact. Ashwin commented that newer buildings had higher construction standards.

"What are the odds of us getting back to the Bodesta Lodge tonight?" asked Allison.

"Let's get ourselves over to that hotel and see if they have any information."

He helped her up the embankment, and they made their way to the hotel. Inside the talk focused on the earthquake with everyone asking the same questions. No one had any answers, but comfort could be found in the safe confines this building provided.

Ashwin left Allison in the lobby and took off down the road to see if the streets were passable. Word was out that the earthquake extensively damaged the area near the airport, resulting in all flights cancelled. Allison sat on the leather couch near the elevator and watched the service man check out the elevator to make sure it continued to be in good working order. She thought about the beautiful evening, of only a few minutes before, as they watched the release of the sky lanterns. How magical that was. She will always treasure that moment, but it worried her to see Ashwin so troubled once they returned to the car. She had never seen him that way, but how well did she know him? What was he about to tell her before the earthquake suddenly interrupted their talk? How ironic that the earth shook her exterior world and prevented Ashwin from possibly turning her inner space upside down. She stood up and walked over to the window. Outside the scene showed overturned trees and a crumbled circular driveway. As upsetting as all of this was, she forced herself to focus on these tangible problems because the unknown seemed too frightening.

Allison glanced at her watch—10 PM. It should be mid-morning in New York. The instruction was to not call Jim yesterday, but no one said anything about the following day. She pulled her phone out of her pocket and dialed the overseas number. Much to her surprise, Jim answered.

"Jim, how are you doing? I heard you're in the hospital."

"Is this Allison? So glad you called. I've been worried about you."

"What do you mean? I'm concerned about you. What happened?"

"Hey, I had a little fainting spell—been working too late and not eating well, that's all. These people here are making it into something more serious."

"Jim, no one in the medical field makes things more serious if they don't have to. What are they suggesting?"

"They've scheduled to put a stent in one of my major arteries—guess there's a little blockage. From what I understand, it's an in and out deal. I'll be fine, but what about you?"

"About me? Everything was fine until the earthquake. Never before experienced anything like that."

"Earthquake? In Thailand? Nothing that I know of has been reported about an earthquake. When did that happen?"

"Try one hour ago."

"An hour ago? Where are you now?"

"Ashwin and I were in a park at a Sky Lantern ceremony just before it happened. We were in his car ready to return to my hotel when the car started to shake like a washing machine on its spin cycle. Right now I'm sitting in a hotel adjacent to the park while Ashwin is checking the roads to see if we can get through."

"Okay, about this Ashwin . . . what's his story?" Jim asked.

"What is it you want to know? He's a fantastic guide and I learned so much from him. He knows a lot about Thailand and has taken me to so many interesting places. I can't wait to show everyone the photos."

"So he's working out well?" asked Jim.

Allison placed her feet up on the stool in front of her. "Uh, yeah . . . why? Whenever I express an interest in something, he has me there the next day. For example, I asked about the school system here, and Ashwin arranged for me to meet up with a headmaster of one of the primary schools. I even observed a teacher instructing 6th graders on ratios. You might say Math was never my strength, so I learned a little something that morning."

"I'm glad things are good, but do you have any concerns?" asked Jim.

"Concerns? No, why are you asking me all these weird questions?"

"I called the other day—did you get the message?"

"No, did you leave the message with the front desk?"

"No, I called your cell, but some guy answered and said you were in the bathroom. Who was that?"

"It must have been Ashwin. That's weird—I do remember hearing my cell ring, but he said it was a wrong number."

"How old of a guy is this Ashwin?" Jim asked.

"Late thirties, why?"

"Well, the agency he works for has been trying to get ahold of him. It seems he's made no contact with them since he started his assignment. Usually he checks in every other day. I guess his family is also concerned because his mother passed away last week."

"Wait a minute," Allison said. "That's impossible. Ashwin told me his mother passed away several years ago."

"There's something else I need to tell you. When his employer asked how things were going, I mentioned how much you enjoyed your ride to the temple on his motorcycle. He told me your guide never rode a motorcycle and most likely wouldn't start at age sixty-four."

"Sixty-four? What? That's impossible. Are you sure about all of this, Jim?"

"That's why I tried to get ahold of you. If that was Ashwin who answered your cell, why didn't he tell you I called unless he didn't want you to know."

"Hey, it's possible there was a screw up. Maybe the agency assigned this other guy to take me around; but with his mother getting sick, Ashwin took the job."

"Sounds reasonable, except his employer referred to this fellow by name—Ashwin."

"Are you telling me that the person who has accompanied me this past month is someone else? Someone no one knows about? I can't believe that. He's such a wonderful, caring guy. That can't be true. Why would he do that, and what happened to the real guide?"

"Allison, carry on as normal and don't let on you know anything."

"Jim, I'm scared. What should I do?"

"Can you get to the police?"

"Things are pretty intense after this earthquake. I'm not sure how responsive they would be? Oh, I need to hang up. He's coming into the lobby now. I'll talk to you later."

"Allison, wait!"

Allison hung up the phone and forced a smile as Ashwin approached. "So how are the roads?"

"We should be okay. Do you want to give it a shot?"

"A shot?" she asked.

Aswhin said, "Yeah, you know—a try?"

"Oh, right—a shot. Sure, let's go. It's been a long day and I'm anxious to get back to my room."

On the way back, all Allison had on her mind was Jim's disclosure that her guide was in his sixties and his mother died a few weeks ago. None of this made any sense. *What was Ashwin about to tell me before the earthquake? Should I take a chance and ask? No, my gut feeling is to not go there at all. Keep everything on an even keel.*

"That was a 6.0 earthquake we experienced which I'm sure caused a lot of damage. We're going in a direction where the roads are reported to be in better condition."

"Good thing there's not too much traffic," Allison said.

"Yeah, that will complicate things soon enough. Was that your first earthquake experience?" Ashwin asked.

Allison nodded her head. "I hope I never go through that again. Do you know if there's any damage around the Bodesta Lodge?"

"I don't think so. According to the news on the radio, most of the heavy damage took place around the airport. Good thing you're not flying out too soon, huh?"

Allison smiled and said, "Yeah, good thing."

The man continued making his way through the rubble until he saw a police car parked by the side of the road. Inside sat two police officers with one of them on the phone. They looked up to see a haggard man staring into their window.

"Are you hurt," the officer in the passenger seat asked, rolling down the window.

"I need help," he said, looking behind him. "They may be after me."

"Who?" asked the officer.

"These two guys who abducted me several weeks ago. They kept me inside what I think might have been a vacant warehouse, but I'm not sure. Anyway, the building took a tumble in the earthquake, and I made my way out of there. I think one of them might be buried under the rubble."

The police officers stared at him as they questioned if his story was real or that of a demented man. "What do you say we take you to the hospital to get checked over?"

"I don't care where you take me as long as it's far from here."

"Okay, get in the back. So, what's your name?"

"Ashwin Willapana."

Chapter 44

STRATEGIZING

"MS. WAGNER, A police detective was here looking for you," the hotel clerk said.

"When was that?"

"Earlier this morning."

"I've been gone all day. Do you have his number? I'll call him tomorrow morning."

"Yes, he left his card." The clerk reached into a drawer, pulled out a card and handed it over to her. "Is Mr. Willapana here also?"

"No, he returned to his apartment. I'm grateful your hotel suffered no damage. Were the tremors strong?"

"Yes, but only a few dishes fell off the shelves in the kitchen. We were lucky."

Allison nodded and made her way to the elevator. When she got to her room, she double locked the door, flopped on the bed, and stared at the ceiling. It started out to be a wonderful morning at the school and ended with the evening lantern launch. The full moon provided the perfect backdrop as the countless lights advanced into the sky, mingling with the constellations.

The night could not have been more perfect until Ashwin mentioned he needed to talk to her. Later her call to Jim only complicated the situation. *Who is this man I love? Was he impersonating someone else? For what reason?* Like a bolt, Allison sprung off the bed.

FREDDIE REMZA

"My Lord, he must be connected with the brooch! That has to be it."

After a sleepless night, the morning could not have come too soon. Her cell phone rang and Allison noticed the number to be Ashwin's—or whatever his name was. The phone rang a second time, third. She collected her emotions and answered.

"Good morning, Ashwin."

"How did you sleep, honey?" he asked.

Honey . . . whoever this guy is called me honey. "Not too well—too much happened yesterday. Did you make it home alright?"

"It was tricky. I would have preferred to stay with my favorite journalist, but she sent me out into the cold."

"I'm sorry, Ashwin, but exhaustion set in, plus I had the start of a migraine. This morning it's full-blown, so I'm begging off today."

"Do you want me to come and take care of you?" he asked.

Allison forced a laugh. "No, I just need some time alone right now."

"Well, okay. It's probably a good idea not to do any traveling with the streets torn up in places."

"Are things pretty bad out there?"

"Yeah, especially near the Wat Rong Khun Temple."

"That beautiful white temple with the skulls and hands reaching from below?"

"That's the one. From what I heard, they closed it because of serious damage. So yeah, get yourself some rest and I'll check on you tomorrow."

"Thanks for understanding," said Allison.

"Are you sure you're not interested in any company? I promise to be good."

"I'll see you tomorrow, okay?" she said, hoping he wouldn't suspect anything.

"Okay, but it will be a long day without seeing you."

Allison ended the call, fell into her pillow and sobbed. "How could this be happening to me? Why did I even let this happen? Who is this guy?" With a clenched fist, she beat into her pillow until all anxiety drained from her small frame.

Allison looked in the mirror at her reflection and didn't like what she saw—eyes, swollen and red. Stumbling to the bathroom, she applied a cold washcloth until she experienced relief from her throbbing headache.

Allison turned on the TV and searched until she came upon the BBC reporting the morning news. The journalist talked about the conflict between the Red and Yellow shirt people and the effects of the prime minister stepping down from office. Next came the news about the earthquake including the areas in Chiang Rai to avoid until the following week. She half-listened until an onsite reporter gave details about the fatal stabbing of a man in his hotel room two days before.

"The police reported the man's possible involvement with Thailand's missing brooch."

He continued to say that the police from both Thailand and Japan were in a cultural property dispute as to who should rightfully claim the brooch once it's found.

She pulled out the card the hotel clerk gave her and dialed the number. "Yes, this is Allison Wagner. I understand yesterday Detective Chaidee arrived at my hotel looking for me. I was gone all day and couldn't call until now."

"Yes, Ms. Wagner, I'll put him on."

"Detective Chaidee here. Ms. Wagner, I trust you are fine."

"Yes, but I need to talk to you about something that surfaced last night, and I'm not comfortable talking about it on the phone. How are the roads to your office?"

"They should be fine. Whatever rubble that fell between you and our office had been cleared during the night and early morning. Things are busy here. Do you mind coming?"

"Not at all—I should be there in two hours."

"Will you be alone?" he asked.

Allison understood the reason for that question but didn't press. Instead she said, "Yes, I'll be taking a taxi."

Two hours later, Allison made her way to the police station, dismissed the taxi, and walked through the front door. In the front hall sat a woman talking on the phone. She motioned to Allison that she'd only be a minute longer.

"Yes, what can I do for you?"

"I'm here to see Detective Chaidee," she said.

"Is he expecting you?" Allison nodded her head. The woman called the detective on the phone to confirm the appointment, and then looked up at Allison.

"Detective Chaidee is down the hall, third room on the right."

Allison walked the length of the hall and stood staring at the door with an opaque window. Written in large script was Detective Chaidee's name. Although this was not her first visit to his office, today was different. Things had changed—not only did she suffer from a damaged ego, but her confidence was badly shaken. She tapped on the door and the detective beckoned for her to enter.

This second encounter with Detective Chaidee allowed her to pay more attention to his physical features. Now that she stood once more before him, she noticed he was rather tall for a Thai, had wide hands, and a large scar over his left eye. She tried to not look at the scar and pretended not to notice, but the detective's observation skills were too good.

The detective motioned for her to sit in the chair across from him. "Three-years-ago a drunken man punctured me with a kitchen knife," he said.

Allison asked, "I beg your pardon? I don't understand."

Chaidee said, "You're wondering why the scar—just telling you a drunk stabbed me with a knife."

Allison blushed. "I'm sorry, I didn't mean to stare."

"It is what it is. Ms. Wagner, have you mentioned to anyone about us having the brooch?"

"I've said nothing."

"Not even your guide, this . . . ," he stuttered, skimming through his notes, "this Ashwin Willapana?"

"No, I never mentioned anything about you having the brooch. As far as he knows, I still have it, but I need to talk to you about him."

Allison went into detail about how preoccupied he seemed the past two days. She described their brief conversation in the car until it was abruptly interrupted by the earthquake. She explained how the guiding agency tried to notify Ashwin that his mother passed away, but Ashwin had mentioned to her earlier that his mother died several years ago.

"You see, nothing adds up. The final blow came when my editor revealed Ashwin was in his sixties. The Ashwin who has been taking me around is clearly in his late thirties. I may be wrong, but I fear he's involved with the brooch."

The detective focused on her every word. "I'm glad you told me this. Late last night two of our officers picked up a man claiming to be Ashwin Willapana. He claimed two guys, whom he believes were working for the Chao Pho, pulled him off the street and kept him locked away in a warehouse."

"What's the Chao Pho?" asked Allison.

The detective gave details about this organization describing them as merciless and quick to take things into their own hands. They could be compared to the mafia."

"Oh Lord, the mafia?"

"I'd say this man had been retained since the day you met up with your guide."

"Ashwin, a member of the mafia?" Allison repeated in disbelief. "I have trouble believing that one—I really do."

"Actually, his name is Anthony. We've had our eye on him for several days now, but then the real Ashwin surfaced and confirmed what we believed."

"Where is this Ashwin?" Allison asked, taking a tissue from her purse to wipe the tears from her eyes.

"I can see he has a hold on you," the detective said.

"I was not only conned, but manipulated. You see, I'm not one to be easily fooled." She looked down at the tightly clenched tissue.

"These guys? They're quite good at what they do. I dislike asking this, but were you in a romantic relationship with him?"

Allison nodded her head. She looked up and said, "But only recently—tell me, Detective Chaidee, where is this real Ashwin?"

"Right now, the real Ashwin is in the hospital. He's undernourished, dehydrated, and covered with bug and rodent bites. When the officers found him, he could barely stand up and stumbled over the slightest incline."

"All this because of a stupid brooch? It makes no sense."

"Yeah, people do all kinds of things for money. The brooch that was slipped in your bag is prized not only in monetary value but also historic worth."

Allison asked, "Where is it now?"

"I can't say too much at this point, but we're working out a deal to do a trade with the Japanese. We're hopeful it will end up in our museum where it should be."

"What should I do? He'll be calling me today wanting to make plans for tomorrow."

"We would like you to meet up with him and carry on as normal."

"I don't know if I can pull that off. How do I know what he's capable of doing if he finds out I'm onto him?"

"Just a minute, Allison." The detective left the room and came back a few minutes later with a man dressed in jeans and a tee-shirt. "This is Detective Wattana, an undercover agent who for the past few days has been shadowing your every move. What we need is for Anthony to admit he's not who he says he is. Any other information you can get out of him will also be good."

"You know, as I think back, my backpack always interested him. After we discovered the pin, he asked if he could keep it. When I suggested that possibly it could be the stolen brooch, he over-reacted and insisted it had to be costume jewelry."

The detective asked, "If it was costume jewelry, why did he want it?"

"He told me no one wears stuff like that anymore, but his elderly aunt would enjoy it."

"I'm sure his aunt would," the detective said in a sarcastic voice.

"Damn, I'm so stupid!"

"No, don't feel that way. Like I said, these guys are good at manipulating people. I can see you're becoming angry and I don't blame you, but you must not show any of that to him, do you understand?"

"What do I do now?"

"I'd say make a dinner date with this Ashwin for tomorrow. When we feel the time is right, we'll take care of the rest. Detective Wattana will continue to trail you. Matter-of-fact, he's had a room in your hotel for two days."

Startled to hear that, Allison took a better look at the guy. "Wait a minute, I thought you looked familiar. Weren't you in the elevator with us yesterday evening?"

Wattana nodded his head and winked. "Been following you for several days."

"I never knew that," Allison said, feeling uneasy over the wink. Embarrassed, she wondered how much he actually saw of their relationship.

Detective Chaidee said, "I'm sure you didn't know that, Ms. Wagner. Detective Wattana? He's one of the best undercover agents we have."

Chapter 45

MONTRI

THE OFFICER THAT stood guard at his door questioned every person seeking entrance to the room. No exceptions—especially hospital staff. People often disguised themselves as a nurse or aide to gain access to a patient, but not with Officer Chongrak. No one got by him.

Montri was in an induced coma so not to put any further stress on his body as he struggled to heal. That morning he showed improvements as he regained consciousness. He had no recollection of what happened after two men broke into his home, made their way into his study, and discharged ammo into his body.

As soon as he was informed that Montri was coming out of the coma, the police chief left for the hospital. They had suspected Montri's involvement in the theft as well as the murder of Sarut. With Keerati locked up, who killed Deng? The chief realized the importance of questioning Montri. After experiencing a near death situation, he might talk.

"Naai Montri, good afternoon. How do you feel?" asked the chief.

"Not so good—who are you? What happened? Where am I?"

"You tell me, sir. According to your house staff, two guys broke into your home and tried to kill you. Do you have any memory of that?"

"No, the last thing I remember was sitting in my study."

"Were you alone?"

"Yeah, except for Princess. She was with me."

"Uh, who is Princess?"

"My cat—Princess is my cat. Where is she? Is she okay?"

Montri's personal bodyguard stood up and signaled to not say anything about Princess' death. The chief nodded and said, "There's no report on your cat, but I have a serious question for you. Who did this?"

The chief made note of Montri's hesitation and pushed a little harder. "Naai Montri, you realize you could be dead right now. Someone out there wants to kill you. I don't know the reason, but you do."

Montri shook his head and said, "No, no idea."

"Well, let's see if I can help you remember. We know there's a connection amongst Sarut, Deng, Keerati and you. Sarut is the man who stole the brooch from a Tokyo jeweler, and Keerati set himself up as a clerk in the same store."

Montri opened his eyes. "What does that have to do with me?"

"We traced phone calls, text messages, and interesting enough . . . we found fur fibers from your cat on all three men. You guys are well acquainted, so don't give me any of your bullshit. Come on, who did this to you?"

Montri closed his eyes for a long minute and responded, "Deng—that son-of-a-bitch, Deng."

"No, that's impossible," said the chief. "Deng was murdered right at the same time as you were being ambushed."

Montri opened his eyes. "Deng is dead?"

The chief said, "Yeah, he died of multiple stab wounds— pretty much a slaughter took place in his hotel room. It's possible someone is waiting for the right moment to finish the job on you. Are you going to keep quiet and let that happen?"

Feeling alone and vulnerable, Montri decided he had no choice but to tell the police chief everything he knew. What did he have to lose—his life? He was on the verge of already losing that. Plus paying back the money looked pretty bleak and the chances of gaining possession of the brooch was almost nil. The situation looked pretty much dead-end to him. So he waved his hand in the air and said, "It was the boss of the Chao Pho. I'm sure he gave the orders."

"Are you part of that organization?"

Montri said, "No, but he offered a deal that seemed sweet at the time. My part was to arrange for the brooch to be taken from the store and hand it over to him. In return, I'd receive over 30 million bahts. Seemed easy enough until that damn Sarut screwed things up and lost the damn brooch. I think the girl has it."

"What girl?"

"Shit, I don't know her name—some American broad. Deng arranged for his brother's friend to get it from her."

"This friend? Is his name Ashwin?" the chief asked.

"No, sounds like that though. I can't remember. Where's my Princess? Send someone to my house to get her."

In an effort to calm him down, the chief patted his shoulder. "Montri, take it easy. I need the answer to that one question. Think hard—what was the name of the person who was to get the brooch from the girl?"

Montri lifted his head and turned to the side as he coughed up blood. The nurse rushed over to help, and then advised the detective to leave because his questions were putting too much stress on the patient.

The chief ignored her warning. "Montri, what was the name of the guy?"

Montri laid his head back on the pillow, closed his eyes and motioned with his index finger for the chief to come closer. The police chief lowered his head and Montri said, "I think his name was Anthony. Yeah, that was his name—Anthony."

Chapter 46

ANXIETY

"HI ASHWIN," SAID Allison, answering her cell phone as she headed towards an established nunnery outside of Chiang Rai.

"Hi, I called your room but no one answered. Where are you?"

Allison took a deep breath hoping to release any anxiety from her voice. "Oh, I'm in a taxi driving to a nunnery. This great opportunity popped up, and I'm on my way to speak to a nun about the controversy over the ordination of Thai women as Buddhist nuns."

"Why didn't you call me? I would have been happy to drive you."

"I considered that, but it was so last minute. Besides, I'd be more welcomed if I were by myself."

"I was hoping to meet up with you today. I missed you yesterday."

"I missed you, too, Ashwin."

"So how did you spend your day?"

"I didn't do much—stayed in my room and slept. That's the only thing that will chase a migraine."

"You mean, you stayed in the room the whole day? Weren't you hungry?"

"No, I ordered room service that evening. Hey, speaking

of food, I'd love to get together for dinner tonight. Could that be possible?"

"Sure, I'll pick you up after you're done with the interview. Give me a time."

"Oh . . . not needed. I have several errands to run, but I'll see you tonight."

After a long pause, Ashwin said, "Okay, how if I pick you up at the hotel around six?"

"That's perfect. Look, I'm almost there and I need to get my questions in order. I'll meet you in the lobby at six." Allison hung up and rested her head on the back of the seat. *How will I get through this?* She was never good at lying— her mother always told her that when she was a kid. She looked out the back window of the taxi and saw Detective Wattana two cars behind her. Pulling out her phone, she called the number he gave her.

"Hi Detective Wattana, Ashwin—or whatever his name is—just called me. I sensed his confusion over why I'm taking a taxi, but I think I did a fairly good job explaining it."

Detective Wattana asked, "Have you settled on meeting up with him later?"

"Yes, he's picking me up at the Bodesta Lodge for dinner tonight at six. I told him I'd be busy interviewing a nun this afternoon. Hey, there's really no need for you to trail behind me. I'll be fine."

The detective hesitated but said, "Okay, everything appears to be under control. I'll be sitting in the hotel parking lot around 5:30."

"Thanks, bye." Allison looked at her watch and asked the driver of the taxi how much longer to the nunnery.

"Another ten minutes."

She closed her eyes. *Lord, help me get through tonight."*

Confused, Ashwin hung up the phone. This was so un-like Allison—the bubbly, American girl who always greeted him with a cheerful voice. He experienced a different side of her ever since the evening of the earthquake. Everything appeared fine until he returned from checking the condition of the roads. She went from acting loving and warm to more calculating and guarded. He understood none of it. She didn't want him to stay that evening and begged off the following day due to a migraine. When he called the next day to check on how she was doing, the desk clerk mentioned she left the hotel that morning by taxi. But when he inquired about her day, Allison told him she had stayed in bed. She even men-tioned she ordered room service. *Something was not right.*

Chapter 47

THE NUNNERY

THE STREET LOOKED like any other with mature shade trees on both sides. Tucked within was a coral colored building that would go unnoticed to anyone passing through. This is where the taxi dropped her off. Chiang Rai was shrouded in smog that particular morning, and Allison was unsure if her stinging eyes resulted from the polluted air or the lack of sleep from the past two nights. Northern Thailand typically had quite a bit of haze during the pre-rain season. The irritating fumes and smoke from the continuous slash and burn taking place in the hill country didn't help. A Bhikkhunis (*Thai nun*) received her at the main entrance.

"Welcome," the nun said as she and Allison greeted each other with the traditional wai.

"Sa-wat-dee-kah, thank you for allowing me to visit."

"Would you like some tea?" the nun asked.

"That would be lovely, kob-khun kha *(thank you)*.

The nun signaled to one of the other nuns to prepare tea while she escorted Allison into a small room furnished with a table and eight chairs.

"You are from America?"

"Yes, I'm in Thailand to gather information for a documentary we are currently putting together on your country's transformation from its ancient culture to the modern world."

"How interesting," the nun said. "How can I help you?"

"I understand there's been a lot of controversy regarding the women in the religious order fighting for equality. Could you explain where you're at with that?"

The woman, dressed in a saffron colored robe, smiled back at her. "Throughout Thailand there are many bhikkhunis living in monasteries. We are not respected by Thai authorities and do not enjoy the benefits that the monks receive."

"Can you give me some examples?" Allison asked, nodding to the other nun who brought in the tea.

"I certainly can. The monks have their own hospital, but we do not. The monks have their own university, but we do not. We also do not receive a monthly pension while the monks do."

"Women everywhere have had to fight for equality," said Allison. "Would it be a correct assumption to say that women have contributed much to the Buddhist religion?"

"You go to any monastery and you'll see it's the women who are the monks' attendants—feeding them, doing their laundry, and tending to their needs."

Allison said, "We experienced the same situation in America, but it's changing now. There's an expression that says for every successful man, there is a woman."

The Bhikkhunnis nodded her head and laughed. "Yes, yes! In Vietnam, Tibet or Taiwan the idea of ordaining Buddhist nuns is accepted. Here, in Thailand, women are not to become nuns, but are supposed to lead the life of a lay person as they serve the monks. What is confusing is when the Buddha was alive, he ordained women."

"So what you're saying is if Buddha thinks it's okay, then Thailand should."

"Yes, exactly," said the nun.

Allison quietly wondered why women in Thailand were deprived of this status. Under Thailand's current administration, female ordination is permitted; but there is this conservative religious advisory group that believes only men can enter the monkhood. They remained quite hostile toward the bhikkhunis.

Aloud she said, "Interesting, so even though it is now okay to be ordained, you still meet up with opposition?"

The nun asked, "Are you aware of the 'Four Pillars' of Buddhism?"

"I am—the monks, nuns, lay men and women."

The nun nodded in agreement. "Many men would like to eliminate the nuns and lay women. So we are trying to bring about change by building a community of female monastics—hoping to pave the way for women to ordain and be ordained."

"How is that going?" asked Allison.

"We must be careful and move slowly. If we seek ordination, we could be accused of impersonating a monk which is a civil offense over here in Thailand. Instead, there's a separate order of non-ordained females called mae chi."

"Yes, I'm familiar with a mae chi who is the head of a Safe House for women in Bangkok. Aren't they somewhere between an ordinary lay person and an ordained monk?"

"Exactly," said the nun. "Do you have time? I'll show you around our place."

After giving Allison a tour of the nunnery, the two said good-bye using the tradition wai. It had been such an interesting morning, Allison momentarily forgot her personal problems. As she looked around to flag a taxi, a familiar Toyota approached. Allison's heart skipped when she realized it was Ashwin.

He pulled the car up, rolled down the window and said, "Looking for a ride?"

Allison had no other choice but smile and get into the car. "Well, this is a surprise. How long have you been waiting?"

"We made plans for this evening, but I needed to talk to you before then."

Allison said, "Alright, this sounds kind of serious."

"There's a little restaurant around the corner. Care for some lunch?"

Thinking it would be better having this conversation in a public place as opposed to inside a car, she agreed. They walked into a neighborhood family-run restaurant, sat down and gave their order.

"You look anxious, Ashwin. What is it you want to discuss?"

Ashwin reached out and took Allison's hand. She experienced the sudden rush of sensations she always felt whenever he touched her. Mixed emotions filled her core as she teetered between love and anger.

"Allison, I'm going to come right out with this. I need to confess that I'm not who you think I am. You see, my name is not Ashwin Willapana—it's Anthony. All I said before—about having been a teacher and my wife dying—all of that is true, but I am not a tour guide. I do not work for a guiding agency."

Allison pulled her hand away. "But why? How is it I'm involved?"

"Please, let me just say what I need to say. I promise to answer all your questions. You see, I was contacted by this man whose brother knows my cousin. He asked if I wanted to make money by showing this American woman around Thailand. I considered that to be a good job so I agreed. Other than tutoring English, not much was happening in my life."

"So why did you change your name?"

"I didn't understand that either, but I was simply following his instructions. I figured why not? Remember when we went to visit the Hill Tribe?"

"Yes."

"Right around then the guy who hired me, contacted me again. He said I was to figure out a way to grab your backpack and find this pin. He said it was hidden inside your bag and implied it was a situation where a friend put the pin inside the wrong bag. I thought that was a strange request and told him I couldn't go into your personal things. When I suggested coming out and asking you about the pin, he went crazy. He said that you weren't to be told anything. He acted desperate and warned that someone higher up would see to his death if he didn't get that pin back."

"At the time, had you realized it was the missing brooch?" asked Allison.

"No, not at first. To be honest, I didn't know about the brooch until I saw the news on TV in your room. I don't own a TV and hadn't seen a newspaper. Then that night in the bungalow when those two men broke in, I realized I was in over my head. At first, it wouldn't have mattered, Allison, but you've become someone special to me."

"I don't know how to handle this, Ashwin—or Anthony—whatever your name is. What do you want me to say? That your deceit was excusable because you didn't know me."

"No, of course not, but I had hoped you'd hear me out and then forgive me. I don't want to lose you, Allison."

"I leave for Bangkok in a few days. Then I fly to the United States the following morning. Truthfully, how could this even work? I'm not living here—my life is in New York."

"Allison, people from different countries marry all the time. They make it work."

"Marry? Who is talking about marriage? Ashwin . . . see, I don't even know what to call you. We've known each other three weeks. That's not enough time to be considering marriage."

Anthony lowered his head. "You're the first person I've had feelings for since Narissa died. I thought you felt the same."

"Anthony, I don't understand what my feelings are. You have to realize this is not a good way to start any kind of relationship." Allison stopped talking as she saw Detective Wattana and a police officer walk into the restaurant. With his back to the door, Anthony didn't notice as they approached their table.

"What's the matter?" he asked.

The detective came in from behind, pulled a gun and said, "Put your hands up in the air and stand away from the table."

Startled, Anthony jumped. He gave Allison a puzzled look but did as the detective commanded. The police officer handcuffed him and took him out of the restaurant. The detective stayed behind and asked if she was okay.

"I had no idea he would be waiting for me when I came out of the nunnery. He said he needed to talk so I thought it better we talk in a public place. I thought you weren't trailing me this afternoon."

The detective said, "I don't take my orders from you,

Ms. Wagner. I waited behind and saw you get into the car with him. We will need a statement from you."

Unsure whether it was the disappointment of what could have been or the release of pent up anxiety, but Allison burst into a flood of tears.

"Are you alright?" the detective asked.

"I'm sorry about this. Can I go back to the hotel first? I need to regain my composure."

"How much longer will you be in Chiang Rai?" the detective asked.

"For two more days."

"Come in tomorrow morning at ten. Right now, I need to get this guy to the station. Can I call a taxi for you?"

Allison shook her head. "Go do what you have to do. I'll be fine." She went to the window and watched the detective get into the car with Anthony in the back. As they drove down the road, the waiter came out with both orders.

"I'm sorry about this, but we won't be eating." Allison put several bahts on the table. "This should cover it."

Chapter 48

CLOSURE

THE TRIP TO the police station did not come without remorse. Allison made her statement on a recorder whereby she gave her opinion that Anthony went into this not fully realizing who he worked for and what was expected of him beyond taking a tourist around his country.

He thought his assignment was to guide me around Chiang Rai, and only later learned he was expected to come up with the brooch. By then, he wanted out of the deal but was told that was impossible. As it turned out, his contact person was Deng, the man stabbed to death in his hotel room.

Impossible to cross-examine Deng, they moved onto Montri. During an intensive interview, Montri confirmed what Anthony told both the police and Allison.

Allison anticipated flying out of Chiang Rai later that afternoon. She wanted to put all of this behind her, but realized that could never happen until she had a chance to talk to Anthony. She took a taxi to the prison where an official escorted her into the visitors' room. Anthony arrived and broke into a wide smile upon seeing who his visitor was—the same smile that won her over the day they met at the pool. The smile no longer had the same affect.

"Allison, thank you for coming. I heard you spoke in my defense. I have no idea how all this will end, but I appreciate what you did."

"No need to thank me, Anthony, I only said what I believed to be the truth. The fact you confessed everything with no knowledge that I already knew . . . well, that held a lot of credibility. I hope you realize that you have a lot of soul searching to do about the decisions you made."

Anthony covered his face with his hands and shook his head. He dropped his hands to the table and looked at Allison. "I made a mess of things. I am so sorry about all of this."

"I'll be leaving Chiang Rai later this afternoon but wanted to say good-bye before I left. I also wanted to tell you this was the first time I mixed work with my personal life. That was a big mistake, but sometimes it's difficult to not let the heart take over." Anthony smiled and reached for her hand, but Allison pulled away. "Anthony, what I felt for you was real. I know that, but I can't let raw emotions direct the path I take."

Anthony asked, "Is it because we both come from two different countries?"

"That could be a part of it, but I can't ignore the mistrust I now have resulting from your dishonesty. I'm hoping in time this hurt will fade; but honestly, it won't ever go away."

"Allison, there are strong feelings between us. What we have is wonderful."

Allison nodded. "You don't seem to understand that our relationship was in its early stages. I now realize much of what we experienced was physical, but there's more to a relationship than that. In time, this sadness we both feel will fade."

"Not for me, Allison. This feeling of loss will never leave me."

"Yes, it will. We are better off leaving things as they are."

The police officer came into the room and told Allison the visitation was over for the day. Allison reached out and touched Anthony's face through the metal bars that separated them. "I've loved you, but the idea of us being together is impossible."

Anthony said, "I still love you. I loved you since that day at the waterfalls. That was when I realized I could no longer go on with this charade. I was miserable, but didn't know how to tell you."

"Didn't you wonder why you were hired to be someone else? The whole situation was wrong from the start."

"I can understand why you no longer want to have anything to do with me, but I had hoped you'd give me another chance."

Allison wanted so much to do that, but her head said no. "Ashwin . . . I mean, Anthony—can you see my problem? I don't even know what to call you. For whatever reason, you agreed to take on someone else's identity which shows me that you are capable of deceit. We all have flaws, but this is a big one."

"But Allison, that wasn't my intention."

"Perhaps not, but as I look back on this month, I'm surprised I came out as well as I did. I had this sense of imbalance right from the start. The plane ride, my time in Bangkok, coming to Chiang Rai—evil continued to follow me. And when I became anxious or worried, I felt I had you to rely on. Do you have any idea how upsetting it is to realize you were a part of that evil?"

Before Anthony could respond, the prison guard walked over to them and insisted their visit was officially over. Allison felt sorry for this person, now hunched over and looking defeated. Gone was that huge smile and confidence she loved. Although she felt miserable, she remained too angry to forgive. Right now she needed to be away from this problem.

"I wish you nothing but good things, and I pray that the mess you are in gets cleared. I want no harm to come to you, but I also need to consider myself. Largone *(good-bye)*."

"Come on, it's time to leave," the officer said, tugging at Anthony's arm. Allison's eyes followed as the guard escorted him to the door. Right before the door closed, Anthony spun around and their eyes locked one last time.

Back in Bangkok, Allison made a phone call to Jim when she learned he was recuperating at home. "Yeah, I'm out of the hospital, but no one will allow me to return to work. I'm kept as a prisoner in my own home."

"Jim, instead of grumbling, consider this a vacation. Once you're back at the office, the stress will return. You have capable people working for you—let them take over for a while."

"I can see you're no help. Hey, shouldn't you be back in New York by now?"

"I had to change my ticket—met up with a bit of a problem I needed to fix."

"Problem? What kinda problem?" Jim asked.

"I'll tell you about it when I'm home on Thursday. Tomorrow afternoon I plan to visit the Royal Barge Museum. You know the brooch someone placed in my bag? It actually depicts one of those barges."

"All the trouble that pin got you into? I'm surprise you even want to see a barge," Jim said.

"Quite the opposite. When you consider how I entered Thailand with a barge hidden in my backpack, how symbolic to end this trip by visiting the Royal Barge Museum."

Jim laughed. "I read a copy of the *Bangkok News* this morning. With all this leisure time, I can actually pick up someone else's paper. It reported the brooch was recovered and is in Bangkok. It also said that the Japanese are going along with a trade in order to avoid a cultural property dispute."

"Yeah, the museum in Bangkok is handing over several pieces of Japanese artifacts in return for the brooch. It's a wonderful solution for what could have been rather sticky."

"Before I hang up, I want to tell you the funding to bring Lan to the U.S. came through. Tell her she better get herself a spiffy outfit to wear to the Academy Awards because this spring there will be a plane ticket to Los Angeles with her name on it. She'll be sitting with our team."

"Really? The funding came through? Oh my God, that's wonderful news! You can't possibly understand how much it means to receive good news."

"Well, I can only guess what that remark infers. Then again, maybe I don't want to know, huh?"

"Yeah, I'll tell you all about it when I see you." *Well, maybe not everything*, she thought.

"Can't wait to get the details. Uh . . . will this give me an ulcer on top of everything else that's going on inside of me?"

Allison raised her eyebrows and rubbed her forehead. "Of course not, Jim. You take care of yourself, and I'll see you when I return."

"When is that again?"

"In two days—see you soon."

"Allison, I'm sorry your relationship with Ashwin turned out the way it did," Lan said.

"Yeah, well his name is Anthony, not Ashwin. Whenever I get depressed there's this simple expression I repeat that helps me get through any disappointment."

"What's that?" Lan asked.

"I tell myself *it is what it is*. This usually comes with its own dosage of magic. If you can't change things, then accept them. I don't know what I was thinking, Lan. I let my emotions take over any rational thoughts."

"Sometimes that's okay to do," Lan said.

"Hey, enough about me. I have a surprise for you, but I'm not telling you until dinner tonight."

"Surprise? What kind of surprise?" Lan asked.

"Not until dinner—now tell me about this Royal Barge Museum."

"Okay, we're heading towards the Noi Canal where the museum is located. It's both a wet and a dry dock. Inside you will see eight barges berthed just above the water. The Thai people believe that every boat has a spirit which they consider to be female."

Allison said, "That's funny—we also refer to ships as females."

"Okay, we're here now." The two girls walked up to the entrance of the museum and purchased two tickets. Inside, Allison realized one barge was more beautiful than the last—each reflecting the intricacies of Thai craftsmanship over many centuries. Several of the barges displayed a figurehead at its prow—one in particular was the seven-headed serpent which symbolized water. Two others had a Garuda, a human bird-like figure, at its forefront. Another vessel had the Garuda dressed in a reddish body.

"I believe this is the barge that the brooch portrayed," said Allison, "but as regal as that one is, I think this one over here is my favorite." Allison pointing to the boat having a monkey at its prow. "I love monkeys."

"That's called a Hanuman," said Lan. "As for me, I like the half-bird, half-ogre."

"Tell me about these boats," Allison said, snapping one photo after another.

"Well, they were built for war. Most of the barges were in bad condition due to deterioration and damage from the World War II bombs."

"Looks like they've been restored to their original beauty."

"Yeah, the current king was responsible for that. Today they are used on special occasions, such as the Royal Barge Procession. It's one of the best events in Thailand and has been taking place for over 700 years. To see these barges parading down the Chao Phraya River is an exotic sight. They are manned by as many as 50 oarsmen and nine other crew members. Each of the oarsmen wear their traditional dress and are in total sync with each other."

"When do they have these parades?"

"Only on occasions such as the celebration of a cultural or religious event. I've only seen one since I've been here. I can tell you the parade is always accompanied by chanting as it passes by the Temple of the Emerald Buddha, the Grand Palace, Wat Po, and finally arriving at the Temple of Dawn. The last one was held when King Rama IX presented the Kathin Robes to the monks at The Temple of Dawn."

After leaving the museum, they headed over to the

restaurant for an early dinner. Allison filled Lan in on several things she did while in Chiang Rai, which left a lump in her throat because they involved Anthony.

"Which was your favorite?" Lan asked.

"Now that's hard to say, but I would have to go with a toss-up between my visit to the Hill Tribe and the Sky Lantern launch. It's difficult to accept how something as special as the lantern launch happened minutes before discovering the truth about Anthony. Wow, it's hard for me to refer to him as Anthony."

Lan nodded her head. "That's understandable. Look at how many days you spent calling him Ashwin. I hope you can find it in yourself to forgive the man. One thing my experiences have taught me is if you don't forgive, you will never heal. Without healing, you'll never completely move on with your life. That could cost you plenty—a happy life and the confidence in new love."

Allison smiled. "Thank you for that, Lan. I promise to not let this set me back."

The two friends waited for the bill in silence—each in her own thoughts. "I don't mean to change the subject, Allison, but do you know what just now entered my mind?"

"I think so. You're thinking about the last time we had dinner together—Yen was with us."

Lan sighed. "It's been hard for me, Allison. I've been told that people are lucky if they have at least five good friends."

"Yeah, we all have friends, but then there's this inner circle of people that we bond with in a forever way. Time, distance, and circumstances can never change that relationship. It's always strong and will never break."

"I know. Something might happen—good or bad—and

my immediate thought is to share it with Yen, but I can't.
She's no longer here."

"I certainly get that, Lan. The best soup is one that isn't
boiled but instead is allowed to brew. That's how it was for
you and Yen. It doesn't matter if she is here with you on
earth or in another place. If you let your mind go quiet, you
can hear her voice."

"That's what I do, Allison. I have to be careful because
Mae Chi has overheard me having conversations while no
one is in the room."

Allison laughed. "I can see Mae Chi now wondering if
she should have the counselor get counseling."

Lan pushed her plate to the side. "We did a lot together—
simple things like taking a walk, sharing stories over a cup
of tea, going to the market. I think about the many times I've
gone to the market with her, but didn't that last day. Perhaps
if I had accompanied her, she'd still be alive."

"That's possible, but most likely not probable. Think
about it, Lan. You could have been killed, too." Allison got
up from her chair and walked to the other side of the table
to offer Lan a much needed hug. "Her physical body may be
gone, but spiritually she will always be with you if you listen
to the small voice inside your head."

"Yeah, I hear the whispers," said Lan. "Thanks, Allison,
you're what I needed today. It will be sad saying good-bye
to you."

Allison returned to her seat and said, "Ahh . . . but not
for long."

"What do you mean? Will you be returning to
Thailand?"

"I hope someday to do just that, but do you remember
how I told you of a surprise I had?"

Lan nodded her head and said, "Okay, are you going to tell me what it is or keep me in suspense?"

"The documentary film we made of Vietnam was nominated for an Academy Award in the 'Best Documentary and Short Subject' category. Do you know what the Academy Awards is?"

"I believe so—is it the Oscars?"

"It is. They are held every spring in Los Angeles, California."

"What a wonderful surprise, Allison. Congratulations!"

Allison laughed. "Oh, that's not the surprise."

Confused, Lan said, "It isn't?"

"Nope—you have only a few weeks to obtain a visa because you are going to the United States to sit with our team at the Academy Awards. We hope your presence will send good karma."

"I'm going to America? But Allison, I don't have the funds for that."

"No worries. My boss, Jim Gallagher, arranged to provide a plane ticket, hotel room, and even took care of all your expenses like the purchase of a new gown."

Lan was dumbfounded. "Is this a joke?"

"It would be a mean one, wouldn't you say? We'll talk later about what you need to do. My office will help you obtain a B2 tourist visa. I've already spoken to Mae Chi and she gave her permission for you to go."

Lan threw her hands up in the air and yelled, "I'm going to America. I'm going to the Academy Awards!" Realizing her outburst, she covered her mouth and apologetically bowed her head to the diners nearby.

"Allison, I can't wait to tell my Uncle Trung and my

grandmother back in Vietnam that I'm going to America. You always seem to be presenting me with gifts."

"Not this time, Lan. This was all my boss' idea. He made it happen."

"Please thank Mr. Jim Gallagher for me, okay?"

"You can do that yourself when you meet him. And now, Miss Lan, I need you to drive me to my hotel. I have this early flight to catch tomorrow. Sad to say, but soon it will be time to say largone *(good-bye)* to Thailand, to its temples, to this land of smiles, and to all that might have been . . . but wasn't."

Do not pursue the past
Do not lose yourself in the future
The past no longer is
The future has not yet come
Look deeply at life as it is.

Gautama Buddha

OTHER BOOKS
BY THE AUTHOR

The Orchid Bracelet

(Book 1 of a two book series including *The Stolen Brooch*).

Excerpt from *The Orchid Bracelet*

He was a seedy type of guy. He parted his hair on the wrong side of his head, a front tooth was missing, and he reeked of body odor. He went by the name of Mr. Swoon. There was nothing attractive about this man except for the wad of money he kept in his pouch. He used it as bait as he wandered into the village located in the central highlands of Vietnam where pine trees covered the hilly terrain. The area was scenic, but the village was poor. Mr. Swoon knew that. Actually, he counted on that.

*Finalist in the *Next Generation Indie Book Awards* (general fiction)

*Finalist in the *ForeWord Book of the Year Award* (multicultural)

Available online at Amazon, Kindle, and Barnes & Noble
www.outskirtspress.com/theorchidbracelet

The Poison Ring

Excerpt from *The Poison Ring*

Piles of dirt stood alongside the road and in the occa-sional empty lot. Wherever lay a patch of land, no matter how small, a vegetable garden was planted with perhaps a cow sitting in the center. Being lowered into this alien world with its diverse culture took time to process. No books, no photographs, and no personal descriptions prepared Liz and Sunita for their first encounter with Nepal.

*Finalist in the *Next Generation Indie Book Award* (multi-cultural)

*Finalist in the *ForeWord Book of the Year Award* (multi-cultural)

Available online at Amazon, Kindle, and Barnes & Noble
www.outskirtspress.com/thepoisonring

The Journey to Mei

Excerpt from *The Journey to Mei*

My alarm clock went off at seven. This is not unusual as it goes off at seven every school day. Normally I groan, stretch, pull the pillow over my head, and pretend the an-noying blast of noise never happened. Today was different. I hopped out of bed and jumped into the clothes that draped over my desk chair. I was excited. Summer vacation would be starting in five hours.

The Journey to Mei is a story of international adoption. This book is a valuable resource that could be given to the adopted child to read and perhaps use as a tool to stimulate discussion. It's also a story that could be handed to the child's siblings, cousins, classmates and friends.

Available online at Amazon and Barnes and Noble
www.outskirtspress.com/thejourneytomei

Ride the Wave

Sequel to *The Journey to Mei*

Excerpt from *Ride the Wave*

Water is amazing. It's the place to be if ever I need to think. It doesn't have to be an ocean—a river or lake will do. Just being by it helps me sort out so many things. A month had passed since the accident and quite frankly, I can't free myself of the guilt. I knew I wasn't responsible. Everyone kept telling me that, but somehow the pain that took root in the pit of my stomach would not go away.

Available online at Amazon, Kindle, and Barnes & Noble
www.outskirtspress.com/ridethewave

Sculptured hands reaching from below at Wat Rong Khun.

Chao Phraya River in Bangkok.

Floating Market

Grand Palace in Bangkok

273

Row of Buddha statues at Wat Pho in Bangkok

Salt Farming in Thailand

Thai Wai Greeting

Wat Rong Khun

Woman from the Long Neck Karin Hill Tribe.

CPSIA information can be obtained at www.ICGtesting.com
Printed in the USA
BVOW02s1958230315

392936BV00003B/7/P